SUNRISE
OVER
FALLUJAH

Also by Walter Dean Myers

Fiction

Harlem Summer

The Beast

Slam!

The Glory Field

Somewhere in the Darkness

Fallen Angels

Nonfiction

Antarctica: Journeys to the South Pole

At Her Majesty's Request: An African Princess in Victorian England

WALTER DEAN MYERS

SUNRISE OVER FALLUJAH

SCHOLASTIC PRESS

AN IMPRINT OF SCHOLASTIC INC.

Library of Congress Cataloging-in-Publication Data

Myers, Walter Dean, 1937-
Sunrise over Fallujah / Walter Dean Myers. — 1st ed.
p. cm.
Summary: Robin Perry, from Harlem, is sent to Iraq in 2003 as a member of the Civil Affairs Battalion, and his time there profoundly changes him.
ISBN-13: 978-0-439-91624-0
ISBN-10: 0-439-91624-0
1. Iraq War, 2003 — Juvenile fiction. [1. Iraq War, 2003 — Fiction. 2. War — Fiction. 3. African Americans — Fiction.] I. Title.

PZ7.M992Su 2008
[Fic] — dc22

2007025444

10 9 8 7 6 5 4 3 2 1   08 09 10 11

Printed in the U.S.A.   23
First edition, May 2008

Book design by Elizabeth B. Parisi
Map by Jim McMahon

To the men and women, now serving, or who have served, in the United States Armed Forces, and to all the families who have anxiously awaited their safe return.

SUNRISE
OVER
FALLUJAH

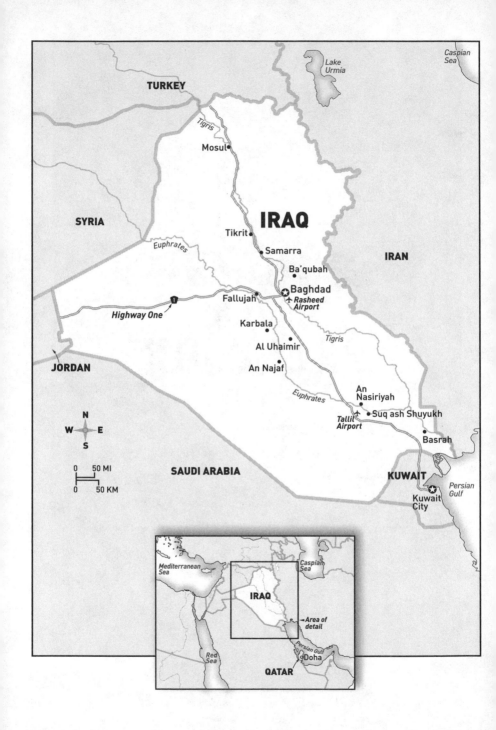

February 27, 2003

Dear Uncle Richie,

When I was home on leave I reread the letters you sent from Vietnam to my father. In one of them you said you were always a little nervous once you arrived in country. We're not in Iraq yet, but that's the way I feel, kind of jumpy. At one of our orientations (and we have at least two a week) an officer said that guys who fought in Nam wouldn't even recognize today's army. We're supposed to be so cool and well trained and everything. I hope so. I was thinking that maybe your eyes wouldn't recognize today's army but I'll bet your stomach would.

I can't tell you where we are right now, but it's less than a hundred miles from the Iraq border. What our army should do is to take photographs of all the military stuff we have over here and then send copies to the Iraqis. That would end things right then and there. I really think the Iraqis will back down at the last minute and hand over their weapons and we'll just have to put in a handful of military police to take care of business while the political people do their thing. I don't expect anybody to be shooting at us.

You were right, though, when you said I would have doubts about my decision to join the army. You joined a war that had already started; I thought this would be different. Dad was still mad at me when I left and it was no use telling him how I felt. You know he had all those plans for me to go to college and whatnot. I tried to explain to him that I didn't think he was wrong about college or even about me studying finance. You know your brother so you know what he said — "If I'm not wrong, then why are you joining the army?" Uncle Richie, I felt like crap after 9-11 and I wanted to do something, to stand up for my country. I think if Dad had been my age, he would have done the same thing. He was thinking about me and about my future — which is cool — but I still need to be my own man, just the way you were at my age.

Anyway, say hello to everybody for me. And if you happen to speak to Dad, please put in a good word for me. All my life I never went against him until now and I really feel bad that he's upset about me joining. Uncle Richie, I remember listening to you and one of your buddies talking about Vietnam in your living room. You were both kind of quiet as you spoke, as if you were talking about some secret thing. That was interesting to me. I hope that one day I'll be talking and laughing the same way about what Jonesy (a guy in my unit from Georgia) calls our adventure.

Well, that's all for now.

Your favorite nephew, Robin

"Gentlemen, ladies, welcome to Doha by the Sea.
I'm Major Spring Sessions and I'm overjoyed to welcome you to sunny Kuwait. If we actually have to enter Iraq, you will be playing a crucial role in achieving our objectives by interacting with the civilian population. There are many different areas of expertise among you but together you make up a very strong team — and that's a concept that will be stressed over and over again — and you have all expressed an interest in the Civil Affairs unit. I'm sure we'll all get along and make the army proud of us." Major Sessions was cute, black, and had a smile that lit up the headquarters tent. She looked sharp in her desert cammies. Jonesy nudged me with his elbow and I had an idea what he was thinking.

"Our entire detachment is made up of about forty-two people and there will be some switching around as we go along. We might increase some teams and decrease others. That's an important concept because what we're going to be doing, as an advance Civil Affairs unit, is to assess future needs. Right now we have one medical team, one construction team, an intelligence team, security personnel, and a flex team that will work directly with the native population. Some of the security people will also be assigned to work with the locals, so you see how fluid the Civil Affairs unit will be. This is an important mission and you're important to it. Don't forget that. Captain Coles will brief you on your assignments, your mission, and your relationship to the Infantry while you're over here. Thank you."

Major Sessions smiled again, pivoted on her right heel, and moved smartly from the small stage.

I had been introduced to Captain Coles when I first arrived at Camp Doha and he seemed all right. Not too gung ho, but not sloppy, either. Tall and thin with blue-gray eyes, Coles always looked sincere, as if he really wanted to know about you and was interested in what you were saying. He waited until Major Sessions left before he went to his clipboard.

"I have everybody listed here but the three new security teams. When I call out your name give me some sign that you're here, that you're alive, and tell me your hometown," he said. "You're not trying out for *American Idol,* so be as brief as you can be. I just need all of you to start connecting names and faces and get to know each other. Evans!"

"Corporal Eddie Evans, Stormville, New York, sir!"

"Jones!"

"Corporal Charlie Jones, Stone Mountain, Georgia, sir!"

"Harris!"

"Sergeant Robert Harris, Tampa, Florida, sir!"

"Kennedy!"

"Corporal Marla Kennedy, Dix Hills, New York, sir!"

"Perry!"

"Private Robin Perry, Harlem, New York, sir!"

Captain Coles looked up at me. "What kind of name is Robin? Your mama didn't know if you were a boy or girl?"

"I think she knew, sir."

"Well, which is it? Boy or girl?"

"Man, sir!"

"Okay, I can deal with that," Coles said. "Darcy!"

"Specialist Jean Darcy, Oak Park, Illinois, sir!"

"Ríos!"

"Corporal Victor Ríos, Albuquerque, New Mexico."

"Nice town," Captain Coles said. "Danforth!"

"PFC Shelly Danforth, Richmond, Virginia."

"Pendleton!"

"Corporal Phil Pendleton, Leetown, West Virginia."

As Captain Coles read off the list of names I looked around to see how many of the guys and the four women I remembered from the flight over. We had all arrived about the same time from the States, which was good. No two-month "old-timers." I was glad to see everybody was wearing name tapes.

"Okay, listen up!" Captain Coles put his clipboard down and

looked us over. "For the time being we're attached to the Third Infantry. If we actually get into a combat phase, the Third Infantry and the Fourth Marines will spearhead the attack. The Third isn't particularly happy taking care of us, but they won't get into our hair unless we screw up and get in their way, which we won't. For the most part we'll be trailing the Third's main combat force by at least a few days. We're going to have a lot of freedom, at least at first, as the planners and shakers back at the Pentagon — or wherever they do their planning and shaking — decide exactly what they want from us. In the unlikely event that Mr. Saddam Hussein doesn't step down and there actually *is* a shooting war, we will not be first-line troops. Basically I think there will be a war because Mr. Hussein, in my opinion, is not wrapped too tight. We, the Civil Affairs team, will be on board to see what the Iraqi noncombatants need so that we can begin the rebuilding process as soon as possible. In case you're too stupid to follow what I'm saying I will run it down for you very slowly and very carefully. If, when I am finished, you still don't understand, I will probably shoot you.

"Operation Iraqi Freedom has four phases. The first was the understanding and assessment of the area. This started way back during the first Gulf War that ended in February 1991. Since that time the Intelligence experts have been studying the area to understand the local dynamics and local problems. That phase is completed. We know what we're facing, what we're doing, and why we're here. At least that's the theory. The second phase is the preparation of the battlefield, which more or less means bombing the heck out of the enemy, taking out his communications, and disrupting his lines of supply. That'll start when the order is given, but that's not our job. The third phase, if necessary, will be the forceful removal of the present regime in Iraq and neutralizing their weapons, especially their weapons of mass destruction. These weapons could include various forms of gas and biological weapons, maybe even nuclear devices. The fourth and final phase will be the building of a successful democracy in Iraq. That's where Civil Affairs comes in. It's our job to assess and start that rebuilding process.

"I'll be point man for our operation and I will answer to Major Sessions. Major Sessions has a nice voice, pretty eyes, and a very nasty disposition. She would not mind shoving her hand up my rear end and tearing out my entrails if I don't keep you clowns on mission.

"Major Sessions answers to Colonel Armand Rose. Colonel Rose would also not mind tearing any or all of us a new one. He's served on the ground in Grenada in 1983 and in the first Gulf War and he's kind of suspect about what we're supposed to be doing, so he'll be watching us carefully. He's going to want to know what kind of a job we can do. In other words, will we be able to make our battlefield successes meaningful. It's as simple as that.

"My personal mission in life is to grow old and grumpy and watch my kids flunk out of school. I need to get back home to get that done and I would appreciate your help."

We left the tent and drifted out into the bright Kuwaiti sun. The intense direct light was always a bit of a shock and I saw guys going for their water bottles. I wasn't sure whether I should drink as much water as possible or try to train myself to drink less.

Since Kuwait was right next to Iraq, I thought things would be tense here, but they're not. Our living quarters are in a warehouse area; the mess hall is really good and it even has a coffee shop. There are also fast food places, a theater, and a library that was built after the first Gulf War. After two weeks in country, I was still trying to get used to the heat and even complaining like everybody else, but down deep this is a little exciting, too. I'm also wondering if there really is going to be a war. There is a huge amount of guys and heavy equipment already here and more being brought in every day.

"Hey, Birdy!"

I turned around and a tall blonde caught up with me. I'm six-two and we were almost eye to eye when she reached me. I glanced at her name tape. Kennedy.

"Say, Birdy, weren't you at Fort Dix?" she asked.

"Yeah, and the name is Robin, not Birdy," I said.

"Whatever," she said. "I like Birdy better."

"Kennedy, I knocked out the last person who got my name wrong," I said.

"Really? I'm impressed," she said; a grin spread across her face. "What kind of weapon was she carrying?"

Kennedy flipped the sling of her M-16 over her shoulder and sauntered off toward the women's quarters.

I had come down with measles at Fort Dix, New Jersey, with only two weeks left to go in my Infantry training cycle. After a week in isolation at the hospital I spent three weeks hanging around the dayroom watching television and shooting pool while it was being decided if I would have to repeat the whole cycle again. I ended up with another training group and then received orders to report to the Civil Affairs detachment at Camp Doha in Kuwait.

I went to dinner in the main mess. The tables actually had flowers and napkins on them and we ate off regular plates instead of the trays we had used at Fort Dix. I grabbed some meat loaf, mashed potatoes, and string beans, and found a table. One of the guys who had been at the meeting with Major Sessions came over and asked if he could join me.

"Sure," I said. The guy was about five-seven with smooth brown skin and a round face. Solidly built, he looked like he could take care of himself. But when I saw his camouflage do-rag and dark shades I knew he was a little different.

"So what you about, man?" he asked.

"Same thing everybody else is," I answered, "getting ready to go to war. What are you about?"

"I'm about the blues," he answered. "You know, the blues is what's real. Everything else is just messing around waiting until you get back to the blues."

"So what are you doing in Kuwait?" I asked. I glanced down at his name tape. It read JONES.

"Yeah, I'm Jones," he said. "But everybody back home calls me 'Jonesy.' What I'm doing here is getting some experience, getting to see some stuff, and saving my money so I can open up a blues club. When I get that club going I'm going to play blues guitar six nights a week. Then on Sundays I'll jam with God because me and him is like this."

Jones held up two crossed fingers.

"Yeah, okay."

"Yeah, yeah. Look, you and me got to stick together," he said. "That way I can watch your back and you can watch mine."

"Okay."

"You play guitar?"

"No."

"You sing?"

"No."

Jones looked away and I got the feeling he had already lost interest in watching my back. He talked some more about the club he was going to open. He didn't sound as if he had much of an education, but he seemed sincere about wanting to play his guitar. He said he practiced it at least two hours a day.

"Yo, Jones, that's good," I said.

"'Jonesy,' you got to call me 'Jonesy,'" he said. "That way I know you looking out."

I liked Jonesy even though I wasn't sure what he was talking about sometimes. Like when he asked me if I was a hero.

"No," I answered.

"You tall — how tall are you?"

"Six foot two."

"A lot of tall dudes are hero types," Jonesy said. "You go crazy trying to watch their backs. You know what I mean?"

"Yeah, but I'm not the hero type," I said.

There were special detachments created for Medical, Construction, and Intelligence. The Medical detachment people were a little older and were led by Captain Miller, a no-nonsense captain who acted like she knew what she was doing. The Construction guys looked like the most fun and I figured that most of them had worked in either building or engineering in civilian life. The Intelligence detachment looked okay but spent most of their time reading through reports from Central Command – CENTCOM – or listening to radio intercepts. Some of them had been through language school for Arabic. Captain Coles said that the rest of us, a dozen or so soldiers, would be working within the villages as part of the flex team.

"That means we'll be doing anything that helps," he said. "And we'll get blamed for everything that goes wrong."

Sergeant Harris, a black soldier who had switched to Civil Affairs from Quartermaster, along with Captain Coles, sorted the dozen of us into three Humvee squads, giving us a choice of who we wanted to ride with. Jonesy said he wanted to ride with me, and Coles said he would, too. That still left a space in our vehicle and Kennedy was assigned to it. I didn't know if I liked her, but I didn't care all that much, either.

"The squads and assignments will change according to the situation," Captain Coles said. "You're assigned to a vehicle mostly so we can hold you responsible for keeping it in good order."

First Squad was Jones driving, Kennedy on the squad gun, me, and Captain Coles.

Second Squad was Sergeant Harris driving, Darcy, another girl, on the squad gun, and Evans.

Third Squad consisted of Love driving, Danforth on the gun, Pendleton, and a really quiet guy named Corbin who had worked in a rehabilitation center in civilian life.

Ahmed Sabbat was our field interpreter. He was American, but his parents were from the Middle East.

We were all up for whatever happened, and everyone had an opinion about what that might be.

"You know, the Iraqis are talking about how they let the UN inspectors in and how their people are suffering from the sanctions," Evans said. "If they were getting ready to fight they wouldn't be doing so much talking. This is March. I'm betting by the Fourth of July I'll be home fishing."

"There's no use watching the news to see what's going on." Sergeant Harris had his feet up on his foot locker. "Saddam is getting ready for us and we're getting ready for him. That's all there is to the thing, man."

"Saddam's clever." Captain Coles's voice was soft, measured. "He has to remember the Gulf War and he's savvy enough to understand that he can't stand up to the United States. No Iraqi general is going to give him a different take on things. If he lets it get to the point where we start going in, he's going to be taken out."

"Okay, I hear what you saying," Harris answered. "But you tell me this, sir. The president is telling him to step down and get out of Dodge. Where's Saddam going to go? Everybody over here hates his butt. He had a war with Iran, so he can't go there. The Egyptians don't like him. Everybody in Kuwait hates him for invading them. Where's he going to go? If he ain't got no place to go, he's got to stay and fight."

"He going to stay and get smoked!" a guy named Lopez said. He was olive-skinned with dark short-cropped hair. The dude looked dangerous. I had asked him what the initials tattooed on his hand — ALKN — meant and he just looked at me and laughed.

"You know where Saddam could be safe?" Sergeant Harris was on a roll. "In the United States. We could put him in the witness protection program. Give him a million bucks so he could live good — maybe a little business — that would be funny. Yeah, he could sell pictures of Elvis on black velvet."

"You really want to get into this war bad, don't you?" Marla Kennedy was playing solitaire on the foldout table.

"Look, Miss Molly. These people need to learn what's going on. You see what I'm talking about? What they understand over here is power." Sergeant Harris glanced toward Captain Coles to see how his remarks were being taken. "They got to see your power. They got to see you take out their cities, kill a few folks. In a way, we're teachers getting ready to let them know what American power is really all about. That's why I'm here."

"What I think" — Jonesy put talcum powder in his boots and shook them — "is that Saddam got a tune in his head and he wants to play it real bad. And when it don't go right he just play it louder. A lot of dudes do that. They call it music, but it could just be war."

"Jones, what are you talking about?" Coles asked.

"Hey, Captain, why are you over here?" Kennedy looked up from her cards.

"I joined the army when I was twenty-two and trying to figure out what to do with my life," Captain Coles answered. "I kept thinking I was going to make up my mind on some career path and then get out. Haven't quite got around to making up my mind or getting out. I feel good about defending my country, about being in Civil Affairs. You know, we bring a human face to war. I feel good about that."

I couldn't tell if Captain Coles really felt good about it or not. He didn't share much with us.

"You think we're going in?" Evans asked.

"As you say, Saddam's backed himself into a corner." Captain Coles nodded as he spoke. "He understands power. If he backs down now, every gunslinger in the Middle East will be after him. So he might as well stay and fight it out."

"Stay and get wasted, you mean." Harris did seem anxious.

Captain Coles stood up. He looked uncomfortable. "I'm going to go speak to Sessions," he said. "She was talking about us pulling guard duty, but I think I can talk her out of it."

"Tell her that Sergeant Harris will take a shift by himself," Kennedy said. "They won't need the rest of us."

"Yo, woman, you got a lot of mouth for a chick!" Harris said.

"Glad you noticed it, Sergeant."

Captain Coles left and Sergeant Harris started flipping through the television channels, seeing if any of them came in clearly. I knew the military channel would, but I didn't want to watch another rerun of the latest speech from the White House. I got up and went out into the clear spring air.

Before arriving at Doha I had imagined being on a desert with camels wandering by and palm trees swaying in the wind. It had taken seven hours to fly from Newark, New Jersey, to Ramstein Air Force Base in Germany, and another seven to reach Kuwait. The place blew my mind. The whole city of Doha was squeaky clean and beautiful. Almost everything was new or nearly new. I arrived on a Saturday morning and went with a bunch of guys into the city. There was every kind of department store you could think about and the street hummed with SUVs. When I saw the Grand Mosque with its golden dome, it took my breath away. One of the guys I was with, a civilian contractor, told me that I would never get used to the architecture in the Arab countries.

"It changes your whole perspective about the people over here," he said.

Nine o'clock this morning we marched to the CENTCOM theater and saw a film about Saddam Hussein. There were at least a thousand guys there, most of them 3rd Infantry dudes and a lot of Marines and Special Ops. Saddam looked like a sweetheart of a guy. Always calm looking, distinguished. In most of the pictures there was no change of expression on his face. In the film he was always seen either shaking hands or shooting a pistol into the air. Then the images changed to the Kurds who were gassed. A woman still had her arm out toward her child. The whole scene looked unreal, as if it had been staged. I wanted to turn away from the bodies lying on the ground. Some looked as if they might move at any moment. Just get up and walk off. I didn't want to see these people lying dead. I tried to get myself mad, but I only managed to feel scared.

The thing was that nobody else seemed scared. A lot of guys acted as if they were pissed and were anxious to get the war thing started. A guy from the 3rd Infantry, kind of small, with almost a baby face, kept talking about facing the Iraqis.

"We need to think about winning this thing and checking ourselves out to see if we really want it. You know what I mean? Because if we really want it we can make it happen," he said. "Those people, the Kurds, laying on the ground, they didn't have a chance. We got the chance. We got to do a gut check and see if we got the will to win."

I didn't know if I had the same will to win as the guy from the 3rd. What I did know was that I wanted to do my part. The officers let us sit around and talk up the war and I thought that they did it on purpose. It was like being in a locker room before a big game.

"I seen a 240 take a guy's leg off from a hundred yards," a big-headed corporal said. "The whole leg came off and the sucker was just laying there on the ground, looking at his leg as he died."

I felt a little sick.

After the movie we went back to our quarters. We had settled down into card games and the usual BS when we got called out to formation. Captain Coles saluted the two officers, a colonel and a lieutenant, who gave us a quick inspection. The colonel had enough gear on to be burning up in the heat. He was making sure he looked tough. I thought about his getting heat rash and smiled but wiped it off my face before he passed by me.

"You people represent the United States Army, and you represent our country and our way of life as well," the colonel said, sounding like he was making a formal speech. "If we go into Iraq the people there will be watching the combat troops, seeing how well they perform their duties as well as how we treat the local population. But the most lasting impression will be of you soldiers working Civil Affairs. You can do a great job over here or you can undo any gains we make by acting without thinking, acting out of fear instead of logic, or acting in a manner that betrays American principles. Years from now, when the people in the cities and villages remember this operation, it will be your faces and actions that they will recall."

Colonel Rose ended the talk with a recording of "The Star Spangled Banner." It was a little hokey, but standing there at attention with all the other soldiers, I did feel a sense of pride.

"I think Civil Affairs is going to be the most interesting thing about this war," Captain Coles said when we returned to our tent. "And maybe the safest if I can convince Major Sessions to keep you guys off patrols. I'm passing out the official vehicle assignments. You're responsible for routine maintenance and cleanliness and you each have to sign for your assigned vehicle. Look over these assignments and memorize them. If we go in you won't be allowed to take any documents with you except maps and your personal identification. I'm assigning the first three security squads."

He handed out the papers and we looked them over. The assignments were the same as he had put on the blackboard earlier.

■   ■   ■

"We'll have different leaders depending on what assignment we're on," Captain Coles said. "Regardless of the mission and who the leader is, we need to think of ourselves as a team. If we reach a position in which we're not only seeing each other but actually sensing what each member of the team is feeling, there's a good chance we'll all come out of this war in one piece. Any questions?"

"So you want to break it down to us one more time?" Danforth asked. "We're supposed to go out and kill the Iraqis and blow up their stuff. Then we help them find their arms or legs, or whatever we've blown off, and patch them back together. Then we all sit in a circle and sing campfire songs, right?"

"You might not be taking this seriously, Danforth, but the Operations people are and they're going to make it work. What this war is going to be about – and we're still not positive it's going to happen – is regime change and destroying the Iraqis' chemical and any nuclear weapons we find. It's not about making the people suffer and it's up to us to let them know that. If Saddam does step down and they turn over their weapons, we can avoid a lot of bloodshed."

"Yeah, okay." Danforth shrugged. "It's definitely good on paper."

The way Captain Coles laid it out, each squad would have one Humvee, consisting of a driver, a gunner, and two other guys. Marla outranked me but she wanted to be the gunner. I liked her and I liked Captain Coles. Jonesy was okay, too. Coles said he would ride with us most of the time, which was why we only had three in our crew.

What we did for the next three days was to sit around and wait and talk about whether or not anyone was going to start shooting.

Most of what we learned was from the television news. There was a VCR in the dayroom and we watched a lot of flicks. They had every war movie ever produced, including three copies of Tom Cruise in *Top Gun*, which I liked. We also watched a lot of training films and spent hours practicing putting on our gas masks. I also noticed that the teams were hanging out more together.

"Hey, Birdy, you know why the mess hall is so empty this morning?" Marla brought her tray over to my table and plunked down across from me.

"How long you going to call me Birdy?" I asked.

"It's empty because half the Hoodlums sneaked out in the middle of the night," she answered. The Hoodlums were what we called the Special Ops guys who went on secret missions in enemy territory. We had asked a few what they did, but they weren't talking. Actually, most of them just grunted.

Marla continued, "Some women from the Engineering Battalion near the post exchange told me. They got them up around two in the morning. They were all blacked up and in every kind of uniform you could mention."

"What were those women doing up?"

"Had to go pee," Marla said. "Did you know women did that?"

Captain Coles came by with a cup of coffee in each hand. "Mind if I join you?"

"No, sir," I said.

"All signs point to go," he said. "If you're going to write any letters home . . ."

Marla spotted Danforth and beckoned him over. He came to the table, turned a chair around, and straddled it.

"Marla heard that the Hoodlums left camp last night," I said.

"They can't be going into Iraq yet." Danforth gestured with his hands as he spoke. "There's no official war."

"They've been going in and out of Iraq for the last six months," Coles said. "They're setting up scouting operations, making contacts, that sort of thing."

"How come they didn't get the Hoodlums to supply security for Civil Affairs instead of us?" Danforth asked. "I mean, some of those Special Forces guys act like they'd consider it a favor if they killed you."

Coles laughed, a big toothy laugh that lit up his whole face. "That's probably why the average Iraqi won't talk to them," he said. He put more sugar into his coffee, tasted it, and pushed it aside. "You guys look like reasonable people. The army probably thinks you might even try to talk to a villager before you killed him."

"There's Ahmed." Marla nodded toward the chow line. "Where's he from? He's in the American army? Those aren't desert camouflage units he wears."

"Cleveland," Captain Coles said. "He's a civilian translator. Try not to kill him if you can help it. They frown on that kind of thing in Cleveland. The army wants him to blend in wherever possible. Be a kind of go-between."

"This be a strange war," Marla said.

"Where you from, Captain Coles?" Danforth asked

"Allentown, Pennsylvania. My family's lived there for three generations back. Before then we were, or so I've been told, in England. Allentown's a good little place. A couple of hours from anywhere exciting. Some of the best food in the world from nearby farms and some of the Amish folk in the area. Where you from again?"

"Richmond," Danforth said. "Right outside of the city, really."

"What's your hometown?" Coles asked Marla.

"Is this the beginning of a war movie?" Marla asked. "Everybody tells about themselves so when they get killed we'll all feel sorry for them?"

She didn't wait for an answer. She stood and just walked away. Definitely cool.

The next morning we watched President Bush give a message to the American people that sounded like it was from a cowboy movie.

The Humvees came and we received ours with the usual military lecture.

This is the finest fighting vehicle in the army of the United States of America, so don't you meatheads go f'ing it up!

Second squad, Harris, Darcy, and Evans, painted a name on their Humvee, calling it *Def Con II*. I was still a little mad at Marla for always calling me Birdy, so I suggested we call our Humvee *Miss Molly*, which was what Sergeant Harris called her.

"Yeah, that works," Marla said.

From: **Perry, Robin**

Date: **17 March 2003**

To: **Perry, Richard**

Subject: **Various**

Hey Uncle Richie,

Just got online for the first time over here. They have a list of about 100 rules about email. We can't say this – we can't say that – all about security. BUT . . . there are 590 reporters (give or take a 100 or so) asking us questions and reporting everything we're not supposed to be saying. No real problem because we don't know anything. I wrote Dad a good letter. Anyway, I thought it was okay. Did you know he doesn't like the internet? He says it "will mature" in another 20 years.

The infantry and the marines are the stars over here. The camera crews follow the guys with the most equipment. Oh, this is not important, but I thought you might find it interesting. They have floors in the tents that look like the kind of floors at basketball games, the kind you assemble. We can't put water on them because when the guys come in with sand on their boots it really messes them up. So we don't have to wash them down. Small blessings. Last thing. The guys from the Arabic television station, Al Jazeera, all look like they could have come from Harlem . . . dark skinned, etc.

If you talk to your brother, aka Dad, you might tell him that I was waiting for a letter from him.

A lot of guys were getting nervous thinking we were going into combat, but most were just excited. It's funny, but as much as guys talk about not wanting to be in a danger zone, I think we really do want it. We want to get home safe, but we want the danger. We were shown films of the first Gulf War over and over, watching planes hit small targets with guided missiles, hearing the voice-overs of guys cheering.

I knew we were building up to it. It was almost like getting ready for a basketball game, reassuring ourselves that we were cool, that we were going to win. It got to be even more like that when the 3rd Infantry Division called a huge formation. It looked like a trillion guys lined up. The colors of the 3rd ID were out front along with the American flag. A few officers spoke, talking about the mission in Iraq and how proud America was of us. Then the main speaker, a tall general with a pistol strapped to his leg, came out and gave the order for us all to stand "at ease."

"We are the best trained, best equipped, bravest, most daring army in the world," the general said. "Soon we will be entering Iraq. If Saddam is smart he will step aside and give the order to allow us to enter peacefully. And we will do so. If Saddam is dumb and refuses to step aside, we have to enter with force, and we will do so. How this war goes is up to the Iraqi army. But they will not be an obstacle to the successful completion of our mission."

Officers moved smartly, looked tough, reminded everybody over and over about how well we were trained. There was something about the speeches that all sounded alike.

Back in the tent, me and Jonesy weren't that sure about our training.

"You think the Third is better trained than us?" Jonesy asked.

"Probably," I said. "I was trained to shoot at targets popping up in a field and they weren't shooting back."

"Most of my training was about diving down when you heard gunfire," Jonesy said. "Dive down, roll over one time, and get up running."

"Where was that training?"

"In the ghetto, my man!" Jonesy said. "We had drive-through restaurants, drive-through car washes, and drive-by shootings. So on a real busy day the brothers didn't even have to get out their machines."

"Yeah, right," I said. "I just hope Marla has enough training to work the squad gun. She could have pulled driver."

"I think she can do it," Jonesy said. "She's got a little gangsta lean to her."

Jonesy was right. Marla Kennedy wasn't somebody you took lightly.

When Jonesy and I got back to our tent Sergeant Harris already had the television on; he flipped channels, looking for news. Harris hadn't found anything official yet but kept saying stupid stuff like how he could tell by the Iraqi minister's body language that they were going to fight.

"Man, these people need to learn something!" he said.

Yeah, and he was going to teach them.

It was still dark when Jonesy woke me, shaking me by the shoulder. I opened my eyes. "What's up?"

"You believe in God?" he asked.

As I sat up I saw that he was holding a flashlight in one hand and a small Bible in the other.

"Yeah, I do," I said.

Jonesy bowed his head for a moment, then turned on his flashlight and began reading from the Bible he held. "Our Father which art in heaven, hallowed be thy name. Thy kingdom come. Thy will be done on earth, as it is in heaven. Give us this day our daily bread. And forgive us our debts, as we forgive our debtors. And lead us not into temptation, but deliver us from evil: For thine is the kingdom, and the power, and the glory, forever. Amen."

I felt awkward. It had been years since I last prayed, and I had never prayed with a friend. Jonesy held up his fist and I touched mine to it.

"What's up, man?" I asked.

"I don't know," he said. "I just got a feeling."

"Like, what kind of feeling?"

"Crossroads," he said.

"What's that mean?"

"There was this blues dude — Robert Johnson — got to the crossroads, met the devil, and they struck up a deal. Sold his soul to the devil for some guitar licks."

"Yeah?"

Jonesy stood up and tucked the Bible under his arm. "I'm just wondering if I need to strike me up a deal," he said. He went back to his bunk, lay down, and turned his back toward me.

In the distance I could hear the roar of planes. I looked at my watch. It was five thirty. The sun would rise soon.

■ ■ ■

"This is not my grandmother." Jean Darcy was pissed out of her mind. "This is my great-grandmother and she is eighty-five years and four months old. Her birthday is the same as mine and I promised to write her and tell her what is going on. She don't understand stupid, and that Colonel King was just talking stupid!"

We had just had a lecture from King, who was in charge of

all Civil Affairs in the area. If what he told us wasn't exactly stupid, it was at least confusing.

"So what do you need to know?" Pendleton asked.

"Who are we supposed to be shooting over here?" Darcy asked. "Because I am not worried about who we're supposed to be getting along with. I figure if they're trying to get along with us they won't be shooting at us."

"Anybody who has on a different uniform than we have on we can shoot," Pendleton said.

"Unless they're Coalition forces talking Dutch or Italian or something else I can't understand, right?" Darcy asked. "And King was talking about if the Iraqis are fighting and things don't go right for them they just take off their uniforms and act like civilians but we're not supposed to shoot civilians." She was on a roll. "Now can you tell me how I'm going to explain that to my great-grandmother?"

"Okay, let me straighten this mess out." Jonesy was soaking his feet in a basin of water. "If somebody who looks like an A-rab shoots you, the first thing you got to do is to pull out your Rules of Engagement card and see what the rules are for the day. Because it could be a Rodney King day and we just all trying to get along and then you don't shoot him."

"You think that's funny but it ain't funny, Jones." Darcy was still mad. "And how about that stuff with the Sunnis and the other people?"

"The Shiites," I said. "Colonel King said there might be battles between the two sects."

"So if they're shooting, you have to see who they're aiming at," Pendleton said. "They could be shooting at each other."

"And Saddam wiped out a whole village of Kurds," Marla said.

"My great-grandmother is not going to understand this crap," Darcy said. "I don't understand it, either. We're over here talking about an enemy we can't identify and friends we're not sure about."

"What bugged me was when Captain Coles asked if we were going to disarm the Iraqis and Colonel King said we weren't," Pendleton said. "He said it would be disrespecting the tribes and we can't do that because we're going to be dependent on them to give us information.

"What we got to do over here," Pendleton continued, "is to kill all of them and let God sort them out."

I turned and looked at him and saw he wasn't smiling. He meant just what he said.

King had been talking about treating people humanely, and with dignity, but we were thinking about how hard staying alive was going to be.

The bombing of Iraq has started. I don't know what it's doing to the Iraqis, but it's filled us with shock and awe. We watched the first impacts on Baghdad this morning on television just before daybreak. The dim images of city buildings suddenly illuminated by explosions that swept across the night sky filled the TV screen with brilliant color. A reporter wearing a flak jacket flinched as the bombs exploded behind him. Some of our guys were cheering; most just watched quietly. It wasn't hard to imagine those bombs falling somewhere near you.

At 0600 we saddled up and went out to the range to test-fire our weapons. Targets were a hundred yards out and each squad took a turn trying to hit them. In stateside training, the shooting was a pastime, something you did because it was interesting but you didn't really like because you knew it meant you had to clean your weapon. Here on the Kuwaiti desert, target practice was suddenly serious.

When it was my turn on the squad gun I was on target when we were stationary but way off when the Humvee was on the go.

"Don't worry about it," Captain Coles said. "When we're on the move it's suppressive fire — all we want the enemy to do is to keep his head down while we get away."

Jonesy wasn't any better than I was, but Kennedy was on the money big-time.

"You do a lot of shooting back in the States?" I asked.

"I guess," she said with a shrug. "My training officer said it just comes naturally to some people."

"You're a lot better at it than I am," I said.

"Birdy, the way you shoot is pitiful." Marla grinned. "Maybe you should just practice making mean faces at the enemy."

I didn't like that. The girl had an edge to her that ran along my nerves all the time. I thought about what my father said: I'd meet a lot of lousy people in the army.

We left the target range and trekked to supply. Sergeant Harris was in charge; he had checklists and made us lay out all of our equipment on the ground.

The supply sergeant, a huge black dude who looked half asleep, gave us a mini lecture on the equipment. When he saw that some of the medical officers weren't paying attention, he stopped.

"My apology, Sergeant," one of the doctors said, throwing the supply sergeant a sloppy salute.

"You don't have to be sorry, sir," the sergeant said. "But if you don't have the right equipment and you get your sorry butt wounded or killed, it won't be funny. And the first time you see somebody lying on the ground with a sucking chest wound where his body armor should have been, you're going to be thinking about getting back here and making sure you have the right equipment. You might be smart enough to be a doctor, but you ain't smart enough not to die."

"I think that's enough, Sergeant," the medical officer said, trying to sound more authoritative.

"No, it ain't, *sir!*" the sergeant said. "'Cause you don't know more than me about being over here. I been here before. I went home. Hope you get that message."

Captain Coles stepped in front of us. "Everybody is responsible for everyone else in this unit," he said. "If you see somebody out there without his protective gear on, speak up. If you see somebody walking away from his goggles, or who isn't taking care of his gear, speak up. The teams going out in the field are too small to have to deal with wounded or killed soldiers. Medevac worked in the first Gulf War, but we don't know what the enemy has learned since then."

We finished getting our equipment together, signed for all of it, then broke for lunch. Me and Jonesy sat together. I had hoped Marla would come over, but she sat with some women from a PSYOP unit. What they did was work on the minds of the enemy. Sometimes they dropped leaflets, sometimes they did nasty little propaganda things, like spread rumors about the enemy's officers. They spent a lot of time trying to figure out what the enemy was thinking.

A small, round Specialist came over and asked if Jonesy and I wanted to join a prayer group.

"I don't think so," I said. "Maybe . . ." I looked at Jonesy.

"No way," Jonesy said. "I'm a blues man. All we believe in is the blues and hard whiskey."

"Sometimes prayer can help you see what you're missing," Small and Round said.

"No interest." Jonesy waved the guy away.

I watched as the SPC went to the next table before I looked

at Jonesy. "Yo, man, you came to my bunk the other night and asked me if I wanted to pray."

"That wasn't me talking," Jonesy said. "That was my testicles talking. *I* ain't worried about dying, but you know how testicles get sometimes."

We were scheduled to move out right after lunch. I didn't feel like eating. Coles pulled out some maps and showed us where we were, north of Kuwait City.

"We're following two Infantry brigades," he said. "We're going to be traveling southeast and then swing around so that we're behind the Infantry all the way."

My stomach tightened. We were actually going into combat.

There wasn't a whole lot of talking as we lined up our vehicles and moved over to the fuel station. Some of the crews turned back their odometers to zero so they could record how many miles we totaled.

The fuel line was two miles long and we had nothing to do but hang out and notice that other units got to fuel ahead of us even if they were after us in line.

"Hey, where you guys from?" I turned to see a roundish sister who looked a little bit like a short Queen Latifah. She was with two other little lady soldiers.

"Harlem," I said. "Where you from?"

"El Paso," the woman said. "I know you never been there."

"These guys from New York have never been anywhere, never seen anything, and don't know anything," Marla said. "Birdy's still waiting for a cab to take him home to his mama. Who are you guys with?"

"Five Oh Seventh." The little blonde's accent was thick enough to laugh at if she had been on television. She crossed her legs, squatted, and then sat. "You guys with the Third ID?"

"Sort of." Jonesy was looking hard at the little blonde. "We're Civil Affairs — trailing behind them, making friends with anybody they don't kill."

"We're logistical support or something like that," the black woman said. The name tape over her pocket read JOHNSON. "We got thirty-two trucks of stuff to transport some freaking where."

"You going north by the Blue Line?" Marla asked. "That's what we're doing. Then 106 to the IHOP, a hard left when we reach Petticoat Junction, then straight on to Disneyland."

"Yeah, that's about it," Johnson said. "I hope this mess is over before we get into it. If you people hear about any parties, let us know."

"You got thirty-two trucks and about how many dudes and dudettes?" Jonesy asked.

"What's a dudette?" Johnson asked.

"Girl dudes," Jonesy said.

"Girl dudes? Okay." Johnson had a nice smile. "We got sixty-six *people*, little man. Each truck got a driver and an alternate. I can drive anything that got more than two wheels."

The third woman in their group leaned against Evans's Humvee. Sometimes she smiled but she didn't say anything. It was a funny trio: a sister, a tiny blonde, and a dark-haired girl who could have been Spanish.

"Y'all get your ROE cards?" the blonde asked.

"What's that?" I asked.

"They gave us these Rules of Engagement cards saying who we supposed to shoot and stuff," she said. "I can't figure out what they mean when they talking 'bout 'Happy Shooting.'"

She passed a card over to Jonesy. He read it, shaking his head slightly as he did, and then handed it back to the blonde.

"According to what I was told, when these people get happy they shoot off their pistols or AK-47s into the air," Jonesy said. "When they do that, we're not supposed to shoot at them."

"Let me see that card?" Marla asked.

The blonde handed it over. "Where you from?" she asked.

"New York," Marla said. "Not from the black part, like Birdy, though. Okay, rule six in the Rules of Engagement. Expect 'Happy Shooting' from the local populace. This shooting is not hostile and should not be responded to as such."

"So if some guy's smiling and shooting in the air," Jonesy said, "it's okay. But then he lowers it a little bit and he's still smiling while he's lighting your ass up, then you can shoot back?"

"It depends," Marla said. "How big is his smile?"

"Five-Oh-Seven!" a captain called out. "Let's go! Let's go!"

The Five-Oh-Seven women piled back into their vehicles and started lining up for refueling. Their trucks were huge and I tried to imagine the little blonde behind the wheel.

We didn't finish fueling up and loading extra fuel cans into the back of the Humvee until late. Captain Coles told us to go bunk down for the night and be ready to leave for the border the first thing in the morning. He had just finished telling us that when a command vehicle pulled up and gave him new orders.

"Okay, guys, mount up! We've got hearts and minds to win!"

We were on our way to Iraq.

Third squad took the lead. Captain Coles rode with them. Second squad with Sergeant Harris, Eddie Evans, and Jean Darcy came next. Two vehicles with medical personnel and Intelligence Ops followed; our squad pulled up the rear.

We traveled across country for a while headed for Highway 1 and started past a long line of MP vehicles. Some Kuwaiti workers waved us off. We waved back. Jonesy was hunched over the wheel, trying to adjust his seat belt by wiggling his butt.

I wasn't exactly scared. My mouth was dry, the way it felt before a big game or an important test in high school. But I was going to be doing something I had never done before. I was going to be in a war.

We rode deep into the night and into the early morning. The Kuwaiti desert, in spots, was beautiful. The rising sun spread like a brilliant egg flattening out. A distance away, we could see small dust storms changing the colors that played along the edge of the horizon. I remembered part of a song by Bob Marley.

Check out the real situation
Nation war against nation
Where did it all begin?
When will it end?

We were in the longest line of vehicles I could ever imagine. It extended as far in front of us as it did behind. Periodically we were stopped for identification check. Once, when a Military Police officer thought we were with the 352nd Civil Affairs Battalion, we were told we were going the wrong way.

"We're attached to the Third." Captain Coles looked over the MP's organization table and found us listed. "Civil Affairs detachment Alpha. Right there."

The Brits were going into Iraq toward Basrah and we were swinging around to get behind the American forces. We went south toward Camp Virginia and then west from there. We were told to pull over and dismount as it grew dark. There was already a makeshift camp in the desert and we pulled into it. Captain Coles told us to inspect the vehicles but nobody was thinking about the Humvees, only the sounds of the big guns booming in the distance. The vibrations from the heavy weapons traveled through the air and I could feel something deep inside my bowels react every time there was an explosion. The scent of gasoline mixed with the smell of sulfur in the warm air.

"Birdy, how far are we away from Iraq?" Marla's face was caked in sand from her nose down. Her eyes and forehead, covered by her goggles and helmet, were clean.

"We could make it there in a couple of hours," I said. "Easy. You want to shake this joint and bust on in?"

"No, what I want you to do is to explain to me who they're

shooting at. I thought the Iraqis would be too shocked and awed to fight," Marla said.

We had to eat MREs, the packaged food we had brought along. I still wasn't hungry.

"Makes me feel like a big boy," Jonesy said. He took off his Molle vest and flopped on the ground, using his helmet as a backrest. Captain Coles told us to stay together and be ready to move out on a moment's notice.

"And don't sleep under the Humvees," he said. "Years ago, in my father's unit, some guys were sleeping under their trucks and when they moved out in the middle of the night they were run over."

"So, Captain, why don't you tell us again what we're going to be doing in sunny Iraq," Jonesy asked as Harris, decked out like a gunslinger from a cowboy picture, came over.

"What we're going to be doing," Coles said, "is testing some of the theories that the PSYOP people think will work. We'll go and smile and ask the people what they need and see how they react. They think they'll be slow to react because they don't want to get killed. But if they don't react right away and we're genuinely helpful to them, then we'll be able to keep them from the battle."

"And the 352nd? That's a whole battalion of Civil Affairs specialists," Marla said. "How come they're headed to Kuwait City instead of to Baghdad?"

"I promised the guys at the mall in Kuwait City I'd send them some business," Jonesy said. "So I sent the 352nd."

"Part four of the program is the most important part," Captain Coles said. "If we just go in and take out their weapons of mass destruction and their regime, then we're just tough guys. But if we go in there and take out their desire to fight us and help them build their own democracy, then we're heroes."

"That's the theory, anyway," Darcy said. She had cut her hair short and looked like a boy with her helmet off. "My great-grandmother doesn't care two figs for theories, so that's another thing I can't tell her."

"There's a lot of theory going on in this war," Coles said. "Theories about what we can do, how the equipment is going to stand up, and how the Iraqis are going to act. If it all works, then this is going to be a textbook war. The big brass doesn't want an established Civil Affairs unit to fail so we're like an advance scouting party. We're testing the water, so to speak."

It sounded good. I knew that Coles was sincere. He wanted to do well, to serve his country, but he didn't want to sound too gung ho.

We were up and mounted before daybreak and were on our way. We reached the border area at 0600 hours. There were hundreds of Kuwaiti soldiers and American engineers at the border. They had filled in the anti-tank traps and had made a path across the border into Iraq.

"From now on, every time you get into your vehicle you're going to be on high alert," Coles said through the radio hookup. "Combat locks on at all times. Don't let anybody approach your vehicle. Good luck."

I didn't feel anything special as we were waved into line to cross from Kuwait into Iraq. I remembered an orientation booklet the navy had passed around talking about how Iraq was known as the cradle of civilization. We were headed into Babylon and were excited.

"Yo, Birdy!" Marla's voice crackled in the intercom.

"What?"

"Check out that line of green on your left," she said.

Me and Jonesy looked over and saw some civilians laying something in a neat line on the ground. "What is it?" Jonesy asked.

"Body bags," Marla said. "Welcome to Iraq."

I could feel my heart beat faster as we crossed the border into Iraq. Marla's pointing out the body bags didn't help it slow down. We were still in convoy formation, with vehicles stretched out forever.

The way I understood it, the Marines were going in first, pushing aside any resistance. Then the 3rd Infantry Division came behind and secured the positions and established Lines of Communication. In some places they would switch and the 3rd ID would go in first and the Marines would follow. It was a kick-ass operation that ran by the numbers. Move in, take the position and establish a Forward Operating Base, then secure the Lines of Communication back to the jump-off point. That's what the sister with the 507th was doing, making sure that the Forward Operating Base was supplied.

"Piece of cake," Captain Coles said. "Just check off the boxes as you go along."

"We need to hook up the television set as soon as possible," Marla said. "So we can get the scores. So far I think it's the Coalition one, the Iraqis zero."

The breaks in traveling came at odd times; whenever anything was happening a mile or two up the road we stopped so we could all move as a unit. It was nearly seven thirty in the evening, and the sun had already gone down, when we were told to pull over and set up a bivouac area.

Marla made a big deal of setting up the television and even convinced Sergeant Harris to hold up the antenna. After turning the antenna around a bit we finally got CNN. They were interviewing a round-faced marine.

"I know we're facing a war on terror and we have to make sacrifices to overcome a determined foe and rid the world of weapons of mass destruction, and I'm willing to do my part . . ."

"If he said he was scared out of his mind he wouldn't get on television," Marla said.

"If they stick a camera in my face I'm going to say the same thing that marine said," Jonesy said. "I ain't never been on television before!"

The newscaster gave the name and city the marine was from. Then they switched to a newscaster who looked like he was on a balcony. There were explosions in the background and he was flinching as he tried to describe the scene.

"You think the bombs are hitting anybody?" Marla said. "I don't see any bodies laying around."

That was true. They were still talking about shock and awe and how many bombs were falling around Baghdad but they weren't showing any casualties. I didn't want to see any, either.

We had parked our Humvee off the road and bedded down around it. The night was hot and we were all sweating. I smelled something bad and thought it was Jonesy but then realized it was me. I thought about getting up and washing, but I was too tired.

■ ■ ■

"We're moving out!" Captain Coles was yelling into the tent. I heard him, but nothing he said made sense. Somehow I got into a vertical position, found the tent flap, and walked out into the brilliant desert morning. There was already a small line in front of the latrine tent so I trailed off toward the back of the squad tents and peed on the ground. I saw Harris across from me. He was making sure that everybody saw his business. Yeah. Sure.

We packed our gear, policed the area, and loaded our extra equipment into the supply vehicle. Jean Darcy came by carrying a plastic tray with her breakfast on it. I saw scrambled eggs, sausages, and potatoes.

"You like people?" she asked, looking up at me.

"Yeah, I guess," I said.

"Jerk!"

Strange chicks joined the army, I thought. Strange and strong.

I looked at my watch. It was only five o'clock. How could any-body be so pissed that early?

Captain Coles came by and told us that we were moving out in thirty minutes.

"You know where we're headed?"

"Dunkin' Donuts in Baghdad," he said.

I looked around for Darcy to tell her no, that I didn't like peo-ple. I didn't find Darcy, but I found Marla helping Jonesy adjust the straps of his vest.

"Hey, look at that sunrise," she said.

I looked to where she was nodding and saw the sun on the horizon and above it a thin red line that stretched endlessly in the distance. There was also sand, rising like a shadow with shift-ing shades of dark brown and orange, coming toward us. Cam-eras were brought out and guys stepped away from the trucks to get clear pictures.

"Jonesy, check this out!" Sergeant Harris called out. He had put a bayonet on the end of his weapon and was holding it up so that Jonesy could photograph him in profile. Sergeant Harris. American hero.

The sandstorm blew nearer and the sky suddenly darkened. The sand, swirling through the hot air, blocked out everything.

By the time the sand hit us it was coming from every direction. There was no place to turn. The fine grains stung my flesh and went into my nose, my mouth. I was breathing sand, inhaling sand, coughing, trying to spit.

"Get down! Cover up!" I recognized Major Sessions's voice. When had she shown up? I found a spot against the wheel of a Humvee and squatted. I thought about my goggles and tried to pull them down but my face was already covered with the fine grit and stinging in a thousand places.

Somebody yelled for us to cover our weapons. I got my goggles down and tried to open my eyes. There was sand on my eyelids; I thought I heard scratching as I opened and closed them.

We settled into the storm. We were not the winners. After the first few minutes of cowering near whatever stable object we could find, we just stayed put and hoped we would outlive it.

I did not want to be here. I thought of the places I could be: Harlem, Philadelphia, Chicago. I did not want to be in Iraq.

The sandstorm lasted two days. Two days of misery and wanting to die. When it ended we were all a mess. There was grit in every piece of gear and caked onto our skin.

"This crap doesn't even wash off!" Marla complained.

"God sent down some shock and awe and you guys folded," Jonesy said.

"And what did you do that was so great?" Captain Coles asked.

"I wrote a song," Jonesy said. "I call it 'I Hate Your Mother Worse Than I Hate This Sand Blues.' You want to hear it?"

Nobody wanted to hear it.

I rinsed my mouth out with a mixture of water and baking soda we got from the medical people. By the time I had done it three times and couldn't feel the grit in my mouth anymore, the squad had the television on.

We watched the news and found out the navy had sent more missiles into Iraq. Buildings exploded in flames and thick black smoke disappeared into the night skies over Baghdad.

In between the bombing coverage and the shots of ground targets being bracketed and then destroyed, there were images of cheering Iraqis.

"They know why we're here," Sergeant Harris said. "They probably don't know what it means to be really free, but they can sense it. You know what I mean?"

"Then again," Coles said, "if they weren't cheering, would they be on television?"

Marla's head snapped up and she looked at Captain Coles. I couldn't tell what she was thinking.

We spent hours cleaning the sand out of our gear, out of our ears, our weapons, our uniforms, and the Humvees. We had to test everything to see if it worked. Lieutenant Nelson, one of the intelligence guys, had an expensive camera and had tried to take photos of the sun through the sandstorm. His camera didn't work at all anymore; he spent an hour cursing at it.

■ ■ ■

We were back on the road headed north when we got the news about the first confirmed casualties. The 507th, the same crew we had talked to just before the dust storm, had bought it big-time.

"They had at least five killed and a bunch captured north of Highway One," Captain Coles said. "They got hit around some place called An Nasiriyah."

"How do you know some of them were captured?" I asked.

"They were on Al Jazeera, the Arabic station," Captain Coles said. "There were feeds to CNN, all the stations. The Iraqis have three of the women."

"Crap! We were just talking to them the other day," Jonesy said.

Marla exhaled heavily, blinked hard, and looked away from us.

This scared the living crap out of me. I thought about the women we met from the 507th and wondered if they were the ones who had been captured. I couldn't imagine someone pointing a weapon at me while I begged for my life. I couldn't think about it — that was all I thought about.

More news about the 507th trickled in. There were at least a half dozen killed, probably more.

At 1100 we were told to pull over to the side of the road, that we were standing down until further orders.

At 1130 we were told we might be moving back to Kuwait, to hook up with the 422nd Civil Affairs.

"What's going on?" Harris asked. I could see he was getting jumpy.

"The best laid plans of mice and men . . ." Captain Coles said. "CENTCOM is trying to figure out what happened to the 507th. They were supposed to be in a safe area. Now they're rechecking the Lines of Communication to figure out just what is safe and what's not."

"Was the 507th moving too fast?" Marla asked.

"I don't know, we'll have to check it out on the news."

Somebody had painted the television in the supply truck in desert camouflage colors. We took it out, hooked up an antenna, and tried to get the news. The only thing we got was static and some ghosts; some officers from the 3rd had a set that was working and they let us come and watch the news. We saw the captured guys from the 507th. They faced the television camera, but their eyes were looking around the room. They looked absolutely terrified.

"What are they looking at?" Marla asked.

It was what we were all thinking.

One of the soldiers, pale, wide-eyed, could hardly sit up. The Iraqis who held him kept asking him questions. The black woman who looked like Queen Latifah, who had been so funny when she was talking with us at the refueling station, was shaking. Her eyes were wide and darting around the room. My stomach tightened as she answered questions about where she was from in the States.

God, please don't let them be killed.

Somebody said it was chow time but Captain Coles came in and told us to mount up. "Eat something on the way if you can. We have orders to head toward An Nasiriyah," he said. "There's still a lot of heavy fighting going on there, but they want our Civil Affairs unit in place as quickly as possible. I don't think anybody anticipated POWs so early in the game."

"So we're going to look for them?" I asked.

"The theory is that if any Iraqis are going to give over the POWs, or tell us where we can find them, it'll probably be to somebody who is treating them decently," Coles said. "Hopefully, that'll be us. They're sending a Bradley with us for protection. I'll be briefed on the way. That kid Ahmed from Cleveland who speaks Arabic is going to ride with First squad, and you'll be right behind the Bradley. Stay in touch with each other and stay alert. Kennedy, you don't have to go if you don't want to."

"Bull!" Marla said.

Coles looked at her, then nodded and headed toward the Bradley.

We started moving out at 1315 hours. We took a position behind the Bradley fighting vehicle, a big tank-looking affair with a mounted cannon.

Ahmed, the interpreter, found us. He had been around but not hanging out with the regular troops. He was thin, dark-haired but light-skinned. He could have been Latino. He shook hands all around and Jonesy asked him how he had learned Arabic.

"My family is from Lebanon," he said with a shrug. "My grand-mother made me learn it."

An Nasiriyah was less than two hours north according to the maps. We started off and matched our speed with the Bradley. Second squad was behind us with two male medics. I wondered if the two women on the medical team had wanted to stay behind.

The day was white brilliant. Inside our vehicle we were quiet. We watched everything on the road. The road itself was a little wider than two lanes. Someone from the Bradley called back to us and told us that the shoulders were soft. Jonesy was riding right down the middle. Occasionally an Iraqi vehicle flew by and we could see the Bradley's big gun train on it.

As we neared An Nasiriyah, the traffic picked up. We were passing people in fields, some in carts. In the distance we heard the sounds of fighting. Automatic fire, big guns, explosions, and a steady chorus of small arms fire. Once in a while there would be a brief lull and then it would start again.

"Air support!" Marla called down. "Two o'clock! Twelve o'clock! Wow!"

Jonesy and I tried to look up out of the right window but the jets had already streaked by. They were really low and the boom made us all jump. I felt a pain in my hand and saw that I was clutching the door lock. I let it go and wiped my hand on my pants leg.

We rolled through the outskirts of An Nasiriyah and into a section of town. The low two-story buildings were painted white or pale green. Dark smoke bellowed from one of them; another was burning. The smell was terrible. I couldn't see any smoke near me but I knew it was all around, making it hard to breathe. Soldiers on the ground formed a ring behind a string of Humvees,

Bradleys, and some big trucks with what looked like communication gear. My heart was beating fast. I hoped I didn't look scared.

We stopped, got out, and moved to where Captain Coles was signaling us. He was standing next to an officer with white hair who reminded me of my homeroom teacher in high school. I saw the bird on his collar, which meant that he was a colonel.

"We're doing a house-to-house search in this area," the colonel said. He pointed toward the row of buildings directly in front of us. "This is a Shiite area, so they're mostly friendlies, but you can't be sure. Captain, get your medical people just to walk through. See if anybody needs first aid. Do a little smiling at them. They told our translators they didn't know anything about our POWs, but we're not going to leave much of a force here, so we need to win a few hearts and minds in a hurry."

The section they were searching was only about a hundred yards deep. Some guys from the 3rd said they had received fire from a rocket-propelled grenade from somewhere.

"So don't fall asleep!" a square-shouldered corporal said.

If we were scared, the Iraqis seemed even more terrified. Some of the men waved white rags in the air, showing they were surrendering. Most of these men were old. The women spoke to us in Arabic.

"Ahmed, what are they saying?" I asked.

"Mostly they're saying they don't want to fight," Ahmed said. "That they're not in the army. Some are saying 'Welcome to the Americans.'"

Me, Marla, and Jonesy got out of our Humvee and walked into the first building we came to with our weapons high, sweeping the rooms, checking for movement. We kicked in the doors, just as we did back in training. But in training I was just trying to get points for doing it right. Here I was holding my breath. Here I was trying not to tremble.

I couldn't tell if the house we were in was an apartment house or one family. It was neat. There were onions on the counter and a mesh bag with eggs. A magazine on the table had a picture of Oprah Winfrey on the cover with something written in Arabic under it. It was a nice picture of her, so I guessed it was an entertainment magazine.

"I got something! I got it!" a voice called out from down the hall. "Somebody get a translator!"

"Ahmed!" I called to him.

"Coming in!" Marla called as we approached the room to let the guy inside know who was carrying the weapon.

Marla went in first and then me and Ahmed. There were three people, an old woman, a boy younger than me, and an old man, sitting on a couch covered with what looked like an old sheet. A small girl stood at the end of the couch, her elbows on the armrest, her dark eyes watching us closely.

The guy from the 3rd, a big, thick-necked sergeant, was holding up a tube. It was an RPG launcher.

"Ask them who this belongs to!" the sergeant barked at me. Did I look like an Iraqi to him?

Ahmed asked the Iraqis and they all started talking at once. The sergeant was on his radio.

"They're saying it was their uncle's and it was here since the war with Iran," Ahmed said. "Nobody knows how to use it."

The sergeant repeated what Ahmed said into his radio. Marla took the tube and sniffed it. She handed it back to the sergeant and he sniffed it.

"Yeah, it's been recently fired!" the sergeant said.

We covered the two old people while the sergeant searched the young guy. I thought he might have been my age, maybe a year either way. He was babbling in Iraqi and broken English.

"I love America! I love America!" he was saying.

Another infantry guy came in and they began tearing the place apart looking for more weapons. The sergeant told us to shoot the kid if he moved.

The old woman started crying and pleading. Marla tried to calm her. Then she took off her helmet and the woman saw that Marla was a female. She tried to take her hand and kiss it. Marla didn't want the woman kissing her hand and tried to get her to sit down. The man, gray-haired and toothless, was babbling away. I felt as if I had to pee.

"He's saying that the boy is good, that he doesn't fight any-body," Ahmed said.

"You believe him?"

"They have the weapon," Ahmed said, with a shrug.

The woman stood up again.

"Sit down!" Marla said, indicating with her hand what she wanted the woman to do.

The woman's eyes widened and she got down on her knees.

Ahmed said something in Arabic that I guessed meant "sit down," but the woman got up and took a picture from the counter. She took it out of its frame and handed it to Marla. Her hands were shaking as she spoke in Arabic.

"She saying that he's her grandson and he's a good boy," Ahmed said when the old woman went on.

"Take him outside!" the sergeant snapped.

We started to take the boy and the grandmother let out a wail that filled the room. The old man fell to his knees and began to pray. The little girl began to wail, too. When the old man started to stand I pointed my rifle at him and he got back down on his knees and held his hands palm-up and began to pray again.

"Tell her we'll take care of her grandson," Marla said.

Ahmed began talking to the woman, who was tearing at her clothes and crying almost hysterically. When she saw Marla put the photograph down she got up and gave it back to her.

"She wants you to think of her because you are a woman," Ahmed said.

We started out and I told Marla to put her Kevlar back on. She was biting her lip, but she got it back on. The 3rd ID guys had the Iraqi kid by one wrist and his hair and took him outside. We reached the street and four or five other infantry guys jumped down from the truck they were on.

They pushed the kid down into the dirt as an officer came over. The sergeant who had found the launcher was explaining what had happened in the house, when a shot rang out.

A gunner on a Humvee spotted the shooter and opened up. The sniper was in a second-story window; I saw the rifle go spinning into the air and his arm fly up as he fell backward into the darkness of the room.

The kid on the ground jumped up and started to run.

The gunners' first bullets kicked up the dust near his feet. The next spun him completely around. The last knocked him backward.

Some 3rd ID guys headed toward the house where the shot had come from. Two heavily armed soldiers walked slowly toward the kid's body lying in the street. I didn't want to see him, but I couldn't help walking toward the still figure.

The boy's body was curled forward, head bent toward his knees. There was a dark stain on the front of his light blue shirt, a triangle of blood spread on the ground in front of him. One hand was closed and one opened, the fingers slightly spread. I felt myself holding my breath. I moved the muzzle of my weapon away from him. It was harder to move my eyes away.

The grandmother ran from the building. She looked heavier than she had in the apartment. Her mouth was open, a black hole in her gray, lined face. Her lips moved but there was no sound. She gestured toward the boy, took a tentative step to him, then stumbled forward and fell on her knees. She looked at him and then up at me. Her anguished eyes pleaded hopelessly. I walked away. Away from the house, away from the body, away from the grandmother. The buildings across the street, the soldiers moving cautiously past them, were unreal through my tears. It was a horror movie badly out of focus, with only the images in my head crystal clear.

We spent the rest of the afternoon in An Nasiriyah. Ahmed did some translating. We talked to some children who gathered around us, pointing at our weapons, waving to us. Some of them imitated us, walking the way they thought we walked. I guess we looked funny to them in our desert camouflage, Kevlar helmets, and Molle vests.

Were they so used to the killing that they could go on with their lives so easily? Did the wailing of the woman for her grandson seem too familiar to them? They were only kids, for God's sake.

The children either wore American-type clothes or long shirts that came down to their ankles. Some spoke to me in Arabic. I forced smiles but my mind was in chaos. The sight of the dead boy had scared me, as had the walking away from him. I looked over at the small crowd of Iraqis gathered around the body. They were wrapping him in cloth.

Some 3rd ID guys came over to where I was standing with some candy and started passing it out.

"They're like all kids," the guy next to me, a stocky sergeant with a southern accent, said. He offered me the box.

"Yeah." I took the box.

"You get used to the killing." He said the words softly. "It don't help much at night when you're trying to sleep, but you get used to it."

March 25, 2003

Dear Uncle Richie,

I'm writing this letter but I probably won't mail it. I probably won't save it, either. Today I saw a stranger die. I saw what the M-16s could do. I don't know why the kid started to run. Maybe he was afraid. But what happened was that he was killed, and we left him lying on the ground. At first I was really sad, depressed. Then I felt myself trying to shut it out. I started by telling myself that he was probably one of the guys who wanted to kill Americans, but that was a dead-end street. It just didn't work. What works is to put it outside of you. To let it be not part of who you are. I know I won't ever be able to talk about it. I wonder if that is the reason you never talked about anything that happened in Vietnam.

On the way back to our base I saw that Jonesy's hand was shaking. Nothing else, just his hand. I thought about putting my hand on his, but I didn't. None of us in First Squad talked about what had happened.

The medical truck was all goodness. So were the medics who deal with Civil Affairs. They put out white tables and took out boxes of supplies. All the Iraqis recognized what was going on and started edging forward.

"You know what they have over here that they don't have at home?" Marla asked me as she leaned against the fender of the Humvee. Her hip was touching mine.

"Arabs?"

"Lame people," she answered. "Most of them look all right, but you see a lot of people with birth defects and things they would have taken care of in the States."

She was right. There were more crippled people and blind people in Kuwait and Iraq than I had ever seen at home. For many of the Iraqis it would be the only medical treatment they'd ever get. The two guys and two women doing the medical stuff treated anything, from chest colds to rashes. It was weird. On one side of the square, there were people washing the ground where the kid was killed. On the other side our medics were looking at sores and passing out antibiotics.

And there were some Iraqis who just stood silently.

The kids began to get over their shyness once they saw adults talking to the medical people. They surrounded us, pulling at our gear, asking for candy, sometimes just trying to touch us. One kid had on a Derek Jeter Yankees T-shirt. I liked that.

I kept my eyes away from the house we had searched. Over and over I told myself that the kid had used the rocket launcher, that he had tried to kill Americans. Maybe he even had already killed Americans, and he was the enemy. In a way I was cool with that. In my head I could deal with his being dead. But it had all happened so quickly. One moment he was alive and he was scared, as I was scared with him and for him. And then he was dead. I had never been that close to anyone who was killed. I had heard the boy talking, had seen his dark eyes darting around the room. Then I saw his body jerking in the dusty street, as if he had already been separated from it. I wanted not to think.

Marla was back up in the gunner's turret and I headed back to the Humvee.

"Yo, Marla, how you doing?" I asked.

"If you see a bus schedule for Dix Hills, Long Island, save it for me," she said. "I'm ready to leave this mother."

"Tell me about it."

We weren't going home, of course. We were still wandering northward toward Baghdad. We weren't at the front of the action and I was glad of that, but there was enough going on where we were to keep us on our toes.

"Who's supposed to be the bad guys here?" Jonesy asked as he slipped behind the wheel of the Humvee. "We got people standing around looking like civilians one minute and then the next they're pulling heat from their closets."

What I wanted, more than anything else, was to go to bed. I felt more tired than I could imagine, as if my very bones were drained of marrow. Captain Coles came over and said that we were changing direction. He seemed jumpy, too. Darcy was with him.

"Where we going?" Jonesy asked.

"The 204th Medical called asking for some help south of An Najaf," Coles said. "That's about a hundred and some miles northeast of here. There was some heavy fighting and the Infantry suffered a number of wounded and a half-dozen KIAs. Their medical unit is dealing with the infantry and the worst of the wounded Iraqis. They want us to deal with some of the minor wounds of the Iraqis."

"We going to do it?" I asked, instantly knowing that we would.

Coles looked at me, then pivoted sharply and walked away.

The medical team attached to us consisted of two physician's assistants, one male and one female, and two technicians. They seemed okay, dedicated really, and they worked well with the Iraqi women and kids. They hauled along a trailer behind their Humvee, and I watched as they loaded up.

"We're moving too fast," Marla said. "How the heck can we fly past these villages and just leave them as if they're not Iraqis and we're not invading their country?"

"I bet this all looks good on paper," Jonesy said.

I asked Marla if she wanted me to take a turn on the squad gun.

"Don't get careless," she answered. She took a drink from her water bottle and swallowed hard.

My throat was dry, too. The water was warm but it felt good in my mouth as I settled down behind the machine gun. I shook my shoulders to loosen up. I wasn't afraid when we were moving. It was a different feeling when we were out of the vehicle and roaming around the villages.

Second squad, with Ahmed along to interpret, was going to lead the way with the medical team next, and then us. The whole route was supposed to be under control of the 3rd. I could only hope it was. Our little convoy of four vehicles took off. Darcy popped up in the Two Squad gun position and waved. Jonesy measured the distance in time between vehicles and eased onto the open road.

I felt vulnerable in the turret, as if every gun had an eye on the end of it that was looking for me. I felt ashamed of what I was thinking.

I wanted my mind on the road and what was happening around me. I turned sideways, trying to see if anything was coming behind me. I kept the gun sights moving along the building lines. We passed one low building with tables and chairs and men eating and drinking. They pointed at us as we passed, and when I pointed the gun at them, one of them opened his shirt as if to dare me to fire at him.

I reminded myself of my mission in Iraq. I was defending America from its enemies, removing weapons of mass destruction from Iraq, and building democracy. If the jerks drinking tea didn't appreciate that, I didn't care.

We drove with as much speed as we could. I was really sorry that I had volunteered to relieve Marla on the squad gun because it was uncomfortable as anything I could imagine. My legs were aching as we drove north along the Euphrates River. The 3rd had set up roadblocks along the way and I was glad to see them. They had put MPs, military police, at some of the places on the roads: It was reassuring to know we were at least going in the right direction.

Occasionally we hit traffic, mostly supply trucks headed in the same direction we were or empty trucks headed south to pick up more supplies. The traffic worried me because I didn't want to get separated from our convoy.

I expected we would pull into An Najaf, find something to eat, and sit around for the rest of the night in whatever facilities they had set up. But as we approached the city, I knew that wasn't going to happen.

The noise from the fighting was unbelievable. If you listened you could tell what was firing. AK-47s, M-16s, mortars, tanks, grenades. All kinds of ways to die in a hurry.

"We're holding up here!" Coles yelled into the radio.

We pulled the Humvee off the road. We were less than a half mile from town. Black smoke billowed up above the buildings and then flattened out and drifted sharply to the east. Bursts of automatic fire came and went, as if there were some dialogue between them that nobody understood. In training I used to like the night exercises. We used tracer bullets along with our regular ammo and you could see them streaking across the darkness toward their targets. But here, so many miles from home, in the gathering darkness, the explosions were terrifying. From where I sat, I could sometimes feel the impact of a shell, feel the shock of an explosion as it traveled through the still night air. I was holding my breath.

Beneath me, in the cab of the Humvee, the radio crackled. We were picking up the communications from the battlefield. Men spoke with a quiet urgency. Tracer fire crisscrossed the city. Brilliant flashes of light illuminated buildings for mere seconds before dying out. I could smell what seemed like oil burning and a sickly sweet odor I couldn't identify.

"Birdy!" Marla pulled on my pants leg.

"What?"

"If you go into town, bring back a sausage pizza and two Diet Cokes," she said.

"I don't think I'm going in any time soon," I said. "You think they'll deliver?"

Coles confirmed it. He told us to hunker down and stay alert. "And keep your body armor on!"

We stayed put all night, taking turns sleeping, or trying to sleep. Jonesy conked out first. Marla worked on eating an MRE in the dark. She said she could smell the whole meal, dry and cold, through the packing.

"Marla, you can't smell it through the packing," I said. "What is it?"

"I can even tell you what kind of cookies they have for dessert," she said.

"I don't believe you," I said.

She shrugged me off and told me to stay alert. I asked her who made her the squad's mama and she laughed. It was a nice laugh.

At ten o'clock in the morning, 1000 hours military time, Captain Coles called to say we were moving out. Marla was outside of the Humvee stretching her legs and had to scramble back in.

"I'm back on the gun," she said.

As we rolled toward the city we could still hear sporadic gunfire. There were lots of our guys around, and down the street a tank stood guard on the corner. Coles called back to us and asked if our map had street names and Jonesy told him that it didn't. I could hear Coles cursing into the radio.

"Contact left!" Marla called out.

I turned left and saw a green car speeding toward us. The Humvee came to a hard stop; I heard the squad guns as they sent bursts of fire toward the oncoming vehicle. The car skidded to a halt and fishtailed slightly; the front wheels ended up on the sidewalk. The doors opened and a group of civilians climbed out, keeping their hands in sight.

"Watch 'em!" Captain Coles's voice came over the radio.

"Contact right! Contact right!" Sergeant Harris.

Panic. We were situated at the end of a long street. On the left the car had stopped. On the right dark figures skirted along the shadows.

The flash of the rocket launcher spread out in a puff and I

could see the rocket trail headed toward the middle of the street. It hit two-thirds short and sent flame first in the air and then rolling toward us. I couldn't see anyone, but I knew where they had been and started firing.

Somebody shot off some grenades and they exploded, lighting up the area they hit for the split second needed to produce eerie silhouettes.

Whack! Whack! Bullets hit the side of the Humvee. I couldn't tell who was shooting at us, but I knew they were coming close. We sprayed the street in front of us and the nearby windows.

There was an explosion behind us and the Humvee lifted off the ground for a second.

"Mortar, right corner!"

I looked toward the right corner and saw two figures. They were carrying a house fan on a stand, not a mortar.

Silence.

"Check the buildings!" Coles's voice was urgent and higher than usual.

My eyes were everywhere, jerking around as I pointed my piece from area to area. "Marla, you okay?" I called to her.

"I think so." Her voice was whispery.

"You sure?" Jonesy asked.

"I'm not shot, so I guess I'm okay," Marla said.

We lit up the area and saw two bodies lying in the street on my side of the vehicle. The car that had been speeding toward us still rested with its wheels on the sidewalk.

"Everybody okay?" asked Captain Miller in the medical truck.

Everybody checked in. When it was my turn my voice cracked badly.

One of the medics had a head injury from his vehicle being rocked by an explosion, but it didn't seem too serious.

"What do we do about them?" a voice came over the radio. "One of them is still alive out there. I see him moving."

He was on my side of the street. Jonesy got back behind the wheel, backed the vehicle up, and moved slowly toward the guy.

"Marla!"

"I'm on him!" she said.

Harris was out of his Humvee, moving toward the guy. He crouched low with his rifle ahead of him.

I remembered Ahmed and was about to ask Captain Coles to get him to talk Arabic to the wounded man when the guy swung his arm up. There was a pistol in it.

The gunman shot wildly, almost as if he wasn't trying to hit us, just making one last defiant statement. Harris shot him more times than necessary. The body had stopped moving with the first shot.

Second squad policed the long end of the street, collecting some weapons from the smashed car. I watched them search the dead dudes. Yuk. We got back in what amounted to a little formation and headed on.

The tension was unbelievable. I couldn't keep my head still. It was almost daybreak and every shadow looked as if it had a gun.

Captain Coles put himself on intercom as he tried to contact the unit we were looking for. He gave our position and in minutes a Bradley appeared to pick us up and lead us to their medical setup.

We reached a café being used as a makeshift hospital for wounded Iraqi civilians. The medics came out and I saw that Owens, who was with the medics, had a bandage on her forehead. A sergeant from the 3rd ID came over and asked if she was all right.

"Just a helluva bump," she said.

"Then get your damned Kevlar back on," he said. "And do it now!"

The medic shot him a dirty look, and then gingerly put the helmet over Owens's bandage. There were wounded civilians, men, women, and children, in the café. The worst off were on stretchers along the wall and our medical people looked at them. We were told to search everybody. The guys searched the males, and Marla and the female medics searched the women. They didn't have weapons.

Only one person had been shot. All the others had either been burned or hit with shrapnel or flying debris. A thin brown man, bald on top, looked closest to dying but had no visible wounds except for a few spots of blood under his nose. An Iraqi who spoke English said that the man had been sitting on a folding chair when a shell hit down the street and the shock of it had picked him up off his chair and thrown him against a wall.

Some of the other wounds were terrible. An old man was lying in a corner on his back. He had a string of beads draped across his palm. His hand and the beads shook uncontrollably. The front of his robe was covered with more blood than anybody was supposed to lose. When the beads fell from his hand I bent over, picked them up, held his wrist, and draped them over his fingers. The old man looked up at me. I don't know if he could see me clearly or not, but he looked.

"Birdy, give me a hand," Marla called.

She had a little girl, maybe eight or nine, whose leg was bloodied. We carried her over to the aid station our people had set up and laid her on the ground. The front of the little dress she was wearing, it might have been her nightgown, was covered with blood. Marla lifted it to see if the girl was hurt bad. She was. An angry wound seeped blood diagonally across her small chest.

None of it was good. I didn't want to be connected with the wounds, or with the dying. It all looked so much better in the training films, when the figures were just silhouettes flickering across a screen. When it was all just a video game. But up close, the smell of blood was connected with real people. I knew that many of them wouldn't make it. They would be dead before the night came, or surely by the next morning.

Then it was noon and somebody said that the 3rd was serving hot food down the street. There was still the sound of sporadic gunfire, but it seemed farther away. I looked for Marla and Jonesy and asked if they wanted to go get something to eat. Jonesy did but Marla wanted to help the medics. I thought of staying, too, but I went for breakfast instead.

We lined up with the guys from the 3rd, had scrambled eggs and sausages. The military cooks were actually using a local Iraqi guy to help them. Me and Jonesy sat down and ate. We took some eggs and coffee back to Marla. Her face was pale with the strain of the work. She ate the eggs on the edge of a cot in which an Iraqi woman was lying. The woman, dressed in black, was facing the wall.

"She okay?" I asked Marla.

"What do you think?" she answered.

■ ■ ■

The portable toilet facilities stunk and the small cabin was filled with tiny flies that bit my butt. But it was the sounds of incoming mortars that shook me the most.

"Hey, man, you could be sitting under a tree and if a mortar hits you it's all over," Jonesy had said.

At first I thought that I just didn't want to die with my pants down around my ankles. Then I realized that it was the noise, the constant booming, that just filled my guts with a trembling sensation. I knew if I heard the boom I was safe because whatever had exploded hadn't hit me. But it was the idea that at any moment it could be all over, that I could be dead or lying in the sand twisting in agony, that filled me with a terror that I hadn't known before. Terror. It wasn't just being scared. It was a feeling that was taking me over. I knew it but I hoped no one else saw it.

When I came out I saw Jonesy drinking a bottle of water. He had his Kevlar pushed back and the water up to his lips. He held a thumb up to me as I approached.

"How you doing?" I asked.

"Keeping on, bro," he said. He pulled another bottle of water from his vest and handed it to me. "Captain Coles just got chewed out."

"Captain Coles?"

"A Third ID guy jumped all over him, man. Chewed him up one side and down the other. The guy seemed so pissed I thought he was gonna shoot him."

"What happened?" The water was cold and delicious. I poured some in my palm and wiped my face with it.

"Somebody said that we had to take prisoners up to PSYOP to be interviewed and the captain said we weren't messengers," Jonesy said. "I guess he was wrong."

I didn't dig the PSYOP guys too much. The ones I had met thought that being in Psychological Operations meant that they were smarter than everybody else. They might have been, but they didn't have to act like it. I had seen the leaflets they dropped over Iraq and the ones they handed out wherever we went. Most were threats with English on one side and Arabic on the other. If you shoot at us we'll kill you, and if you're friendly we'll help you build a new nation — that kind of thing.

"If it was up to me I wouldn't be taking them no place," he said. "Not after that scene." He half lifted his empty water bottle to point to a place behind me.

I looked to see what he was talking about and saw guys putting the bodies of dead soldiers into a truck. Four men were taking the dead, two soldiers to each body bag, past the others who were standing at attention. The bodies seemed light as they loaded the litters into the back of the truck. A heavy Iraqi woman, dressed all in black, glanced at the operation, then hurried down the street. In a narrow street, small brown kids stood against the walls and watched. I wondered what they were thinking.

"It's tough to go down so far from home," I said.

"My moms couldn't take that," Jonesy said. "That would kill her faster than it would kill me."

A image of my mom, sitting at our kitchen table in Harlem, flashed through my mind. If I were killed she would cry, I knew. It would hurt her so much, and as I stood watching the ritual of gathering the dead, I felt sorry for her. I knew what Jonesy was saying, that the dying hurt everybody.

I wondered what my father would think. Would he blame me for dying? Would he say I should have listened to him? I wanted to talk to him so bad. There wasn't anything special I had to say, just that I thought what he wanted for me was okay. Maybe that I loved him. I took out my pen and started to write a note to myself to tell my parents that I loved them. It was BS. The part about reminding myself.

There were three prisoners. Second Squad took two of them and we took one, an old man. He was nearly bald, with patches of woolly hair on the sides of his head turning white. He was the same color as me, too. Thin, square-shouldered, slightly stooped, the old man looked too small to be considered dangerous. He was scared of us. He tried to smile but only showed a small row of bad teeth.

Ahmed rode with us. Third Squad took the point, we were next, and Second Squad followed us.

"Stay close and stay in contact." Captain Coles was subdued. He had had his ass handed to him by the officer from the 3rd ID and it showed.

We mounted up and moved out. I got the map coordinates for the FOB and went over them with Jonesy. He asked Marla if she wanted to drive and she said no.

"I want to be up so I can see what's going on," she said. "And if I'm up there I don't have to make small talk with you dudes."

Good. Marla was coming back.

The prisoners' hands were held together with plastic strips. The two prisoners in the other Humvee had cloths over their heads but ours didn't.

"Hey, Ahmed, ask him why he was doing whatever he was doing," Jonesy said.

Ahmed said something to the guy but there was no answer.

Ahmed hit him in the forehead with the heel of his hand, snapping his head back, and the guy looked first startled, then angry. My rifle was between my legs and I turned slightly so that it was pointed at him.

The old man spoke in Arabic and I looked at Ahmed. Ahmed asked something and the guy answered. His voice was soft and he talked with his head down. I wanted him to speak louder even though I didn't understand Arabic.

"What's he saying?" Jonesy asked.

"He's saying that he's been a good man all of his life," Ahmed replied. "He's made his Hajj and does God's will. He says he's an old man and doesn't know why we want to kill him."

"Why are we taking him instead of some of the others?" Jonesy asked.

Ahmed talked to the man again. This time his voice softened and I wondered what he was saying, because whatever it was changed Ahmed's attitude toward him. Ahmed had just rapped the old guy in the forehead, but now I could definitely hear a change in his voice.

The man answered, then looked away out of the window. He was looking at a road he had probably traveled all of his life. Past familiar rocks, past a burned-out building, maybe even past people he knew.

"He says that the Americans found an AK-47 in his house," Ahmed translated. "He said it was a Russian gun that he bought years ago to protect himself. He says he wanted to protect himself from robbers, and he didn't expect Americans to come to kill him."

"Tell him we didn't come to kill him," I said. "That we're trying to build a democracy over here."

"You bombed my village," the old man, his head down, replied slowly in English. "First you shoot into my house, then you come to the door."

"Where you learn to speak English?" Jonesy asked.

"I drove a cab in London for twelve years," answered the old man. "When I had enough money to buy a house for my family, I came back to my country."

"You're going to be all right," Jonesy said. "We don't hurt our prisoners."

"My house had holes in the walls," the old man said. "I am away from my family. Is this all right?"

"Your ass could be dead," said Jonesy.

We drove the next miles in silence.

It was all pretty confusing. We had been attacked. The guys who had fired on us didn't know us, and we didn't know them. I thought of them getting up in the morning and having their breakfast. Perhaps they had talked about the war. Perhaps they had imagined themselves fighting heroically against us. Now they were dead and the meaning of it was somewhere in the thin smoke that rose over the buildings.

There were lots of vehicles on the road: Bradleys, big trucks, all headed north. We passed Iraqis going about their business on the highway. Some of them just stood by the side of the road, watching us. There was a man and a boy on a cart piled high with old furniture, being pulled by a donkey. We passed a tank that had a sign on its side: JOHN 13:15. I asked Jonesy what it meant; he didn't know.

We reached a command post set up in a private house. An MP took the old man from us and put a hood over his head before leading him away. I hoped they were going to treat him gently.

The 3rd, according to Captain Coles, was headed toward Tallil Airport, which was southeast of us.

"Yo, Captain, is the Third leaving a couple of companies when they take over a place to make sure it stays safe?" Jonesy asked. "They moving so fast they're going to have one dude left when they reach Baghdad."

"That's the point," Captain Coles said. "Hit hard and hit fast."

"Yeah, all that's good on paper, sir," Jonesy said. "But one time I hit a guy hard and fast and knocked his tooth out. Then he commenced to kick my butt long enough for him to have to take a lunch break."

What I thought was bothering Jonesy, and what was definitely messing with my mind, was that it was hard to tell who the enemy was, and with our soldiers moving from place to place so quickly, it was getting hard to tell where our friends were, too.

We picked up a new Intelligence officer, Captain Phil Nelson, and two other Intelligence types. We were supposed to go from the FOB, which was nothing but a few tents in the sand, to a mining area about fifteen to twenty miles away.

"Is this a hot zone?" Captain Coles stood close to Nelson as he spoke.

"That's what we're going to find out," Captain Nelson said. He was short with a huge round head and big blue eyes that made him look like a baby in uniform. "This place has been inspected by the United Nations a hundred times, but what I'm hoping for is that we can find some civilians who can give us a feel for the area, let us know if they're glad we're knocking over Saddam."

"Any friendlies there now?" Coles asked.

"A marine detachment," Nelson said. "They're telling us it's safe for us to go in."

"You're looking for civilians; do you speak Iraqi?"

"I speak Arabic," Nelson said, looking about as white as a human being could look.

The Intelligence guys supposedly knew where they were going and would lead the way with Second Squad. Captain Coles rode with us. Inside the Humvee the captain was mumbling to himself.

"Something we should know?" Jonesy asked.

"The chain of command is getting weak," Coles said. "If you listen to the air traffic, you hear a lot of people trying to find out where their units are."

"I thought they were hitting fast and hard?" Marla chimed in.

"If you're in a fight and you're winning, it's fine," Captain Coles said. "But if something looks fishy and you need some backup in a hurry, it would be good to know where the cavalry is."

"And the way I figure it, you can never tell when you're going to need some backup in a hurry," I said.

"This reminds me of when they started a happy hour in a bar in my hometown," Jonesy said. "It was a colored bar and they ain't never had a happy hour. Some folks thought they was gonna get free drinks. When they found out that they had to buy a drink to get a free one they got to fighting and tore the place up. That's what's happening over here. They don't know if they should be getting happy or tearing us up."

Marla was on the squad gun and I tapped her knee to get her attention as Jonesy pulled the Humvee out onto the road. I thought she might be tired. She kicked me with the back of her heel.

"Yo, Marla, I'm a friendly!" I called to her.

"Mess with my leg again and I'll shoot you through the top of your head," she answered.

"Yo, Jonesy, is Marla weird or what?" I asked.

"Hey, man, we all weird," Jonesy said. "Or do you always do drive-bys in the name of democracy?"

We were going south again to meet up with a company from the 3rd ID. Captain Coles had the GPS system going and was comparing the coordinates on the screen with our maps. That made me feel a little better because there weren't any map landmarks that I recognized. There were some American military trucks on the road, mostly supply units, and a few British units. There were Iraqi vehicles as well, older trucks and an occasional overcrowded bus. Captain Coles started talking about what was probably going on in his hometown and we figured out that the time difference was eight hours.

"It's three in the afternoon here and back home they're just getting up," he said.

"Contact ahead, they're moving to one side!" Marla's voice was crisp, hard.

I felt myself tensing. For a moment I closed my eyes, then realized what I was doing, and opened them again. I felt my hand sweating and wiped it on my pants leg.

Please, God, don't let me do anything stupid.

"What do you think?" Captain Coles asked.

The first two Humvees had already passed an old wagon. Its right side was broken down and it leaned precariously. One of the Iraqis was unhitching the two old mules that had been pulling it, while two other men argued with each other.

"They don't look like hostiles, sir," I said.

"Keep moving, Jonesy," Coles said.

Jonesy had slowed to a crawl, and started edging along the left side of the road when the wheels started slipping. There were a number of curses as the Humvee slid along the shoulder and into the marshy area.

Jonesy revved up the engine and tried to get us out. Nothing.

The other Humvees slowed when they saw us stop. Coles got on the radio and told them what was going on. The Humvee in front of us stopped sixty yards down the road and Second Squad backed up for security behind us.

"Keep your eyes open, Marla," Jonesy said.

Jonesy frantically spun the wheels, but the Humvee just slid deeper into the marsh. Coles got off the radio and started cursing again. He was really good at it, too.

"Nobody's got a tow chain," he said. "If they try to push us out we'll all be stuck here."

I got out and sank into a foot of warm, stinky mud. It smelled like human waste; I wanted to gag. I slogged my way up to the road until I was on solid ground. Captain Coles came out next. Jonesy and Marla followed, sinking thigh deep in the slop.

"What the hell we going to do?" Jonesy asked. "No way I'm walking back."

"We'd have to destroy the vehicle if we left it," Captain Coles said. "Let me try to get it out. Keep an eye on our guests."

There were three Iraqi men, two young guys and an older man. They were looking under the wagon and pointing.

Captain Coles got into the Humvee, turned on the engine, and we watched as the back end of it slipped even farther. The Iraqi men started talking to one another and one of them climbed onto the wagon.

Jonesy and I had our M-16s ready and I stepped a few feet away from him. The Iraqi that had climbed into the wagon, one of the younger guys, came out with a rope. He started our way.

None of us spoke Arabic, so we had to figure out that he meant to tie a rope to the Humvee and pull it out of the marsh.

"We could call back to the base and get another vehicle out here with towing equipment in a half hour or so," I said.

"Or whoever is watching us could get a vehicle of Arabs over here in five or ten minutes," Jonesy said. "We'd be sitting ducks on foot. There's nothing to get behind."

I smiled at the Iraqis, or at least pushed my face forward into what I hoped looked like a smile, and reached for the rope.

The Iraqi held his hands up and then started toward the Humvee. The other young guy went out into the goo with them and I remembered the box of grenades we had left behind in the Humvee. Wonderful.

The two men left their sandals on the road, lifted their long shirts, and waded through the mud to the back of the Humvee. They found the tow hook and tied the rope to it, and then held the rope high while they came back onto the road.

Then the oldest Iraqi went and got the mules.

"Birdy, this is embarrassing!" Marla said as the guy tied the rope around the mules' halter.

"Gahhh!" he yelled. The mules started to pull.

Jonesy got behind the wheel and started the engine.

A few more Iraqis, two older guys, and a woman with three children stopped to look. One of the men was hollering out something and trying to show Jonesy which way to turn the wheel. It took fifteen minutes before the Humvee cleared the mud.

We thanked the Iraqis and offered them ten bucks in American money, but they turned it down. There was a lot of smiling and bowing and I could see that the Iraqis were pleased with themselves. Here we were, the conquering heroes stuck in the mud, and here they were, rescuing us.

Back in the Humvee we were very embarrassed and smelled like dog crap. Marla cleaned her hands with disinfectant gel and wiped them off on me. The Iraqis cheered us as we started off.

We reached Shuyukh, the place we were supposed to be, and found the other squads.

Sergeant Harris came over and, as soon as he got a whiff of us, stopped and backed off two steps.

"Man, y'all smell baaad!"

"Shut up, Sergeant," Captain Coles snapped. He was trying to wipe the bottom of his fatigues off with hand wipes.

Harris went back to the other squads and soon they were all around us, offering helpful comments about personal hygiene. Jean Darcy asked us if we had some kind of secret weapon.

"We're in the same unit, so if you got something good you should share it," she said. "I think you're like clouding the enemy's mind or something with that stench."

Marla blamed the whole thing on Jonesy.

"I can't handle the turret, lead the way, and drive at the same time," she said.

"You could at least change them when they make poo poo in the pants," Jean said.

Captain Coles tried to smile but couldn't.

We were at the Shuyukh site for an hour, while the Intelligence guys talked to some locals. I found out they were looking for weapons of mass destruction and this was one of the suspected sites. They didn't find any weapons of mass destruction, but they did find a crate of American cigarettes.

On the way back to the base the stink got worse and Captain Coles said we had better wash good. "Maybe even get antibiotics or something," he said. "God only knows what we were wading through."

When we hooked up with the guys from the 3rd we found it was the Signal detachment. They had trucks full of communication gear as well as dozens of portable generators. We were given a choice of what we could do. We could go back to the bivouac area that the headquarters element of the 3rd ID had set up outside of An Nasiryah that night, or the first thing in the morning.

None of us could stand the smell any longer so we decided to stay the night.

Field showers are usually cold but the water had been warmed enough by the sun to make these all right. I washed and thought about what my mom would have said if she had seen us being pulled out of the marsh. I was sure she would have laughed.

"Yo, Birdy, you know all this part of the world is in the Bible?" Jonesy asked.

"If you say so." I was on the ground with my gear under my head.

"You go to church back home?" he asked.

"Sometimes. You?"

"My father's a minister," he said. "But I don't go."

Jonesy had a portable radio and turned it on. He put it on his chest but was soon asleep and the radio fell off. When he rolled over on it, I thought he would wake up. He didn't. It had been that kind of a day.

April 4, 2003

Dear Dad and Mom,

Things are going well here. We have met very little resistance. The Infantry guys and the Marines are catching it a little but my unit is still cool. I think we are helping the Iraqis, but even more than that, I think we are showing them that Americans are good people, and that we don't want to hurt them.

Iraq is weird — kind of an odd mix with old stuff and new. Some of the cities look as if everything was built a few months ago, but other places could be directly out of the Old Testament. I guess that sounds silly because I don't know what the world looked like during the Old Testament, but it's what I imagine.

We did have some people take a few shots at us but nobody in our unit was injured. When the Iraqis shoot at Americans, there is a terrible price for them to pay because what we have to shoot back with is overwhelming. The only problem is that it is hard to know who the bad guys are or if there are really any bad guys. I don't know what it will be like later on. It depends, I guess. If they respect us and accept democracy, then everything will turn out all right. I heard a guy from one of the infantry units say that this is a camel-tank war. They have the camels and we have the tanks. The whole thing should be over soon, which is good.

I will try to get copies of pictures to send to you. There are reporters everywhere. They are allowed to come along on the missions and even film in combat zones. They let the Arabic newspeople come along, too. There are a lot of ways of looking at what is happening over here, I guess.

Mom, Dad, I love you both very much and miss you as well. Your son, Robin.

P.S. This girl in our squad, Marla Kennedy from Long Island, calls me Birdy, and now everyone is calling me Birdy. I don't mind, though.

April 12, 2003

Dear Uncle Richie,

It's over! I didn't think I would be so relieved, but I am. Everybody here is celebrating. We rolled into Baghdad early this morning and people on the street were waving to us. Whoa! It's like winning the Super Bowl or something. We picked up a Marine escort and they asked us if we wanted to go to Firdos Square, which is like the main square in Baghdad, I guess. We said yes, of course, and they took us to where the statue of Saddam was torn down.

We're bunking down in an office building. It had air conditioning before the war but the electrical system is down big-time. Jonesy found something that looks like a guitar but an Iraqi called it an oud. Jonesy is trying to play the blues on it.

We're all kind of relaxed. There were casualties, but none as bad as what I thought might happen. I think the 4th Marines took the most hits. There is talk that they had more guys killed than the papers or television mentioned. Some guys from the 4th came here to pick up Quick Clot bandages. They said it wasn't for them, but for some of the Kurdish fighters from the north. To tell the truth, you can't tell the players over here without a scorecard. There are Iraqis all over the place — it is their city and everything, but who knows what they are thinking. I asked Ahmed if the Iraqis are really glad we're here and kicked out Saddam. He said he couldn't tell because they were afraid of him. Him and us, too. I guess.

I think they were glad to see us. Otherwise wouldn't they have fought more? I don't know how many Iraqis were killed or wounded. They don't count them except in the After Action reports, and then I think it's more of a guess than anything because a guy in the 3rd said that the Iraqis always drag away their bodies. I know they could have fought more because we are finding huge amounts of shells, ammo, and stuff. Some of it's old and nobody is paying much attention to it but there's tons of the stuff around.

There's looting going on, too. Guys with wheelbarrows piled high with furniture, office machines, and anything else that isn't nailed down.

Anyway, I'm sure everybody at home is glad the war is over. Yesterday (or the day before, I couldn't tell) the Iraqi 5th Corps formally surrendered. There are rumors that we could be going home within two weeks. I think we'll have to serve a full six months before they start rotating us back. I just hope they start counting the six months from the time we first landed in Kuwait.

I wanted to write to Dad and tell him about the war being over but he is still acting sour about me being in the army. I received the letter Mom wrote and he added a note that only said that he was glad I was safe. I bet Mom told him to add that. It's funny, but one of the reasons I'm glad that I didn't get killed or wounded or anything was that I didn't want Dad to say "I told you so."

Good-bye for now — Robin

P.S. Another rumor is that they have found a mountain of poison gas canisters and some other suspicious material. I guess those are the weapons of mass destruction that everyone was talking about.

"Yo, Captain Coles!" Jonesy spotted Coles coming down the wide lane behind the main buildings.

Captain Coles turned in our direction and then headed toward us. He had a smile on his face and I knew that he understood how pissed we were. We were at some Iraqi military school not far from Rasheed Airport. The school was modern and only had a little damage from the invasion. But they had brought in Port-O-Potties and lined them up in the school's courtyard and our First Squad was painting them. The other CA Squads were off except for a little work they were doing in the sleeping area because they were going to be on patrol in the evening.

"Jonesy, you're doing a good job," Coles said.

"Sir, I don't want to be doing no good job," Jonesy said. "I'm supposed to be a warrior, not painting outhouses."

"They're inspecting the sewer system for hidden weapons and

bombs," Captain Coles said. "As soon as they make sure they're safe, and operative and secure, we can abandon the outdoor toilets."

"This is big-time wrong, Captain," Jonesy said. "Big-time wrong."

The real deal was that the guys from the 3rd ID and the 4th Marines were bopping around Baghdad and getting on television. They were there when they tore down Saddam's statue and all the Iraqis were cheering. That was only right, I thought. They were the ones who did all the fighting.

Baghdad is a trip. It's a beautiful city with wide, clean streets and modern cars zipping down the highways. The sky is low and huge and so blue it's almost purple. The Tigris River has a mix of vessels, some large, some small with one or two people. There is a feeling of peace about the place most of the time, but then there is the distant chatter of an automatic weapon or the dark silhouette of one of our planes streaking across the sky and once again you're reminded that there is a war going on.

We painted the Port-O-Potties bright colors and Marla found a camel spider in the one she was splashing a bright red. When we finished painting we went to the Quarters Area and found the other squads, including Medical, cursing up a storm because somebody had made them line sandbags along the walls.

"If the war is over, how come we have to line the walls with sandbags?" Pendleton asked.

You did what you were told to do in the army, so the question wasn't even worth answering.

The first few days in Baghdad were super cool and typical army days in that we didn't do anything except sit around and watch television so that we could tell how wonderful we were. Most of the guys they interviewed were from the marines but we were all happy. There was talk about fighting here and there, and some of it was serious, but we were cool. The word came down to hire as many Iraqis to do little jobs around the camp as we could. They were all searched when they came to the gates in the morning and didn't have that much work to do during the day. They left just after chow time in the evening.

"If we don't win any hearts or minds at least we can win a lot of gums and bad teeth," Jonesy said, pointing to the guy that had been assigned to us. "He just sit around and smile at us all day."

Jamil Sidqi al-Tikrit was supposed to be Saddam's fourth or fifth cousin. He spoke a little English and was somewhere between one hundred and two hundred years old, or so it seemed. He went around all day straightening up the bunks and sweeping the floors. He smelled like garlic and cigarette smoke and his hands, spotted and brown, shook the way old people's hands do sometimes.

"It's good to have us a slave," Pendleton from Third Squad said.

I didn't dig that too much and neither did Jonesy. We didn't say anything but Pendleton caught our attitude. He came over to me later and showed me a letter he had received from his wife.

"These are my girls," he said, laying photos of two redheaded girls, about three or four, on my duffel bag.

I nodded and looked away. From the corner of my eye I saw Pendleton shrug and pick up his photos.

Jamil said he spoke English, but when we talked to him he mostly just nodded. When Ahmed showed up with a bag of chocolate bars we asked him to ask Jamil what he thought of us invading his country. Ahmed questioned him in Arabic and Jamil answered him.

"He wants to know what you want him to say," Ahmed said.

"We want his honest opinion," Marla said. "What does he think about us coming in and knocking off Saddam Hussein?"

Ahmed spoke to the old man again in Arabic.

"When you kill a camel it is better to cut off the body than the head," the old man said. "If you cut off the head then the camel doesn't know what he is."

"Birdy, you figure out what that means and I'll give you a dollar," Marla said.

She kept her dollar.

■ ■ ■

Morning. I was still tired when I heard Captain Coles call to us. He said something about a meeting in the mess tent.

"How come they didn't tell us last night there was a mess tent?" Jonesy asked.

We found it was the officers' mess and there was fresh coffee, eggs, sausage patties, and pastry. Captain Miller and Barbara from the medics were already there. Marla and Jean Darcy were the last to arrive; Marla came over and sniffed me.

"Not bad," she said, smiling. "I was looking for you last night. I thought we could shower together and wash each other's backs."

The girl is messing with my mind big-time. I'm beginning to think that she doesn't believe I know much about women, which is true, but I don't like women knowing that.

Harris was going on about how he had served a tour in Qatar after the first Gulf War. Jonesy asked him how he had liked South America.

"Qatar ain't in no South America, fool!" Harris was incredulous at what he thought was Jonesy's stupidity. He went on drawing imaginary maps in the air with a stubby brown finger. But he didn't give us any more war stories, so Jonesy did his job.

Major Sessions came in with a colonel. Short wide dude with gray eyes and a big forehead. She gave an informal introduction to our crew. The colonel's name was Opdyke.

"As you know, sir, we're sort of out there taking notes and observing to see how our CA Special Ops might need tinkering," Major Sessions said. She was looking fresh, well rested.

"Well, I have a great deal of hope for the Civil Affairs operations in this war," said Colonel Opdyke. His voice was raspy and I wondered if he worked to make it sound that way. "I was one of the planners that suggested sending a CA unit up front early in the campaign. Give us a head start on the last phase of the overall operation, building a democracy. We build the right democracy and we're going to stabilize the whole Middle East. That's going to end the terrorism, end the violence, maybe even be an end to war. I don't know, but I think we're going to try. This is the aim of the commander in chief, it's my aim, and it damn well better be yours."

Captain Sessions started applauding, so we all did. The colonel went on: "We've got a little situation between An Nasiriyah and Tallil Air Base. Just south of there. They're Shiites, and that's good, but apparently the air force sent over some A-10s on a Close Air Support mission and they took out a school. Killed some civilians. A few children. This is a war and collateral damage happens. That's a fact of war and a reflection of what is known as the 'fog of war.' Nothing happens perfectly. Bullets fly. Bombs fall. People stand up at the wrong time."

Captain Miller started squirming in her seat about halfway through the talk. Her head rolled back when the colonel turned to Major Sessions and asked if we had any females to send to the village. When it was over and we were outside sitting on some piled-up fuel cans, Miller was close to tears.

"How do you kill somebody and then talk about how sorry you are?" she asked. "And what was that bit about asking for a receipt?"

"If they take the money we have to get a receipt for it," I said.

"And you feel good about this?" Miller asked, pointing at me.

I felt myself shrugging, but I didn't know what to say to her. Finally I got out a "no," but I don't think she was convinced.

"The thing is," Miller went on, "is that we don't need to compromise. Maybe somewhere, somebody has to compromise, but we don't. If we're supposed to be putting a human face on this war, then we need to seriously figure out what that means. We can't make it right by giving these people a smiley face."

"Birdy is compromising, ma'am," Marla said. "We're doing the best we can with what we got."

Yo! Marla got my back! All right!

Major Sessions had a brief discussion with Captain Coles, showing him the location of the school, and then left.

"Yo, Captain, that's a hand-drawn map," Jonesy said. "You sure they know where this place is?"

"They bombed it, they should know," Captain Coles said. "Okay, we'll take First Squad and Second Squad. I'll take the money. Get Ahmed ready, too. Look, Miller, they probably do need medical help, too."

"Yeah, sure." Captain Miller said. "And should we put on our veils?"

"We need us some blues in here," Jonesy said, and started singing.

Well, the bombs are falling, yes the bombs are coming down
Baby, them bombs are falling, they really coming down
Sometimes they on target, and sometimes they runnin' wild

But I'm so glad they ain't falling on my mama's child
And that's the truth!

We started clapping for Jonesy. The guy could really sing. All of a sudden his dream about that blues joint made sense.

I thought about what Captain Miller had said as we convoyed past a construction crew setting up what looked like a fuel depot. I thought the colonel had been right. Nothing was as neat as it looked in the movies or on television. War was sloppier, faster, and more violent. The noises were louder than I had thought they would be. The sounds of shells hitting a target, the heat, and the vibrations from the impact seemed to go through me. After a while the vibrations were there even when nothing was going on. It was as if, little by little, I was bringing the crash of war inside me. As if, little by little, the war was becoming part of me. Maybe the smiley face wasn't for the Iraqis. Maybe it was for us.

It took only an hour and ten minutes to reach the area that the A-10 had hit. There was a small building that could have been a mosque, very plain looking, and about fifteen two-story buildings. Most of the buildings had been hit and two of them were nothing more than a pile of rubble. There were two Humvees patrolling the area, just tooling through the streets.

"Italians," Coles announced. "I don't know how we convinced them to send actual ground troops, but they are part of the Coalition." That got all our interest and I was hoping we could meet them. We drove around until we found what could have been a school. Half of the top floor was blown away. A line of pockmarks ran across the front of the building at an angle; where the line met the door, there was a huge chip in the cement. The top of the front door was intact but the bottom was gone.

A group of women sat to one side in the shade of a tree. They were cutting up strips of cloth and rolling them into small bundles. Ahmed went over and spoke to them. One of the women turned and pointed to a low building about fifty yards away. There was writing on the walls and a circle that looked like some kind of logo.

"Birdy, go with him," Captain Coles said as Ahmed started for the building.

"Birdy?" I was surprised. "That's my official name now?"

Captain Coles laughed and checked out my name tape. "*Perry*, go with him," he said.

I caught up with Ahmed, who told me that the local chief owned the store we were headed toward.

"You understand everything they say?" I asked.

"Just about," Ahmed said. "But the woman back there pretended she didn't understand anything I said."

"They don't like us over here, I guess."

"No, it just means that they don't trust us," Ahmed said. "Whatever else we deal with, that's going to be part of the picture."

We got to the store and found a really fat man sitting beside a pile of shoe boxes. There was clothing in the small store; most of it was American-style clothing, some Iraqi stuff. I thought about buying some Iraqi clothing and taking it back home. Mama would like that.

Ahmed started talking to the man in Arabic. The guy didn't answer. There were coins on a table near him, and as Ahmed spoke, he pushed them around with one stubby finger. Finally, after a while, Ahmed stopped talking and the man looked up at him, then away. He didn't look at Ahmed when he spoke.

I wished I knew what the guy was saying. He was very calm as he spoke, very deliberate with his words. He didn't gesture with his hands but kept pushing the coins around the table. Ahmed spoke once in a while, and his voice was low, matching the Iraqi shopkeeper's.

"What's he saying?" I asked.

"He's saying the mothers of the dead children don't want our money, they want their children," Ahmed said. "I don't know if he wants me to beg him or something. I don't know."

"Ask him if he's refusing the money," I said. "Tell him if he is, we'll just go."

Ahmed spoke to the guy again and he answered.

"He wants to know if you're my commanding officer," Ahmed said. "I told him no and now he wants me to go get Coles."

"You should have told him I was your commanding officer and the most dangerous man in the army," I said.

We went back to the Humvees. Marla, Jean, and the other

noncom woman were already with the children. Captain Miller was talking with the women.

"She speak Arabic?" I asked Captain Coles.

"A little," he said. "What's the situation with their chief?"

"He's playing it cool," Ahmed said. "He was kind of chewing me out in a calm way. Asking me stuff like if I thought the money was going to make up for the death of the children. I didn't answer that. Now he wants to see you."

"Which means that he'll probably take the money," Captain Coles said.

As we started back toward the store the guy appeared at the door. He called to some of the women and two of them — I figured they were the ones who had lost children — came over.

Inside the store the man spoke to the women. Ahmed said he didn't understand what they were saying, that they had switched to a dialect he didn't know. The women started yelling at us.

"You don't need to speak Arabic to understand what they're saying," Ahmed said.

He was right. We stood there for about ten minutes while they screamed at us. One woman spit on the ground in front of my feet. Captain Coles told Ahmed to offer up some more apologies, and Ahmed did.

"It's not going to do any good," Ahmed said.

"No, but do it, anyway," Coles said.

It was the Iraqi shopkeeper who put an end to it. He put his arm around the shoulders of one woman and spoke to her softly. The women left and we gave the man the money. He signed for it and then we left.

I didn't know how much money we gave them. It looked like a couple of thousand dollars. I didn't feel good about it. Everything the Iraqis were saying was right. We couldn't buy an end to their grieving, or an end to their missing their kids.

The Italians came over. They shook hands all around. One of them asked in English if I was an Iraqi. He knew I wasn't. I guess they thought that was funny. But they seemed like okay guys, eager to try out their English. One of them said that he had been to the United States.

"Bayonne, New Jersey," he said. "I took the bus off New York and live with my cousin two weeks at Bayonne. I go to New York three times."

Captain Coles had gone to Rome on his honeymoon. He mentioned that and one of the soldiers congratulated him and patted him on the back.

The Italians' vehicles were smaller than ours and didn't have squad guns. The Italians were more casual than we were, too, and I noticed that none of them were wearing body armor.

We mounted up and Captain Miller told us that one of the women said that there were children playing near the school when the plane attacked it.

"She was pretty pissed and I can't blame her," Miller said. "There's a hospital behind the school. It's a wonder they didn't attack that."

"You know, Miller, I bet those guys flying that mission that day are as sorry about what happened as you are," Coles said. "Nobody wants to kill innocent people."

"I don't think so, either." Miller pushed a strand of hair away from her face. "But we learn to let ourselves off the hook pretty fast when we do, don't we?"

"Well, I . . ." Captain Coles started to say something but changed his mind.

I really wanted to know what he was going to say.

"Hey, Captain Coles!" Marla was on the intercom.

"What?"

"You think Birdy is an Iraqi?"

"Could be," Captain Coles answered. "He's very dark."

We drove for another few minutes when we saw the ambulance about a hundred yards ahead of us. It had the cross on the side and two guys standing by it.

"Contact straight ahead," Marla said.

The ambulance made a quick U-turn; the back doors opened and two guys came out.

"RPGs!" Jonesy shouted; he braked to a skidding halt.

My heart jumped and I heard Marla send a burst of machine gun fire toward the guys with the rocket-propelled grenade launchers. Captain Coles screamed into the radio that we were being attacked.

"Watch out for more bandits!" he yelled.

Me and Ahmed piled out and got to the right side of the road, which was higher. The fire from the squad gun must have spooked the guys ahead because they split and went to either side of the road. It couldn't have been more than a hundred yards away.

I went to one knee and brought my piece up to my shoulder. The scope was full of dust and I fired looking over the barrel, panning across the road.

One of the Iraqis was sitting on the ground. He wasn't firing. I saw him push at his legs as if he were trying to get them to move. Then he fell backward.

The other Humvee pulled up with Darcy on its squad gun. Both our guns were trained on the ambulance; we could see the smoke and sparks where the bullets hit its side. Another moment and someone was calling a cease-fire. Nothing moved near the ambulance.

"Mount up!" Captain Coles shouted.

We got back into our Humvees and rolled up cautiously, checking all around us for bad guys. When we got near the ambulance it was riddled with holes. Now both of the guys were on the ground, either dead or badly wounded. The ambulance driver was older than the ones who had started the attack. He was slumped over the wheel. From where I sat I couldn't see any wounds, but I saw the holes in the windshield.

Ahmed picked up the attackers' weapons and then looked in the back of the ambulance. He stood stock-still for a long moment. He was going to the door when Captain Coles yelled at him.

"Let's get the hell out of here!"

Ahmed got back into the Humvee. He threw the two RPGs into the back and held up several vials of something.

"There's a dead guy in the ambulance," he said.

Jonesy got back on the middle of the road and pushed the Humvee as fast as it would go. Marla hung on and told me to grab her leg so she wouldn't bounce out, so I did.

We didn't slow down until we hit the first MP checkpoint. He waved us through and we went the last mile or so to our quarters at regular city speed. My legs were weak when I stepped out of the Humvee.

"Check your weapons," Coles said. "Make sure the safeties are on."

As I checked I saw that I had skinned the knuckles on my right hand.

"See you guys had a little fun!" A wide-faced corporal looked at the side of Second Squad's Humvee.

I looked and saw a neat line of bullet holes. Who had been shooting at us? Had one of our own guys shot our Humvee?

Marla came out over the top and slid down the side of Miss Molly.

"You think that was an ambush? Something they planned because they knew we were coming?" she asked me. "Some serious payback?"

"I don't think so," I said. "They didn't know we were coming to the village. They didn't know when we were going to leave. I think they just saw us and took a chance."

Ahmed still had the vials of drugs and gave them to Captain Miller. Captain Coles went to Major Sessions to tell her what had happened. Jones fell across his bunk, facedown.

"You okay, Jonesy?" I asked him.

"When you playing the blues you always know where you going," he said. "You hitting them same chords your granddaddy hit and you singing about them same old blues. You can jazz it up a bit here and there, but sooner or later you coming back to the bad times. That's what's going down over here, Birdy. Sooner or later, man. One of them crazy suckers is going to hop out from behind a bush or jump out a tree, get lucky, and that's going to be the end of my butt. Right now some sucker is probably got a bullet with my name on it under that dress they be wearing."

Pendleton from Third Squad asked what had happened at the school. Jonesy stammered as he tried to tell him.

I could hardly remember what had happened. Somehow the moment was already lost. Nothing had happened and the only thing that had ever happened in my entire life was the time on the road. Had it been two minutes? A minute? A few seconds? People had tried to kill me. Maybe I had killed one of them. What else could matter?

Captain Coles said that the Iraqis had broken the rules of engagement when they used a Red Crescent vehicle to attack us.

"If they shoot my ass and they broke the rules doing it, does that make me less dead?" Marla asked.

I was dog tired. My shoulders ached. The sand on my face and neck scratched my skin as I pulled off my T-shirt. The bunk was hard, but anything was better than standing up.

A dream. I was riding along some highway in the back of a truck. Then it stopped being a truck and was an ambulance. Suddenly the ambulance/truck stopped and I got out to see what was going on. The road was covered with a low dust cloud. I could see the sun playing in the swirls a few feet in front of the ambulance. Looking up beyond the cloud I saw a group of soldiers. They had lifted their guns and were pointing at me. Somehow it seemed that I would be all right if I didn't move. I tried to stay as still as possible, but then I moved and could see the fire from the muzzles of the guns. I was hit and panicked. No matter which way I turned I couldn't get away.

When I awoke I was sweating. I had thrown my blanket off onto the floor. I got up and thought about going out to the Port-O-Potties, but I went back to bed and pulled the cover over my head.

What got to me was that I didn't think any of the attacks against us were being planned in any big way. It was just some guys sitting around with weapons, maybe even weapons we had given them, and talking about what was going on. Then, if they had gotten themselves worked up enough, or mad enough, they attacked whoever came along. It didn't make any sense to me and I knew that wasn't good.

May 3, 2003

Dear Uncle Richie,

Things are going pretty well here. I'm getting along really well with the squad. We understand things about each other. Probably the most important thing is that nobody is perfect, but that's okay, we're tight with each other. We were sitting around the other day talking about an incident on the road and Jonesy asked if anybody had been scared. Nobody remembered being scared, but we all remembered being scared after it was all over. We couldn't even tell if we had been in danger or not. Ahmed pulled a muscle in his butt and limped for two days.

Mom sent a package with salami and American cheese. I don't particularly like salami but it was from home. I wrote to Dad and asked him to send me some photos from home and the neighborhood and instead he sent a picture of Morehouse College in Atlanta. I guess that's supposed to be a hint or something. I think when I get out I'm going to apply to some liberal arts colleges in New England or maybe Johns Hopkins in Maryland. I heard that they had a pretty relaxed program but well respected. Finance seems so far away from where my head is now.

By the way, Mom said that her hip is really bothering her when it rains. Is that something serious that I should be worried about? Maybe you should tell her to take care of it. Pop has good medical coverage, so I don't think that's the problem. More like Mom is "being strong" as usual. Did you read where the Iraqis sent a mortar shell into our HQ zone? No one was hurt but a television reporter packed up his bags and left THAT DAY! We all laughed but would have gone with him in a heartbeat.

Supply got a batch of laptops in and we're trying to steal one so we can email back to the States. The computers are supposed to be for field communications and they're watching them pretty closely but . . . keep checking your email!

Robin

We had been sitting in our base, which Jonesy called Forward Base Beale Street, for two weeks and I was getting to like it. Rumors had started again that we were going to be rotated back to the States before summer started and that sounded good, too.

I was also getting used to hanging out in Baghdad. You could tell it had once been a beautiful city, and in many ways it still was. But how you saw the city depended on where you were. We had all taken turns going into the presidential palace, which was as fancy as I could imagine. Marla said it looked like an old movie set.

The main streets in Baghdad are wide tree-lined roads that are well laid out. There are parks, squares, and markets off the main drag. When we weren't sightseeing we hung out or cleaned our equipment. It was boring, but boring was getting to be real good.

We were cleaning our weapons when Marla and Major Sessions came into the room. The major gave us the signal to stay seated. She was wearing a 9-mil strapped to her thigh. Very sexy.

"We have a request from the local people of Ba'qubah for medicine for their sheep or goats or something," the major said.

"We need to get a team up there to see exactly what they need. And we need to know what they're thinking about us. We believe these villagers are mostly Sunnis and there's been some talk they have ties to the Sunnis in Lebanon."

"Are we Civil Affairs people or spies?" Jonesy asked.

"Soldiers." Major Sessions's voice dropped a few tones. "That's why you'll do what you're told, *soldier*."

"Yes, ma'am."

"We've got a guide who will introduce us to all the hot spots in the city," Marla said.

"And you'll be escorted by security from the Third ID," Major Sessions went on. "So try to look like soldiers. The Medical Squad and Marla's squad will go. Keep your eyes open and get back safe. You move out at 1100 hours."

As soon as Major Sessions left, we all turned toward Marla.

"Did you volunteer us for this crap?" Jonesy asked.

"I volunteered you to invade Syria," Marla bad-mouthed back, "and Major Sessions volunteered you for this trip to Disneyland."

The security guys from the 3rd included a gung-ho-looking first lieutenant named Maire who came over and said something about "getting the show on the road." He had the coordinates and said it shouldn't take us more than fifty minutes to reach the place.

"I'll take the lead vehicle," he said. "My guys will be second and last. Your two vehicles will stay in between us and stay in touch. If anything breaks out you'll listen for my orders. Capisce?"

We capisced and Marla took out her notebook, in which she wrote down everyone she didn't like. She was filling that notebook up in a big hurry.

Ahmed rode with us to translate; we all gave him high fives as our small convoy started out.

Three days earlier a suicide bomber had blown up a truck in a northern Baghdad neighborhood. Two marines were injured and several Iraqi policemen were killed along with a bunch of civilians. Every time we passed a slow moving truck I tensed.

We reached the northern end of the city and started to pick up speed. Ahmed was in the middle of a story about his brother playing Little League baseball back in Ohio.

"I tried to teach him how to hit," he said. "But no matter what I told him, all he could hit was little ground balls back to the pitcher."

"You should have told him to keep his hands back," Marla said. "That's why he doesn't hit the ball solid. He lets his hands get too far over the plate. He keeps them back until the last minute, he'll hit the ball solid."

"How do you know that?" Ahmed asked.

"Because I can hit, numb face!" Marla said. "How do you think I know it? Anybody from Long Island can outhit anybody from — where did you say you were from? Nowhere?"

That was kind of hard on Ahmed and he shut up. I wanted to say something to ease the tension a little but couldn't think of anything.

We passed an outdoor café where men sat at the tables, watching everything that happened. I imagined them calling in to some Iraqi headquarters, reporting every move we Americans made.

Outside of Baghdad the vehicles from the 3rd picked up speed. Iraqi trucks careened off the road when they saw us coming toward them. No one wanted to mess with the American army. They had seen what happened to people who confronted the Infantry.

We reached Ba'qubah at 1230 and I remembered that I had packed water but nothing to eat. I told Jonesy.

"Don't worry about it, man," he said. "We'll just trade the Racks some ammo for raisins or whatever they be eating over here."

Right.

Lieutenant Maire came over and asked Ahmed to find out where the animals that needed the medicine were. Ahmed said they were probably in the fields and waved toward some low hills in the distance. Maire looked at him, then looked at me.

"Tell this guy to remember whose side he's on," he said.

"He's American," Jonesy spoke up. "You didn't know that, sir?"

The lieutenant looked Ahmed up and down and then walked away. Creep.

Maire set up his security positions. Marla got up on our squad gun and Victor, who was with our medics, got upside on their Humvee. All in all we had twelve guys from the 3rd and eight guys from our unit, so I thought we'd be okay. The Iraqis never seemed all that anxious for a direct confrontation.

Maire sent some of his men through some of the nearby houses. Everything looked cool. Captain Miller and the medics were walking around and Marla told me to go with them, which pissed me off.

"Who put you in charge of security?" I asked.

"So don't go with them," Marla said. "Let them walk around by themselves and maybe get killed, okay?"

I walked with them.

Ba'qubah looked like Greek villages I had seen on National Geographic TV. The people were thin, old-looking. That was a funny thing in Iraq. You could tell who the important people were by how fat they were. Most people were thin, but all the muck-a-mucks looked heavy.

I was thinking again about Marla, about how she seemed to act and think more like a soldier than I did. It was a weird combination, a foxy-looking lady as tough as she was. I was wondering if she was really that tough inside or was it all an act when Owens, who was up ahead of Captain Miller and me, came back to us in a hurry.

"There are wounded people in the house up ahead," she said.

Lieutenant Maire started giving orders and backing us out toward where the Humvees were parked. I felt a familiar tension in my gut and had to keep my hand tight against the side of my weapon to keep it from trembling.

We moved back to a defensive position and watched as a squad of guys from the 3rd moved up.

The area we were in didn't have that many buildings. It was away from the small cluster of two-story houses, and I knew it could have been an ambush. There was a small grove of trees off to my right. The branches seemed silvered and shimmered in the heat.

"No problem! No problem!" Ahmed was waving his hands in the air.

The guys from the 3rd let him through their line and listened as he talked. I couldn't hear what he was saying from where I was, behind the First Squad vehicle, but I could see he was pretty excited.

A sergeant said something to Ahmed and let him lead as they went forward. They went into a house, which was painted white and gleamed in the afternoon sun, while other soldiers looked through the windows. A moment later they came out. The guy from the 3rd had lowered his piece. I guessed he thought things were cool.

Lieutenant Maire took Ahmed over to an older man and began a three-way conversation with Maire doing most of the talking. He screamed at the man in one breath and then at Ahmed in the next. Captain Miller got into the conversation and soon Maire was screaming at her. The guy could curse up a blue streak.

"Birdy!" Marla called down from the squad gun position. "Go see what's happening!"

Lieutenant Maire was getting into it with Captain Miller and I pulled Ahmed aside and asked him what was going on.

"The guy who asked for help is a village elder," Ahmed said. "He said before that the animals were sick, but it's really wounded people."

Technically, Miller outranked Maire, but he had taken charge of the mission.

"You can do what you want, *Captain*," Maire was saying. "But I'm moving my men out now!"

"Have a nice trip, Lieutenant." There was a calmness in Captain Miller's voice. She turned to Owens and said, "Bring the medical supplies."

Lieutenant Maire knew that we might be helping wounded guys who had attacked Americans. There was also the possibility that the whole setup was some kind of trap. That wasn't anything Captain Miller didn't know, too; she had just made a decision to help whoever she found.

The afternoon sky was dazzling white above the small village. The room we entered was dark and smelly and for a moment I was blinded by the contrast. There were only a few candles lit against one wall.

When my eyes became accustomed to the darkness I saw that there were mats lined up along the floor. There were a few women on them, but most of the bodies lying side by side were children.

"What happened?" I asked Ahmed.

"The fedayeen," Ahmed said. "They came and said everybody in the village had to fight against the invaders. The fedayeen knew the villagers were mostly from minor tribes and they didn't care about them being killed. Anybody who refused to fight would be shot. They even gave the children guns.

"They put a bomb on the road and told the children to shoot when they saw an American convoy passing. The children didn't know how to shoot but they fired the guns."

"Who made them shoot?" Marla asked. "The feda-*what*?"

"They're guerrilla fighters," Ahmed said. "They don't have rules. No uniforms. They use any kind of weapons they find and just kill whoever is their enemy."

"Including children?" Marla said; she turned away before Ahmed could answer.

Captain Miller had started attending to the children. Jonesy set up a portable light and I saw that there were fewer kids than I had thought at first. I counted seven. One body was completely wrapped and I figured that kid was dead.

"The convoy that passed here was marines," Ahmed said. "When they heard the firing they shot back. The convoy was moving very fast. The bomb didn't go off so they never stopped, and none of them were injured. The fedayeen, there were maybe nine of them, had two trucks, old army trucks, and after the marines had passed they went down the same road. But first they beat some of the children. Even ones who had been wounded."

"Why didn't they tell us that in the first place?" I asked.

"Would we have come if we knew that there were wounded Iraqis here?" Ahmed asked. "Or that they had fired on Americans?"

None of the children were crying. Kneeling, I looked at one small, round-faced boy of about eight or nine as Captain Miller examined him. A woman sat on the floor next to the child. Miller opened the child's shirt and he tried to stop her.

"I know it hurts, baby," Captain Miller said. "I know it hurts."

The woman reached over and opened the boy's shirt.

The wound was in the crease between his chest and shoulder. The area was dark and swollen. Captain Miller took a pair of scissors and cut away more of his clothing. His arm, a child's arm with round, doll-like muscles, was darker than his chest.

Captain Miller closed the boy's clothing and turned to the next child. The woman grabbed Miller's arm and looked into her face.

"I'm sorry," Captain Miller said, and moved away.

Captain Miller and Owens treated the kids as best they could. Ahmed talked to some of the women.

"The child who is wrapped died this morning," he said.

"Where are the men?" Jonesy asked.

"Some the fedayeen took them with them," Ahmed said. "Some were killed. Others are hiding. It's all hard for them."

Seeing the wounded kids made me feel like crap. This wasn't what the whole thing was supposed to be about. It wasn't what I wanted in my life, but I knew I didn't have a choice. I saw Jonesy talking with one of the kids. Then he sat down, took off his helmet, and started beating on it slowly. Then he started singing a slow blues song. The kid didn't have any idea what Jonesy was doing, but he seemed to like the singing and the dark American soldier sitting next to him.

I said hello to a small girl, her face half hidden by a scarf. She tried to smile. Captain Miller had bandaged the side of her face and I could see the girl wince as her mouth moved.

Outside Ahmed took off his jacket and started helping a man digging what I thought would probably be a grave. We waited until it was deep enough for a small body, and then we started loading up.

Lieutenant Maire hadn't pulled his men out after all. He watched, a cigarette dangling from his mouth, as Captain Miller gave out the bandages and some painkillers to the women.

"How do you know there aren't a dozen enemy fighters hidden somewhere near here, Captain?" Maire confronted Captain Miller. "How do you know those bandages won't go directly to them?"

"I don't know, Lieutenant," Captain Miller said. "Isn't that wonderful? To be able to do something with nothing more than the hope that it's the right thing? Isn't that wonderful?"

On the way back to the base, Ahmed, his clothes dirty with dark sweat stains under his arms from digging, thanked us.

"Hey, we're in the same army, bro," Jonesy said.

Ahmed nodded but didn't say anything. That was the way things were getting to be. There were things you said and things you didn't.

I thought about the fedayeen forcing the children to shoot at marines. They were lucky that they hadn't been accurate, that the marines hadn't taken the few minutes it would have taken to wipe out the area, or hadn't called in Close Air Support to blow the building apart. The face of the boy with the chest wound came back to me. I had asked Captain Miller if it was possible that he would make it — she just shook her head.

"No, he's going to die," she said. "Right now we don't have the facilities to take care of them."

"So we just let them die?" I asked. "Even if they're children?"

"Even if they're children," she said.

When I was a kid, maybe eight or nine, I wondered why God made the insides of people. Why not just make solid people that could do the same things we did instead of all the little parts, veins, arteries, hearts, and things that could go so wrong. Why didn't God just keep it simple?

From a distance, say the eight feet between eyes and television screen, or perhaps at the silent impact of a long-range missile hitting a neatly framed target, combat seemed so simple. There was good and there was bad and the clear distances between the two held their own comforts. But as those distances narrowed, as they came within the range of smell and the feeling of warmth as a shell hit a target or the gentle shaking of the ground beneath you that stirred the constant fear within, the clarity disappeared.

I had seen Ahmed digging the grave for a stranger's child. There was something that Ahmed knew that we all knew: The children belonged to all of us. It was a message the heart wanted to sing.

"Hey, Marla, what you think it's like getting shot?" Jonesy had taken off his boots and was soaking his feet in a basin of water. "You think it really hurts a lot?"

"The thing to do is to get Birdy shot first," Marla said. "He's good with words. He can tell us just how it feels. Right, Birdy?"

I didn't answer, but Jonesy did it for me. He strummed the oud he had found and sang a song he made up called the "Got Shot and It Hurts Like Hell Blues."

Back to Baghdad. You have to go through a maze of cement barriers to come into the main areas, and a private engineering company was putting fences around the place. But our quarters are okay.

There are a lot of private security companies protecting the Iraqi bigwigs. They're mostly white, but there was also a group of sort of short guys who were dark.

"They're from Chile," Victor Ríos said.

"We need scorecards," said a big guy from the Civil Affairs construction crew who had brought over our mail. "That way at least we can tell who all the players are."

"I don't care who the players are," Jonesy said. "I just need to know who don't like my brown butt."

I got a catalog from a shoe company in Florida, two offers for credit cards, and a letter from Mom.

The letter made me feel bad even before I opened it. Mom seemed so far away; home seemed so far away. I hadn't thought much about being away since we started the march to Baghdad, only about what I was seeing around me, and staying alive. I decided to save the letter for after supper.

Victor Ríos, who wasn't exactly chatty, cursed aloud as he read his letter and I knew I didn't want to know what was in it.

Marla stuck her head into our tent. "You studs decent?" she asked.

We were all dressed and she came in with Owens from the Medical Squad. They were carrying a portable television. Jonesy was out taking a leak, so they sat it on his bed.

"Where did you get that?" I asked.

"Traded it from the Arabs for two tanks and a portable fox-hole," Marla said. "We have one in our tent, so we'll trade you this one for your collective souls."

"Yo, Owens! Ríos got a Dear John letter," Harris said. "You need a new boyfriend?"

Ríos, who is the meanest-looking guy in the unit, got up on one elbow and gave Harris a look that would have chilled ice water at the freaking North Pole. "I didn't get no Dear John letter," he said. "My woman don't want to leave me."

"So what you cussing for?" Harris asked.

"My brother's got my mother all upset because he wants to join a gang," Ríos said. "If I was home I'd bust him upside his head."

"In a way, you already belong to a gang," Owens said. She sounded cultured but looked unsure of herself as she tugged at the shoulder of her T-shirt. "We're like a big gang."

"Yeah, man, but people respect what we do," Ríos said. "We have a legit purpose. You go banging on the street and you don't have no win, you either going to jail or you going to end up dead. If I get nailed over here, everybody is going to say I was okay. Nobody is going to look at my mother and be turning their heads. You know what I'm saying?"

"Yeah, I hear you," Owens said. She had got the television on and we watched as a distorted image moved diagonally across the small screen. "But this morning Captain Miller was saying she wasn't sure what we're doing over here."

"Hey, Jamil, what you want America to do over here?" Harris called to the old Iraqi man who sat in the corner. It was the right question, but I didn't think that Harris gave a damn about the answer.

"I can tell you only what we want to do," Jamil said. "We want to live in peace and worship Allah in peace and walk down the streets in peace. Islam is a religion of peace, true Islam. This sounds simple but it's not. We have Allah in our hearts, but sometimes it's hard to hear the true voice when the stomach is making so much noise. Americans can't under-stand that."

"Yo, man, you people got oil over here," Harris said as Jonesy came back into the tent. "If you got oil, you ain't got nothing to worry about."

"Where is my oil, my friend?" Jamil stood up, opened his shirt, and turned slowly around. "Where do you think I'm keeping it?"

"Close your shirt," Marla said. "You're getting Owens upset."

We turned to the television and worked at getting the news. The news was important to us. We gathered around the set, all of us edging closer, turning away as we saw things at times that we didn't want to see, or that we knew weren't true.

The broadcast started with images of Iraqis in Baghdad waving flags, and celebrating. Humvees and tanks rolled down the streets past smiling children. There was a quick cut to a poster of Saddam Hussein on which somebody had drawn horns.

The press conference was the usual: a general talking about our progress. There was a map with arrows on it.

"Anyone see Ba'qubah on that map?" Owens asked.

No one did. All we saw was that we were the winners. Our side had won and the Iraqis were glad that we were there. I looked over at Ahmed. He was watching the television intently.

"Ahmed, what do you think?" I asked.

"How do I know, man?" he said.

"You got to listen to the president," Harris said. "He's got a plan and we're just following it."

"Harris, you can suck up without even having anybody around to suck up to," Marla said.

"Yo, Miss Molly, you're lucky you a woman." Harris stood up, feet apart.

"Looking at you," Marla said, "I can believe it!"

Marla and Owens left. Luckily they didn't take the television with them.

The guys rapped for another half hour, then started scrounging around for food. The 3rd had set up kitchens and anybody could eat there, so we got some hot food. Not bad. Definitely better than MREs.

May 1st, 2003

Dear Robin,

I have just come from Thursday night services. They were wonderful and everyone prayed for all the young men and women over there. I was watching the news this morning and saw that tanks headed into the city over there. The people look friendly enough and they were smiling on the television. I saw the women were not wearing veils or anything. I thought they wore them all the time.

Things are going well over here. Well, almost well. I told Sister Jenkins from church that you were in the army and she said she didn't believe me because you were too young. She had the nerve to tell me that right to my face! Then she told Wanda (Rett's cousin) that she had heard you were in jail. You would think that as old as that woman is she would be a little less evil. She says she has arthritis but I think it's just the meanness gathering in her bones.

Two little stores down the street closed. Some of the people are worried that white people will move in and take them over but I don't care, because the stores needed fixing up. Something is also finally being done with those buildings on Lenox Avenue.

LaKeisha, Edie Law's oldest girl, was talking about dropping out of school, which was supposed to get me all upset. I told her to go on and drop out because they need some more people serving up them hamburgers and sodas for minimum pay.

On the television I saw a church in Alabama, a white Baptist church I think, gathering food and stuff to send to the boys overseas. Do you need anything? Do you want the church to send you anything? You tell me and I will do everything I can to get it to you.

Robin, I love you more than anything and pray to God for you to be safe every night. Please take care of yourself. You were always the brave type, but I want you to be careful and remember those who love you at home.

Your father is not watching his high blood pressure and I need to get on his case but I don't want to hear his mouth about me nagging him. You know he still thinks he's nineteen. He sends you his love and says for you to be careful over there.

Your loving mother, Jackie

I lay on my cot and felt exhausted. It was the way I was always feeling lately. I was up too high too much of the time to really relax. I thought about what Mama had said, that I was the hero type.

No, Mama, I'm not the brave type. Not over here where the booming goes through you, where explosions in the distance shake your whole body. It's hard to be brave when you can stumble across a world of hurt around any corner, where dying becomes so casual you don't even notice it sitting next to you.

Even though the war is supposed to be over, there is still fighting in and around Baghdad, and the sounds of bombing just outside the city at night are awesome. It is like a thunderstorm in the distance. When the night sky lights up, our guys cheer, but it scares the crap out of me. The booming is far away, but it's inside of me, too. It's not so much the noise, it's like something shaking in my chest. The president said that our mission has been accomplished. But there are still guys getting killed, and Captain Miller said they were only counting guys who died on the spot.

"A lot of them are being rotated back to Germany or the States and might not make it down the road," she said. "And nobody's talking about the wounds over here. Blast wounds are terrible."

"They covering stuff up?" Marla asked.

"I don't think so." Miller shrugged.

"They just making sure they talking in the sunshine," Jonesy said.

"Jonesy, you only make sense about fifty percent of the time," Marla said. "Everything else you say is beyond me."

Jonesy grinned.

But maybe he and Miller were right. Maybe more people were dying than made the news, but I didn't want to hear about it.

When we patrol north of Baghdad, outside of the safe zone, we see a lot of dead Iraqis. This morning we found two civilian cars, both riddled with bullets, both with bodies still lying in them. A small crowd of men, some weeping, some talking quietly, stood around the car, waiting for the ambulance to take the bodies away. I keep looking away from the dead because I don't want to see them. When I do look I see that the dead are not like human beings anymore. They are not neatly laid out but twisted at obscene angles on the side of the road. Sometimes there are mourners. They sit near the bodies, wailing and tearing at their clothes. They hold their hands up to the sky, as if asking, *Why is this human being lying here?* I know that human beings are not supposed to look like this. Sometimes there are just body parts lying along the side of the road. At first I felt a little bit ashamed at how scared seeing bodies makes me, but I notice that everyone in First Squad stops talking when we come on that kind of scene. We do it in public, but this is a private war.

We have the war on two radios. Jonesy has the news on all the time on his little portable. On our squad radio we listen to the 3rd ID guys. They sound efficient except for every once in a while one of them will comment on how something got blown away. They have so much firepower that even they are impressed.

We found out that the guys from the 507th were rescued.

"They said the girl Lynch might have been raped," Coles said.

"She's lucky she's alive." This from Jonesy.

"Shut up!" This from Marla.

I looked at her to see if she was kidding. She wasn't.

For a week we did nothing but hang around the zone. The television guys in the area were interviewing soldiers and some Iraqis willing to talk about how well the Americans had done. Jonesy went around our squad tent pretending he was interviewing guys, holding his flashlight in front of them.

"I would just like to say that we did it all for Mom's microwaved apple pie!" Jean Darcy said.

"Hi, Mom!" This from Victor.

"I'd like to thank all the little people who helped make this war possible," said Evans. "Without you I wouldn't be where I am today."

"Right now I'm talking to Corporal Danforth," Jonesy said. "Where you from, son?"

"Richmond, Virginia!"

"This your first time in a combat zone?"

"No, I worked as a guard in the mall downtown across from the Marriott," Danforth said.

"Which was rougher?" Jonesy asked. "The mall or Baghdad?"

"If I had had my body armor, the mall would have been a piece of cake," Danforth said.

Funny thing. Pendleton was embarrassed when Jonesy spoke to him.

"I'm not too good at talking," he said.

"Who you want to give a shout-out to?" Jonesy asked.

"My lovely wife and two daughters, Kayla and Karen."

"Don't ask Birdy anything," Marla said. "You'll just give him a headache."

Jonesy signed off the news, then went into a commercial for Muddy Waters energy drink. It was funny.

■　■　■

Another week of sitting around. Jonesy practiced his blues and he was good at it. We did equipment maintenance, and when the supply room was restocked, we replaced anything that looked too hard to clean. It was the sand, mostly, that really screwed things up. Jonesy made a list of things that he liked about Iraq.

"The weather is good," he said. "I don't mind the heat. And I like Baghdad, but they could build them a few more bars."

"They don't drink over here," Ahmed said. "It's against their religion."

"And I like the kids," Jonesy said. "If I was running this war, I would take all their children, bring them back to Georgia, and teach them to play the blues. Now, you ain't never heard of no blues army. Am I right?"

"Right," I said.

Jonesy went on about what he liked and what he didn't like about Iraq. What he didn't like was people that he didn't even know shooting at him. "This is the drive-by capital of the freaking world!"

What I liked about Iraq at the moment was that I wasn't involved in any of the heavy fighting. From what I heard on the radio and from guys passing through, all of the fighting was rougher than what was making the news.

Marla and Barbara came by and asked me if I wanted to go shopping with them.

"We're going with a group of Third ID chaplains up to a mosque just north of the city. It's supposed to be safe," Marla said. "You want to come?"

"Yeah, okay. We riding shotgun?"

"No, the chaplains have their own security," said Barbara. "Captain Coles said we can take one Humvee. We're going to stop at a market on the way back and then at a PX they got set up in one of Saddam's palaces, so make a list of things your guys might need."

I actually got a piece of paper and started asking guys what they wanted. But after the first guy said what he wanted, which was the horniest girl in Iraq, it got stupid big-time. Danforth from Third Squad was the most stupid when he said he wanted a girl with three breasts.

"Why don't you go tell Marla that," I said.

The chaplains — two Asians, a black woman, and a white guy about forty — seemed like good people. They said they had been invited to the Shiite mosque by one of the local religious leaders.

We got into the Humvee and Marla told me I could get up on the squad gun if I wanted.

"If we're going shopping, I guess the war is really over," I said.

The 3rd ID and 4th Marines had secured an area in downtown Baghdad they were calling "the Bubble." It was like a "don't stick your head up after dark" zone for the Iraqis. The military's Central Command was bringing in all kinds of communications equipment, computers, and Global Positioning Systems and setting it all up in reinforced buildings within the area. The chaplains were from the 3rd and they shook everybody's hands before we took off. Our route was northward through the city and just out of it to the Al Kazimayn mosque. One of the chaplains told us it was a Shiite mosque and the Shiites were friendlier to us.

"Saddam is Sunni," he said.

The mosque was huge but delicate and probably the most beautiful building I had ever seen. The chaplains met the imam who had invited us. The imam asked us to leave our weapons in the trucks.

"They'll be fine there," he said.

The 3rd ID guys wouldn't leave their weapons and decided to stay outside of the mosque. Marla, Barbara, and I left our weapons locked in Miss Molly and went on a tour. I wasn't sure if the man who led us around was an imam or something, and didn't want to ask him. Nothing that he was telling us made any sense to me because he was speaking about people who had been in the area or were buried at the mosque centuries before and I couldn't keep up with the names or dates.

We spent nearly an hour in the mosque and then were invited to lunch. I didn't think we should go and leave our weapons in the Humvee and neither did Marla. Barbara said she didn't care but decided to go back with us anyhow.

We mounted up and made the trip alone back to Baghdad. It was only a few miles and took about twelve minutes before we spotted the first American patrol. We got ID'd and a marine lieutenant offered me two laptop computers and a lifetime pass to Yankee Stadium in exchange for Marla and Barbara. Marla thought it was funny, but Barbara got uptight about it and cursed a blue streak as we pulled away. We met up with another marine Humvee, told them we were headed for the Bubble, and asked if they minded if we tagged along. The driver said no but he was surprised that we were armed.

"I thought Civil Affairs people didn't carry weapons," he said. "Like chaplains."

"The difference," Marla said, "is that the chaplains think they've got an in with God and don't mind dying. We've got a few problems in that direction!"

The marine patrol moved slowly. The guys were young and one of them was eating a sandwich, which reminded me how hungry I was. We were in sight of the palace and I was explaining to

Marla why I didn't have a list of things to buy when a Humvee across the wide avenue blew up.

The marines opened fire immediately, scattering the people on the sidewalk and forcing cars to a screeching halt. The driver ahead of us spun his Humvee sideways, nearly tipped the thing over, and headed for the burning vehicle. Barbara was driving and she made a hard right, and stopped a few feet from the burning Humvee.

Three marines were already out and were trying to pull their comrades from the vehicle, which was now completely engulfed in flames.

"Look out for snipers!" a marine officer yelled.

I started scanning the windows and the rooftops, pointing the squad gun at anything that could possibly be a threat. A few of the marines fired at nothing in particular. They were just keeping everyone's head down.

Then I saw it. A marine was carrying the upper part of a body – I could tell it was an American's by the uniform – to another vehicle. They were producing body bags from somewhere and in minutes the dead marines were off the street.

I retched and was a heartbeat from vomiting. I could feel my mind closing down. It was too much to take in all at once. The explosion that had rocked the Humvee. The sudden bursts of gunfire. Marines leaping out of their vehicles ready to fight. The body of the dead marine.

There was a wounded Iraqi, a heavyset man who had been

carrying a bag of oranges, lying on the sidewalk. The marines searched him, then lifted him gently and moved him against the side of the building. Barbara went over and looked at him, kneeling by his side until two Iraqi men came up to them.

The marines put out the fire and then took out the equipment from the still smoldering hulk of the damaged Humvee. The vehicle, lying on its side, was just a dark shell, like a huge prehistoric animal with flames licking at its blackened ribs.

"IED." Barbara's voice was high and a little panicky as she got back to our vehicle. "Two dead. The Iraqi is going to die, too. They didn't stand a chance."

I had heard about the IEDs, the improvised explosive devices, but I had never seen the damage one could do before.

Two other marines were wounded and I saw their medics tending to them. The others in their unit did a quick sweep of the street, but they didn't find anybody they could identify as the trigger person.

The whole thing was over in a heartbeat. The marine patrol had been coming down the street, the IED had exploded, and now people were dead. There was no confrontation, no blurred figures flying across the busy street, no one to chase down for revenge, no one to be mad at.

A wide-eyed young marine, face smudged from the smoke, came over and told us they were leaving and that we had better get back into the safe zone. The tears on his face had traveled through the grime and stopped halfway down his cheek.

"Sometimes they take potshots at people coming to help," he said. "Even their own people."

"Did you see what exploded?" Marla asked.

"I don't know." The marine looked away. "I might have. Just a paper bag about twenty feet in front of the vehicle. They plant them and set them off with cell phones. I don't know. I might have seen it. They were good people. Good marines."

We were all dripping sweat when we got back to our base unit. Barbara and Marla came in with me. Harris was sitting on a field chest in a towel and made some stupid remark about women coming into the men's quarters.

"We met up with a marine patrol near Zarah Square," Marla said. "They weren't more than fifty yards ahead of us when they got wasted by an IED."

"Anybody . . ." Jonesy didn't finish his sentence.

"Two marines got it and an Iraqi," Barbara said. "One of the wounded marines is in deep, too. It blew off part of his hand."

"I didn't see that!" Marla said.

"He was just sitting there, numb," Barbara said. "The marine medic gave him a shot which put him right out, then put a tourniquet on the arm. I hope he doesn't lose it."

Pendleton asked what had blown up and we told him about the paper bag. He got up and punched the side of the tent. I knew how he felt. The whole thing was a nightmare. The blast had completely destroyed the marine truck and it wasn't even a direct hit.

After Barbara and Marla had sat for a while, talking about

the IED, trying to make some kind of sense of it, they got up and started to leave.

"You okay, Birdy?" Marla asked.

"Not really," I answered. "I don't know if there's going to be an okay anymore."

May 9, 2003

Dear Dad,

I know that we have had our differences and everything, but I want you to know how much I really love you and respect you. I never felt that you were wrong in anything you were saying, only that I had to learn everything you know on my own, even if it hurt sometimes. I really appreciate all that you have done for me and taught me over the years and think that it will come in handy in the long run.

Things are going well over here. The people are glad that Saddam Hussein is no longer in power. Some of the Iraqis who are Sunnis are not as sure about what is going to happen because most of the people in this part of Iraq are Shiites. The Civil Affairs guys will have a larger and larger role now that the fighting is over. There are still some disturbances going on but I think they are just the die-hard fanatics. There is also a lot of looting going on. Jamil, the old man who works in our tent, says that there are not many jobs available. As soon as we get into the rebuilding there will be plenty of jobs and then democracy will really kick in and we'll win the peace as quickly as we won the war. At least that's what the officers are saying and I kind of believe them.

Please take care of Mom and don't let her worry too much. I'm bunking down in the Bubble, which is the Safe Zone, and it is nowhere near the areas where the Iraqis can get at us. Also, the only people who do regular patrols are the Infantry and the marines and some Special Forces guys. Most of the time I play bid whist or watch television. Easy life, right?

Your loving son, Robin

Any time a guy gets a large package from home, everybody gathers around hoping it's something to eat. So when Victor Ríos from Second Squad got a humongous package, all the CA people came over to our tent to see what was in it.

"I don't know what's in it," he said. "It ain't from my people in Albuquerque."

"That's not the point," Barbara said. "The point is that it might be edible. Open it up!"

"Yo, it could be a chemical weapon or something," one of the construction guys said.

Victor looked at the return address. It was from Wyoming. "I bought a toy monkey from Wyoming on eBay," he said. "But it was like a little thing, man."

"A monkey?" Jonesy pulled his head back and squinted his eyes. "You mean like a cheep-cheep kind of monkey?"

"When I was a kid my abuela gave me a monkey to wear around my neck," Victor said. "It wasn't more than an inch high and it was carved in ivory. She said it would bring me luck. I never got shot as a kid, so when I saw the monkey on eBay I made a bid on it."

"Open it up," Jonesy said.

Victor didn't like any attention and I could see he was embarrassed as he unwrapped the package. Sure enough, it was a monkey. Big sucker, maybe four feet high. It was a real monkey, only dead and stuffed.

Harris started cracking up big-time and some of the construction people got on their headsets and started calling people over to come see Victor's monkey. Meanwhile, Victor was uncomfortable but reaching that point where being uncomfortable was going to spill over into being mad.

"I'm not eating him," Barbara said, and started off.

Captain Miller had heard that something was going on and came to take a look. She examined the monkey and announced that it was an African vervet. Victor was shaking his head; when he found the letter that came with the monkey he started reading it and then threw it down. The construction guy, a big, round-faced dude who looked about twelve, picked it up and read it.

"'I am so proud of you boys and what you are doing for our country,' it says. 'So I am sending you this monkey instead of the smaller one you won in the eBay auction. Enjoy!'"

"Some people are just stupid!" Victor was really mad.

"Who's the monkey going to ride with?" Marla asked.

"Why don't you shut up?" Victor said.

"No, really, who's he going to ride with?" Marla asked again. "First Squad'll take him!"

Victor looked up at Marla to see if she was putting him on. I looked at her, too. She wasn't. She was leaning over, taking a good look at the monkey.

"You can have him!" Victor said.

Okay. To me the monkey looked creepy. I don't like dead things and the monkey was dead but he was on a stand with a rod up his back so he didn't look — well, maybe he looked dead because you knew he was dead but his eyes were open. He was grayish brown and the front of his face was black. Marla seemed really interested in the thing, though, and after asking Victor if she could really have it, took it away with all the packaging.

There was a ball game on television, a rerun of the Mets' sixth game against Boston from 1986, and we watched that, but all the time I was thinking about Victor wearing a monkey around his neck for good luck.

The rest of the day went smoothly and when we went to chow I asked Marla if she really wanted the monkey to ride with us.

"Who? Sergeant Yossarian?"

"Sergeant who?"

"Yossarian," Marla said. "That's the name we gave him."

"He don't look like no A-rab monkey to me," Jonesy said.

"That's not an Arabic name," Marla said. "It's from a novel

about World War II called *Catch-22*. Yossarian was the central character."

"Well, Oprah Winfrey got her name from the Bible," Jonesy said. "So I guess we can have a monkey with a name from a novel."

That made as much sense as Jonesy usually made.

We got back from chow and the nets to put over our tent flaps had arrived. We had asked for them so that we could keep the flaps open and maybe catch a breeze. We had one air-conditioning unit which we could hook up to the generator, but the generator made so much noise and messed up the air so much we didn't use it. But nobody wanted the flaps open at night, so we decided to wait until morning to put the nets up.

I told Victor that the women had named the monkey Sergeant Yossarian and that the name was from a book called *Catch-22*. Victor said that it was stupid to give a monkey a name. I thought he just didn't want too much attention.

"Hey, women do that kind of thing," I said.

■　■　■

"Why do we have to do this?" Captain Miller was pissed, as per usual.

"I think the brass is handing us around because they're trying to sell some of the old-timers on the idea of Civil Affairs," Captain Coles said. "Everybody knows about us, but for some of the unit commanders it's still a hard sell. They think we're just propaganda for the press."

"We've built an army around the concept that we're more macho than anybody in the freaking world," Captain Miller said, "then when we screw up an operation you send the women out to make nice-nice."

"We don't know if they screwed it up." Jonesy was putting on his Molle vest and checking his ammo. "We know they bombed a target and some civilians were killed. But the way the people fighting us dress, they could have been soldiers, too."

"If they're sending us," Marla chipped in, "they screwed it up."

"One of our planes might have taken out one of their Red Crescent ambulances," Captain Coles said. "It'll probably be on Al Jazeera for the next six months."

I remembered the time we were attacked by guys hopping out of an ambulance. They were in an ambulance, in civilian clothes, and still had fired on us. I thought about the marines who were killed on the road back to the Bubble, and suddenly I didn't want to leave the tent.

We took First and Second Squads and the women from the Medical Squad with Captain Miller complaining at the top of her voice. I guess that was the way she handled things.

We loaded up three Humvees; one pulled a "water buffalo," a 400-gallon water carrier that could be hitched onto the back of a truck. Coles drove the Humvee pulling the water and the two medics rode with him. Ahmed went along to interpret. In the seat next to me, dressed up in a Molle vest with sergeant stripes, was Yossarian.

Jonesy was behind the wheel and it took us an hour and a half to reach the village, which was just outside of Al-Uhaimir. I didn't know how anybody could live in such a desolate area. Signs of war were everywhere: burned-out vehicles, spent shells, trees that had been hit by bombs and now seemed to twist their way out of the pockmarked earth. The most impressive thing around was a huge terraced mound that looked like something from another world. We stopped to take a closer look at it. I heard Ahmed calling it a ziggurat; the redbrick mound seemed almost to shimmer in the bright sunlight.

"The ancient Mesopotamians built shrines on top of them," Ahmed said. "Read that in the guidebook."

"That's one of the spooky things about this country," Marla said. "Half of the stuff here was built within the past two or three years and the other half has been here for five thousand years."

When we reached the area we were looking for, it was 1300 hours. There were some military trucks, including some water buffaloes, and thirty or forty soldiers. Coles talked to them and found out that the people in the village didn't want to have anything to do with us.

"They're not sure if they're afraid or just pissed off," Coles said.

"Who are they?" Marla asked.

"The 422nd," Coles answered. "They're repairing some damage to the village's water supply." The 422nd Civil Affairs Battalion was the main CA support group attached to the 3rd Infantry. They had regular missions and their own agenda while we were just a "flying squad." First Squad had all talked about trying to switch units once things calmed down.

"Did anybody talk to the local sheik?" Miller asked.

Captain Coles shrugged.

Miller saw some Iraqi women and started toward them. Ahmed went with her, and me and Jonesy followed a few steps behind them. Marla, who had dismounted, went back to the Humvee.

"Yo, Birdy, check out Miller," Jonesy said.

Captain Miller had taken off her helmet and was running her fingers through her hair as she talked to the women. She had said she didn't like being paraded as a woman but she understood that it did make a difference.

I saw Miller talking directly to one Iraqi woman. The captain nodded a few times, and then came over to us.

"We're invited into one of the houses for tea," she said. "One of the women speaks English and I think she's an American."

Captain Coles said he wasn't going in, which surprised me. He told me to go in with the two medics, and Marla.

"How come you don't want to go in, sir?" I asked.

"I think you can handle it," Coles answered.

What was happening, I thought, was that the humanity we were supposed to be showing the Iraqis was wearing thin. I didn't know who my enemy was over here, what rock he might pop out from, from which window he might shoot. I didn't know which of the figures in robes down to their ankles were praying for peace and which were planting bombs on the side of the road.

Half of the electricity in the entire country was out, and even the electricity that was supposed to be all right didn't work most of the time. The house was small, two floors, but the top floor looked too small to be a regular living space. We went into a room that was lit by an oil lamp and whatever light came through the window.

The woman who directed us to the low tables was young, maybe thirty at the most, with a thin, pleasant face that would have been pretty except for the sadness in her eyes. I thought she could have been an American. She didn't have much of an accent as she asked us to be seated. One of the other women brought a large pot and placed it in the middle of the table. The smell of tea, very strong, quickly filled the room.

"Do you want to search my house?" the first woman asked me. "I see you are looking so hard."

"No," I said.

"You speak very good English," Captain Miller said.

The woman nodded.

We were served the tea in glasses and I remembered my grandmother telling me how she used to go down from Harlem to the Lower East Side when she was young and drink tea from glasses instead of cups.

"We were told that there were children injured here," Captain Miller said. "We're very sorry."

The woman spoke to the others, who all turned and looked at Captain Miller. Captain Miller looked back at each woman in turn.

"You say I speak good English," said the woman who had invited us in. "My name is Halima Telfah. My friends call me Hali. I studied at the University of Washington in Seattle for three years and got my degree in biology there. I learned English at the university and at the hotel I worked in to support myself. The Hotel Meany. I thought it was a funny name for a hotel.

"I was very respectful of Americans. I thought you were a wonderful people. You were so free you didn't even know what to do with your freedom. Your women are free. Your men are free. Your children are free. I had so much respect for you and for your country."

"We have respect for your country, too," Marla said.

"I don't think you even know my country," Halima said.

"Can you tell us what happened?" Captain Miller asked. "Were there children injured?"

"When the fighting started — when the invasion started — the young men who lived here, there weren't many, debated among themselves what they should do. They didn't know why you wanted to kill them. They asked that question: 'Why do they want to kill us?'

"They decided that they would put themselves at your mercy. They would wait until you came and see what you would do. Then some Ba'athists came and told our men it was their duty to fight and save their country."

"The Ba'athists?" I asked.

"The Nationalist mob," she said. "Saddam's party."

"Did they come in a Red Crescent truck?" Marla asked.

"No, it was just a regular truck. I think on the side it was painted something about soft drinks. The Ba'athists said that our young men should go to the capital to get orders. They belonged to the local reserves but they wanted them to go to the capital because there was so much talk about surrendering to the Americans.

"We made cakes for our men and packed fresh fruit into bags for them to carry to Baghdad. We cried with them and laughed with them and told them to be careful. The children . . ."

She stopped and put her fingertips to her mouth as if to feel the weight of the words that were coming out. Then she took a deep breath and continued.

"The children were excited. They are only children. Every event is great for them. The men all got into the Ba'athists' truck and the children waved them good-bye. An American plane flew over-head. One of the men, I think it was one of the Ba'athists, shot at it. The plane circled. The children watched. The truck started down the road carrying our sons and brothers and husbands. The plane circled and dropped one bomb or fired one missile or some-thing. It hit the truck and there was a great explosion.

"The plane flew away. It had done its duty for the war that day. The truck was only three hundred meters down the road. We ran toward it. The children ran faster. But there was noth-ing left but pieces of bodies. One little girl began to scream. The horror of it swept over them all but one little girl whose brother was in the truck. She found what was left of him and tried to pull him home.

"Are they hurt, you ask? Yes, they are wounded deep inside. It is not something children should see. The Americans have come and the killing has begun," Halima continued. Her low, flat voice was barely above a whisper. "There is so much killing that there is no place left in our hearts to hold our grief or our anger. Now the children are asking the same question as their brothers: Why have you come to kill us?"

"I'm sorry," Captain Miller said. "I'm very sorry. Is there anything we can do to help?"

"Treat our lives as if they are as precious as your own," Halima said. "That's all we ask."

I felt torn in a hundred directions. The sadness in Halima's voice bothered me, but then I thought about the village men who had been killed, and remembered her saying that they were going to Baghdad to get ready to fight Americans. There was a lot less room in my heart for grief, too. I thought Halima knew what I was thinking, because she kept looking in my direction.

"Are you ever going back to America?" I asked.

"Who knows?" she said. "I don't dare make the predictions I made when I was a child."

We finished the tea and went outside. Captain Miller asked again if there was anything we could do and Halima asked if we had any toothpaste. We didn't but Miller said we would get her some.

"Since the bombing began, it's become such a luxury to brush your teeth," Halima said. "I feel guilty just thinking about it."

There was a boy standing in a doorway. Nine, maybe ten, and thin, he leaned against the side of the open door. The sun slanted across his legs and I saw that he was barefoot. Under one foot there was a soccer ball. I made a kicking motion and held my hands up. He looked at me for a long moment and then gently nudged the ball in my direction.

I walked over to the ball and kicked it back. Another boy came out of the shadows, followed the ball to where it had rolled against the wall, and kicked it back to me. They couldn't help being kids. No matter what happened, they were still children.

I remembered Sergeant Yossarian and motioned for the first kid to come over. He went with me to the Humvee and I pointed inside. He looked and jumped back quickly. Then he looked again. He reached in and touched Yossarian on the arm and saw that he didn't move. The smile on the kid's face was brilliant. White teeth in a brown face enjoying a moment of ridiculous peace. Yes.

He turned toward the houses and called out.

I don't know where all the kids came from, but there were soon seven: five boys and two girls, and one of the boys was chattering something in Arabic. One by one they looked into the

Humvee and the braver ones touched Yossarian. Then the first kid turned to me and spoke in Arabic.

"He wants to know if you play football," Ahmed said.

I knew he meant what we called soccer in America and I told Ahmed to tell him I knew a little about the game.

"Omar says he wants to play a game against the Americans," Ahmed said.

Okay. It was me, Jonesy, Captain Coles, and two guys from the 422nd against five Iraqi kids. We set up goals about fifty feet apart. Some of the Iraqi adults came out and stood on the side. One woman sat at her window with her arms on the sill. It reminded me of the black women in Harlem who would sit in the windows and watch the kids playing in the street.

The Iraqi boys were either better than we thought they should have been or we were worse. Much to the amusement of Marla, they scored at will past a lunging Captain Coles. We were weighed down with body armor and combat boots; the Iraqi kids, barefooted and dressed in light shirts, flew around us. We played for nearly thirty minutes before Coles, mercifully, said we had to leave.

Omar, the boy who had been standing in the doorway, said something to me, making sure it was loud enough for Ahmed to hear.

"He said any Iraqi could beat an American any day," Ahmed said. "And maybe you could get the monkey to play next time."

I said that next time we would win. It was something to say.

I patted the boy on his head and he pushed my hand away and stood up straighter, almost defiantly. Okay, I could deal with that.

The soldiers from the 422nd seemed like really good guys. They said that they would try to build a goalpost for the kids when they finished getting the water pumps working. We let the villagers empty the water buffalo. They brought out jars, buckets, even a few pots, and took as much water as they could carry.

Back to Baghdad. I was glad to be back in the Green Zone, back to feeling safe. Coles read us his report. It said that there was no "friendly fire" incident, and that the village guys could be called enemy combatants.

It all looked good on paper, but I knew that Miller would have trouble with it. I was beginning to understand where she was coming from. She didn't have any easy answers, but she didn't need them.

Back at the tent Jonesy peeled off his boots and socks and collapsed on his cot. His feet stunk so he poured some water on them. "Yo, Birdy, how'd you like playing against those kids?"

"It was okay."

"I really liked it," Jonesy said. "That's what I want life to be about."

"I thought life was going to be about the blues," I said.

"I'm going to be playing the blues at night," Jonesy said. "I got to find something to do in the daytime. That's why I'm over here."

"So what do you think of these Iraqis?" I asked.

"It's like my uncle Herbert used to say." Jonesy propped himself up on one elbow. "You don't need to be around nobody you got to watch all the time unless you making love to them. And God know this Georgia boy ain't making love to nothing over here."

Sergeant Harris and Jonesy got into a stupid shouting match that almost ended up in a fight. We were watching some cop program, the usual stuff with police dealing with low-level street crime. The cops were picking up prostitutes and Harris said that in a way most women weren't much more than whores.

"They get a man to support them and then they just sit back and watch television," he said.

"Yo, man, you got to show more respect than that," Jonesy said. "Your mama is a woman."

"No, you got to watch yours," Harris said. "I'm a sergeant, fool!"

"You also sounding like your brain is AWOL," Jonesy said. "We over here fighting with women."

Harris jumped up from where he had been sitting, pushed Jonesy up against the wall, and drew his fist back as if he was going to punch him. I grabbed Harris from the back and spun him around while Victor and Evans jumped in front of him.

"I'll kill you and that little jerk!" Harris was spitting as he talked.

"Hey, we're over here together, man," Evans said.

"You going to grow you some eyes in the back of your head?" Jonesy was still against the locker as he shouted at Harris. "'Cause you're gonna need them!"

"Why? Why?" Harris balled his fist up again. "You going to sneak up on me? Huh? Huh?"

"No, because your butt is in a combat zone and you going to need somebody to be watching your back," Jonesy said.

"I don't need you!" Harris spat on the ground and then pushed by me toward the door.

Nobody said anything. We had all seen it but there wasn't anything to do but to get over it. I wondered if we would.

"You could report him," Evans said.

"Or shoot him when he goes to sleep," I said.

"Let it go," Jonesy said. "Every dog gets his day."

We sat around for a while, each of us thinking how we would have handled the situation. I knew that most of us wouldn't have had to. Harris had picked the smallest dude in the unit to jump on. There was no way he would have done it back in the world.

I hadn't thought about it much, but Jonesy was right. We needed one another to get out of this war alive. We needed one another and a whole lot of luck.

When Harris came back in, Pendleton told him he was wrong to be hitting a member of our unit.

"You want a piece of me? You want a piece of me?" Harris stood up, glowering at Pendleton.

Pendleton was a big, slow-talking white boy who could have broken Harris in half and everybody knew it. We just waited until Harris got his thirty seconds of showboat time and sat himself down again.

Some of the guys in our unit got along well. The others were okay but they didn't hang out much. But we were all living through the same things, seeing the same fighting, feeling the same moments of boredom and terror. We were used to looking for one another in the mess tent, and expected to see one another in the mornings. There wasn't any room for any BS.

Coles came in just after sunset and told us that we were going to be escorting some Intelligence guys out to a place in the Rusafa district before daybreak in the morning. He asked if anything was wrong, and after Jonesy said no, we all said no.

"Look, I'm really not volunteering you guys," Coles said. He looked around a bit more. He knew something was wrong but couldn't figure out what, so he left.

Morning came long before it was supposed to. We were barely dressed when Coles came into the tent. He looked around to see that we were all dressed and ready to go, and then brought in the two Special Ops guys who were with the Intelligence Unit. Darcy and Marla came in with them.

"Guys, this is Lieutenant Davis, and this is Corporal Lawler," Coles said. "They'll explain the mission."

Lawler had a square head and a short haircut. He looked like a Nazi from an old World War II movie. "We got some information from the confession box that we thought we should check out," he said.

"The confession box?" Darcy sucked her teeth and looked away.

The confession box was a booth the Intelligence Unit had set up. They paid the Iraqis who anonymously visited the box for information on insurgents. Most of the information intelligence got was bogus. But every once in a while something valuable was passed on.

"Anyway . . ." Lawler went on, "the information is that there's an IED factory in the Old City area. We're going to pay a surprise visit and see what we find."

"Who's translating?" Coles asked.

"I will be," Davis said.

Marla rolled her eyes up and away.

"Look, let me give you people a few clues." Davis's jaw tightened, which made a white line across the bottom of his face. "We won the 'stand up and fight' war. That was over when we reached Baghdad. This is different. We're getting guys killed every other day by roadside bombs. These people here have been at war for the last twenty or so years. Before they invaded Kuwait they were fighting with Iran. Intelligence estimates that there are over two million unspent artillery shells and mines spread across Iraq. Each one of them can be rigged into an IED. If one percent of them worked — *one percent* — they could kill twenty thousand of our people. Are you with me?"

"Hey, man, you want to catch the next train out of here?" Jonesy asked.

"They've got the weapons. And yeah, they're crude, but they can kill you just as effectively as a sophisticated weapon. They've got the weapons all over the country, and the technology to arm them is spreading. That's where you come in. We've got guys to jump over tall buildings and run through fire. We've got guys who can shoot the balls off an anorexic flea. We need some soldiers with people skills and with insights. And from what I've heard, that's what you bring to the table."

"So we're going to be looking for these shells?" Marla asked.

"If we can find artillery shells that would be good," Davis said. "But we're looking for the people who have the technology. If we find electrical wires, detonators, clock assemblies, cell phones, then we'll know we're getting close."

"Cell phones?"

"They hook the cell phones up so that when the phone receives a signal, it sends an electrical impulse to a detonator instead of the ringer," Lawler said.

"So if you come across an IED, and the guy who put it there sees you" — Jonesy was scratching his crotch — "all he got to do is to make a call and he got your number?"

"You got it," Davis said.

More scary crap. We started putting on our gear and I made sure all my body armor was strapped down tight. I had heard about IEDs being wired up for remote and even being thrown off a bridge, but it looked like it was getting more and more high tech. It was like the Iraqis were getting better at killing us and we were standing still.

"What happened between you and Harris?" Coles asked Jonesy as we mounted up.

"Nothing."

"It didn't sound like nothing," Coles said.

"Hey, Captain, if I go to the confession box and tell you what Birdy dreams, about how much can I get?" Marla leaned against the side of the Humvee with one foot on the ammo can.

"If it saves lives, Marla, it's worth looking into," Coles said. "I'd rather meet up with an IED on my terms rather than on the bad end of some nineteen-year-old kid making a name for himself at my expense."

Headquarters had set up a booth for Iraqis to complain or make suggestions. The guys in the 3rd ID started calling it the confession box because the soldier taking the information sat on one side of a wall and the person giving it sat on the other. If they gave us any useful information about insurgents or plots, we would pay them for the information. Word got around Baghdad quickly and every Iraqi that needed a few bucks was showing up with a long story — or a short one — about how he had seen three guys plotting to take over the Green Zone or building a weapon of mass destruction. It got to be such a joke that one guy actually said that he had seen someone put explosives inside a goat and it was going to run wild through the barriers.

We were set to go but I had to go back to pee and so did Coles, so First Squad was the last one ready.

An Infantry squad from the 3rd went with us, split into two Humvees, one in front of the convoy and one in back. Their vehicles had iron plates on the sides.

"Birdy, hold Yossarian's hand," Marla said. "He gets scared when we go out in the middle of the night."

We headed east and then circled back around the Green Zone toward the Old City section. We had been told that the Iraqis who were pretty well off lived in Old City before the war. The Iraqis who were really rich lived on the outskirts of the city in walled homes with guards.

Jonesy was half humming, half singing something and I asked him what it was because it didn't sound much like the blues.

" 'Survivor'!" he said. He was always rocking when he drove and also hunched forward toward the wheel. "When you were peeing, Marla said that was the monkey's theme song. Destiny's Child put it out."

I could hardly see the monkey's face because somebody had put a helmet on its head. I hoped God wouldn't think it was funny to let me die sitting next to a monkey.

The first Humvee driver knew his way pretty well and we reached the Old City area in quick time. We stopped, killed the engines, and were told to dismount and get our night-vision goggles ready. Crap. Iraq is dark at night and the only thing you're going to see with the night-vision goggles is something that's trying to kill you. The streets where we had stopped were narrow; perhaps a Humvee could get through but there was no way we were going to take a chance. If some guy popped out with an RPG in those narrow alleys you were toast.

The houses usually had a courtyard behind a fence. The fence was locked with either a dead bolt or a bar across the entire door and if you had to bust through, you woke up the entire neighborhood. Once you broke through the fence, if you couldn't climb over it, you had to find the door. That would be a tough mother to crack as well.

"They act as if they're living in New York City!" Jonesy had said.

I didn't have a comeback for that.

The officer from the 3rd placed his men at each corner of the house. I felt like peeing again as I watched them crouch into position. Two of their guys went toward the outer fence. They knelt together for a split second and then one of them went over. I held my breath for a long second, and then saw the front fence open. So far, so good.

The Humvees were on the outside perimeter of the operation. If the thing went down wrong we were to retreat to the vehicles. I thought of Marla in the turret. She had the squad gun ready and her nine cocked.

"Watch those index fingers! Watch those index fingers!" The officer from the 3rd's voice was a loud whisper.

I checked my finger and took it out of the trigger housing. Don't kill anybody who didn't need killing.

Me and Jonesy went with two Infantry guys, one of them carrying a ramming tool, to the left side of the house, and Harris and Victor went to the right, looking for side doors. We found one and the Infantry guys went up to it and pushed gently. Then they clicked into their radios, knelt on one knee, and waited.

I got down on one knee and Jonesy squatted. I heard the voice in the radio and the infantry guy stood, waited a second, then hit the door with the tool.

BAM! Nothing.

BAM! It broke partway. I imagined whoever was inside reaching for their AK-47. *BAM!* The door broke open and the two Infantry guys moved in quickly, one to either side of the room. I was scared shitless as I went through the door and to my left. The room was lit up as the night light flooded the room, making the whole place seem kind of a spooky green through my goggles. I pushed them up onto my helmet.

The rooms were in a circle around a hallway. In the hallway there was a stairwell, not much more than a ladder going up to the second floor.

The Infantry dude yelled something. It might have been Arabic or I might have just misunderstood him. He fired into the wall, and the next thing he called out I knew.

"Americans!" He was up the stairwell in a heartbeat and the guy with him was close enough to run up his back.

They were screaming at the tops of their voices, trying to take command of the situation. By the time the first two had reached the second deck three more Infantry guys had come in. One went up the ladder while the other two started checking out spaces on the ground floor.

"These guys are scaring me and they're on my side!" Jonesy said.

There was more shouting upstairs and then a guy shouted down the well. "Control!"

"Clear on the first floor!" was the answer.

Two minutes later one of the Infantry guys came down followed by two men, two women, one of them holding a baby, and three small children.

Their officer came in, checked as they sat the Iraqis down in the inner hallway, and sniffed his approval. Then he told the men to start their search.

"Check the upper floor first," he said.

The two Intelligence guys from the 422nd came in and started talking to the Iraqis. There were a lot of shrugs and palms-up gestures indicating that they didn't know what we were talking about. One of the men kept squinting toward Davis, who was doing most of the talking, and I could tell Davis was repeating the questions, slowly and deliberately.

"What's he saying?" Coles asked.

"He wants to know who's going to pay for his door," Davis

answered. "He says he doesn't know anything about any weapons. He's an accountant but we blew up his bank."

"Man, this is just a wild-goose chase," Harris said. "We just busted up some more damn doors and almost killed some more people for nothing."

They finished searching the top floor — I could hear them throwing things around — and then came downstairs. The baby started crying and the woman who held it began to rock her gently. The woman was pretty. I couldn't tell how old, but she had huge eyes that I would have loved to have been looking into under different circumstances.

The two men kept shrugging their shoulders and shaking their heads. Once in a while they spoke to each other and Davis would yell at them to stop. The older woman was crying softly. She didn't answer any questions and looked away any time Davis spoke to her. It was as if they couldn't believe what was happening to their lives.

Davis asked questions for another fifteen minutes and then asked us to search the Iraqis. He told us to get one of the women to search their women.

Coles called Marla and told Jonesy and Harris to stay with the vehicles until she got back. Harris muttered something under his breath and left with Jonesy. God, I didn't like that sucker.

I also didn't like searching people. I had been stopped on 136th Street once, just outside the Countee Cullen Library, by two plainclothes cops who had searched me. I knew what it felt like.

Embarrassed that I had to stand there with my hands in the air while strangers patted me down and went through my pockets, humiliated because they were assuming power over me and I couldn't do a thing about it. I felt I knew how the Iraqi men felt as I searched them. They were just wearing shirts, nothing under them, and I could see they didn't have any weapons on them. Davis saw it, too, but he was taking out his embarrassment on the enemy.

Marla came in and she searched the women quickly and found nothing.

"I'll get his name and address so we can compensate him for the damage," Davis said.

We stood around while Davis took the guy's name and address. Davis asked the infantry guys how much damage there was upstairs and they said none.

"Go check," Davis said.

Marla was looking around in the kitchen area. She stared at a wooden tub.

"We'll make sure that everything damaged is noted so we can pay for it," Davis was saying to one of the Iraqis. "I'm sorry that we disturbed you."

The man was shaking his head in disgust.

"Captain Coles," Marla called. She lifted a hand full of flour and let it fall through her fingers.

"Dumplings of mass destruction?" Coles asked.

"No, just flour," Marla said, lifting a handful and letting it run through her fingers. She did it again. "And detonators."

Everything stopped. Marla pulled out some of the cord and Davis told her to stop. I went over and looked at the tub. There were thin light blue tubes visible; each had two wires, one red and one yellow sticking from one end.

"Jesus! Oh, Jesus!" Davis was visibly shook.

I looked at the Iraqi man who had been shaking his head. Now he was standing with his head down, biting his lip.

Davis told Coles to post the CAs as security. As we went out, the other Infantry guys piled into the house.

I couldn't wait to fill Marla in on what had happened.

"You mean they had finished searching and I was the only one that found the stuff?"

"The only one!" I said.

By the time the 3rd guys had brought out the two males, blind-folded and cuffed, and got them into their vehicles, I could see a streak of light in the distance. It was almost a new day. The sound of the muezzin, calling the Islamic faithful to their morning prayers, lifted eerily across the rooftops.

"Hey, Marla, that was just luck, right?" I asked as we turned the Humvee around to head back to our camp.

"No, I like to cook," she said. "One foster home I was in had me doing most of the cooking. I didn't mind it. But nobody smoothes the flour out like that on top. That's all show-and-tell, man."

I'm not going to live through this war. These people around me, Marla, Jonesy, Victor, Pendleton, even Harris, they're all better soldiers than I am. I would have never noticed that flour. Not in a thousand years.

But I felt good as I undressed and fell across the bed. I hadn't been shot at, and First Squad had found the detonators. Maybe we had even saved some lives. But then I started thinking about the Iraqi women, one crying and one rocking the baby. I remembered how bad I had felt for them, only to find out that they were in a family that probably would have killed me if they had had the chance.

Then I started thinking about Marla in a foster home. What was that like? She was so open at times, but she gave only glimpses of who she was.

The word came down that some supply officer got promoted to lieutenant colonel and Major Sessions, who thought she was going to get the promotion, got passed over. I didn't care but I thought Marla, who was all into being a woman soldier, would. She didn't.

"She's humping behind a desk," Marla said. "I haven't seen her out here ducking bullets or playing hide-and-go-seek with Pablo."

"The whole promo thing's political," Coles said. "Once you get up to captain you have to start kissing butt to move up. Either that or you're in a hot zone and everybody above you gets nailed."

"They'd have to send an IED by mail back to Mama Sessions to get her," Marla said.

Okay, so we all had the 411 and so here comes Major Sessions into our squad meeting looking like she just stepped out of a fashion magazine and talking about how good a job we've done.

"We've been asked to help a woman find her son," Major Sessions said.

She went on about how, in what she called "all the area conflicts," it was easy to lose track of people and how we were showing our humanity by helping the Iraqi woman find her son.

She gave us some details. The kid was fourteen and belonged to a tribe that we were trying to influence, and that even if we could confirm that he was dead it would be cool because then they could have a decent Muslim funeral. All the time I was trying to imagine her with no pants on and her pistol strapped to her thigh. She added that she would be coming along with us.

"I'm not holding the blanket," Marla said when Major Sessions had left the tent.

"What's that mean?" I asked.

"Darcy told me she went with some woman captain to mass and when the captain had to pee she made Darcy hold the blanket on the side of the road," Marla said. "So if Major Sessions has to pee, you're going to have to hold the blanket, Birdy."

"I'll hold it," I said. "I want to see what she's got under those fatigues, anyway."

"You got a girl back home?" Marla was sitting on an empty MRE case loading up canisters of ammo for the squad gun.

"Sort of."

"Sort of?" Marla turned to me with a big grin on her face. "What does 'sort of' mean?"

"It means she's his old lady but she doesn't know it!" Jonesy called from across the room.

"It means that we talked and she said she was going to — you know — be my old lady and write and stuff and we'd make all the big decisions later," I said.

"Birdy, the only letters you're getting over here are from your mother," Jonesy called.

"Jonesy — up yours!"

"No, really, Birdy." Marla folded her fingers and laid her chin on them. "You can tell me. Are you sleeping with this girl?"

"How come that's your business?"

"Yo, Jonesy, we got to make sure that Birdy gets home safe," Marla called out across the room. "He's a virgin."

"Marla, you know, the last person that put their nose into my business —"

"Oh, yeah, what kind of gun did she have?"

I didn't mind Marla getting on my case. I would have minded a few weeks before, but now it seemed cool. Like family.

The big deal about our mission was that the kid, Muhammad Latif Al-Sadah, was the son of a Sunni imam. Only we weren't to mention the Al-Sadah part of his name because it meant something and some other tribes might want to hurt him. We were getting more and more of that kind of talk. There was fighting going on between tribes, fighting between Sunnis and Shiites, and even between people living in different cities. It was like going into a neighborhood to stop crime and then finding out that most of the crime was about what gang you belonged to and nobody really wanted to stop it.

The kid had been out on the streets of Baghdad past curfew and just disappeared. We were going to search the hospitals, detention centers, and the morgues. I knew he might have been shot and that if we found him at all it would be in one of the makeshift morgues they were setting up all over the city. Every day Iraqis were being killed in Baghdad. Our army killed some of them. The ones we killed were mostly guys who attacked convoys or thought they could fire off a quick shot from a window. Sometimes Iraqi men were killed when they were out past curfew. Nobody could tell if they were trying to find something to steal or if they were really up to something.

The coalition forces had won the hot war and the newscasts kept telling us that we were in the stabilizing and rebuilding phase of Operation Iraqi Freedom, but the situation was getting hairy. I couldn't understand what the Iraqis were about, or what they really wanted. The television coverage showed interviews with them, always men and usually, according to Jamil, Kurds, talking about how glad they were that Saddam Hussein was overthrown. It was Jonesy who had the question we all wanted to ask.

"If all the Racks are so happy with what we doing over here, who the hell is shooting at us and laying out all the IEDs?" he asked.

Nobody had the answer. We did know that when they lined up to fight against our Infantry guys, they went down hard. For every one of the coalition people that got killed, there were from five to ten dead Iraqis. Maybe even more. Dead Iraqis didn't show up on the late news.

When one of our guys was killed we got the body off the streets quickly. We even washed up the blood. When the Iraqis were killed it took a while for an ambulance to come and get the body. There would always be other Iraqis around, friends, mourning and crying, sometimes swearing revenge. I didn't know what they did with the bodies. I had heard that, according to their religion, they had to bury them within three days. A guy in the 4th Marines told me he had seen a bunch of dead bodies packed in ice in one of the morgues. He said the sight of it was something that would stay in his head forever.

"Yo, man, the Euphrates River looks blue and the Tigris looks green," Jonesy said.

We were headed along the Tigris toward the Republican Hospital. They had snatched Ahmed from our unit for the week and sent him over to where they were setting up a jail or holding pen at Abu Ghraib. We weren't supposed to take Jamil with us because he was a civilian, but we gave him five packs of American cigarettes and he came along.

The hospital hadn't been hit during the bombing or in the

fighting that followed. But it was shoddy, as far as American standards were concerned, and available only to the richer people.

"A poor man in Iraq might never speak to a doctor," Jamil said. "In the West you complain about the cost in dollars. In Iraq your life is always in Allah's palm."

We were waiting in the third-floor office area for the hospital administrator to talk to us. We waited nearly thirty minutes, with Major Sessions sending first her aide and then Jonesy to remind the Iraqi staff that there were Americans to be dealt with. I felt a little bit ashamed of her. She was tough, but it was easy being tough when you had all the cards.

The Iraqi who showed up was a tall, thin man in a white jacket.

"May I help you?" he asked.

Major Sessions told him about the kid we were looking for.

"We have a morgue attached to this hospital," he said. "We are trying to put together a list of people we have identified who are in other morgues or buried. We can go over our lists — When did he disappear?"

"On April fourteenth," Major Sessions said.

"So long ago?" the Iraqi answered. "We were overwhelmed during that period. It was all triage — very selective, very much —"

"Check to see if he is here!" Major Sessions interrupted the Iraqi. Her voice was flat, hard.

The Iraqi inhaled sharply, as if he were startled, and nodded. "Of course," he said. "We will see. Please come with me."

The elevator wasn't working, so we walked down two flights of stairs to the basement morgue. The staff was working in blue overalls. Some wore surgical masks. One of the women wore a burka and a surgical mask. The smell was strong enough to knock you down. I thought I was going to puke.

The bodies were stacked in shelves, wrapped in cloth. Most had tags that I thought were ID. Some of the bodies were short, maybe only three feet long; I guessed they were either children or body parts.

The Iraqi who had brought us downstairs spoke to a woman in Arabic and she glanced at us before leaving the room. Through the doorway I saw her go up a flight of stairs.

"None of these bodies have been here that long," the administrator said, "but since we don't know if the boy is dead or when he might have died, we can't tell much from the dates. Please feel free to look around. You can also see how successful the Americans and British have been in dispatching your enemies."

The administrator was showing us what dying was about, what it looked like up close. Major Sessions looked around her, as if she needed a place to hide. Jamil found a chair for her and she sat. The major looked smaller sitting there, and for a moment I felt sorry for her. Just for a moment.

"Can't we just look at the records?" she asked. "An American hospital would have records."

The woman I had seen go upstairs returned with a huge book

and put it on the desk against the wall. Jamil started looking through it, turning the pages, shrugging now and then, sometimes stopping to look at a name.

The smell when we entered the morgue area was terrible, but as we breathed in the foul air it got worse and worse. A male attendant handed Marla and Major Sessions masks. Marla put hers over her face, but Major Sessions didn't. Instead she got up, took two steps toward the door, and threw up.

There were two other morgues to check. We dropped Major Sessions off in the Green Zone and me, Jonesy, and Marla went with Captain Coles and Jamil.

"Yo, Marla, you looked pretty cute in that surgical mask," I said. "It looked as if you were wearing a burka."

"What do you say we don't check any more morgues," Marla said. "We'll just say we did."

Captain Coles wasn't going for it until Jamil told him it wasn't any use.

"We don't know what he looked like in life," Jamil said, shrugging. "And the records just say things like 'male body' and give some suggestion of how old the person might have been and how he came to die. Sometimes there is a name and address if they found identification on the body. But . . ."

"But what?" Captain Coles had his head to one side as he looked down at the shorter man.

"A lot of time the papers are taken by people who need them more than the dead person," Jamil said.

That was enough for us to decide not to go to any other morgues.

We went to another hospital and an aid station. None of the doctors or nurses or whoever they had working there were interested in helping us.

"One more dead boy is not of great importance when so many are dying," Jamil said with a shrug. "The hospital workers don't think you're doing anything but wasting their time."

We did see some horrendous wounds in one of the hospitals. There were men with limbs amputated, the bandages wrapped around the stumps of arms or legs. Sometimes they would be bloody. Relatives were in the wards, and even in the emergency rooms, comforting the patients.

"Doesn't say much for sanitation," Jonesy said.

"Jamil, are they bringing in insurgents to these hospitals?" Captain Coles asked.

"Sir, they are bringing in Iraqi peoples," Jamil said.

I'd been to American hospitals. Even the worst ones looked like palaces compared to the Iraqi hospitals.

We took a break near a bridge and watched the MPs search the people, cars, and trucks going over it. A busload of school-children rolled by; they waved at us.

"Jamil, what you thinking about all of this?" Jonesy asked our interpreter. "You glad to see Saddam go?"

"Come back and ask me the same question in one year and I will tell you," Jamil said. "We knew that Saddam was Satan, but we could recognize his mustache and learn to smile when he walked down the street. Who will be the new Satan?"

A guy with a cart of fresh fruit came down the street and we stopped him and bought some. Jamil negotiated the price, which must have been pretty good, because after the guy gave us the fruit he was smiling. We mounted up and Coles said that we were going to go to only one prison.

"When we got here the place was empty and all the cells were open," the captain that ran the prison said. "The Iraqis had let them all out. I'm told the tanks were down the street and the prisoners were running out the side gates. Murderers, thieves, lunatics, everything. They let them loose. I guess the theory was that they'd make trouble for us the same way they made trouble for the Iraqis."

"Who's in here now?" Coles asked.

"Whoever we pick up and don't know what to do with," was the answer. "We're not sure if they're POWs or criminals or what. I think Central Command is trying to decide that back in Kuwait."

"Can you ID any of them?" Coles asked.

"Most of them," the captain replied. "They're people we've caught at checkpoints with weapons in their cars, some with RPGs, a few who were looting. We were going to turn the looters over to the Iraqi police, but they didn't want them."

The captain got two corporals to go through their records looking for the fourteen-year-old Muhammad. They came up with five possibilities.

"Muhammad is the most common name over here," one of the corporals said. "And half of them discard their ID and tell you that they're young so you won't put them in prison."

They got the five guys out and Jamil took each one aside and talked to him.

"This is a creepy-looking place," Marla said, looking around at the grimy walls and barbed wire. "Even for a jail."

"I was in jail one time in my life," Jonesy answered. "For being drunk in public and I wasn't even drunk."

"Then why did you go to jail?" Marla asked.

"I went into a store in Atlanta and shoplifted a pair of sunglasses," Jonesy said. "Just when I started out the door, two cops came in and scared me so bad I nearly fell down. Then I started acting drunk, staggering around the store, and when I had the chance I ditched the sunglasses."

"And you went to jail for that?" I asked.

"Four hours," Jonesy said. "Them was some thirty-dollar sunglasses. I could have got sixty days for them."

The kid that Jamil brought over looked more like twelve than fourteen. He was a slight kid, with big eyes and a broad smile. He was jabbering away in Arabic a mile a minute and Jamil just nodded.

"He said he was out after curfew because his family goat had been killed by the bombing and he had seen a goat wandering around in the streets," Jamil said. "He was trying to get the goat back to his house when the British caught him. They turned him over to the Americans."

"You believe him?"

"No, he was probably out stealing," Jamil said. "But he's the right child."

Captain Coles had to clear permission to release Muhammad and put in a call to his commander, a lady general. It took nearly an hour to pull off, but finally the captain came and told us we could take Muhammad. The kid was so glad to be leaving the prison, he kissed all our hands and praised Allah over and over again.

"He says he loves Americans," Jamil said.

Coles called Major Sessions and told her what had happened. She told us to bring the boy to headquarters.

"If she tries to take credit for finding him, I'm going to put a boot so far up her butt she's going to be sucking toes for a week!" Marla said.

"Then you can take Muhammad's place in the jail," Coles said.

We took Muhammad to Major Sessions, who already had a press conference set up. That pissed us off. Then they wanted to know who actually found the kid, and when our squad was singled out they took Marla, hat off so her blond hair was showing, and interviewed her.

"How did it make you feel when you found Muhammad?" The reporter was wearing his "this is serious" face.

"Pretty good," Marla said, trying to downplay the whole thing.

"'Pretty good,'" the reporter repeated as he turned away from Marla toward the camera. "For American soldiers this rescue mission, reuniting an Iraqi child with his parents, is just part of the day's work . . ."

We got back just in time for supper. Jonesy started interviewing Marla again, holding his spoon up as a mike.

"Yo, Miss White Lady, how you feel rescuing a poor little Racki boy?"

"It's *Ms.* White Lady," Marla said. "And I feel so glad to have done my part to save the world from evil and introduce a little boy to the joys of the free world. And if I see his little ass on the street after curfew, I'm going to shoot him."

We kept Muhammad overnight and took him back to his village the next morning. Captain Coles asked Major Sessions if she wanted to go along. She said no. Marla made some more promises about what she was going to do to the major, but actually we were really glad Sessions didn't go with us.

Some women who knew Muhammad spotted him the moment he stepped out of the Humvee and started calling for his mother. She came out and we went through the whole bit of thank-you and hand-kissing again. It felt good to see people happy with something we had done for a change.

Hey Uncle Richie,

   I am online again because they have set up a whole bank of computers for Headquarters Company and the press. The press can chase us off any time they want, which sucks. The guys in Headquarters Company sit and write letters to their friends. No big deal. I see the Yankees are kicking butt again and with Jeter out. We're going all the way this year! We had a guy try to kill himself today. Captain Miller said that's happening a lot. Guys are getting spooked with the IEDs and the way the Rules of Engagement keep chang-ing. Sometimes the rules – we get them on what they call ROE cards – can change in the middle of the day. My friend Jonesy said he was chasing a suspected sniper down the street and had to dial his cell phone with his other hand to figure out if he could shoot him or not. Mama is always asking if she can send me anything. I don't know how her money is with Pop in and out of the hospital with his high blood pressure. If her money is good will you have her send me some toy dolls? They don't have to be expen-sive. We have little trucks and things for boys and the girls don't mind them but . . . I was just told I have to get off the computer. I hope there's a curse on this machine and that it gets this big-nosed sucker standing over me reading as I type and I don't care if he is a Company Orderly. Love – Robin

Jerry Egri was a Polish-American guy assigned to our unit for one week until he got his regular assignment. He was going to be the liaison between the American troops and the Polish soldiers who were fighting with the Coalition Forces.

"What did you do back home?" Jonesy asked.

"I taught kindergarten in Cleveland — not really in Cleveland, in Shaker Heights," Jerry said. "Shaker Heights is like Cleveland dipped in gold paint."

"You didn't like that?" I asked.

"These kids were so pampered they made me change the rules when I taught them how to play soccer so they wouldn't get hit with the ball." Jerry laughed.

"You taught soccer?" Jonesy was lying on his bunk and pulled himself up on one elbow.

"Yeah. I played in Poland before I came to the States," Jerry answered. "You guys have a movie on this base?"

"How good are you?" Jonesy asked.

"Whoa!" Marla pushed next to me on the foot locker. "Jonesy, don't tell me I'm going to hear what I think I'm going to hear."

"Damn straight!" Jonesy said. "He's here for a week. We can kick some Iraqi butt before he goes."

Okay, so we got a dynamite team together. It was me, Jonesy, Marla, and Victor from Second Squad, and Third Squad with a promise to Pendleton that he could play goalie. Darcy and Evans said they would be our cheerleaders and even Captain Miller said she'd come to see the game.

Captain Coles radioed the 422nd and in less than an hour they called back with the news that Omar would set the game up for the next Friday. Jerry was going to teach us the basics and play with us.

"We need a few thunder kicks," Marla said. "Shock and awe, baby! Shock and awe!"

We set up a practice area and started assigning positions. There were defenders, forwards, centers, the whole works. Soccer was a lot more complicated than I thought it was. The bad part was moving the ball. If you stopped to kick it somebody was on top of you and it didn't go in the direction you wanted it to go. If you tried to kick it while it was moving it might go anywhere.

"You gotta concentrate!" Jerry said.

I could see the frustration on his face the first day, especially when a few of us missed the ball entirely. And any time Jerry wanted to come over and take the ball from us, he could. He could just work his feet better than we could. Finally, he stopped us from trying to move the ball up and down the field and just put us in a circle and had us kick it around to one another. By the third day we were almost getting it. Victor was pretty good, and so was Ahmed.

"You're not bad, Perry," Jerry said to me. "Somewhere between Ronaldinho's grandmother and my dog."

Yeah, thanks. I thought we were getting it. We could actually pass the ball to one another and, as long as Jerry wasn't too close, move it some. The week had been slow; the 422nd was moving into Baghdad and taking over the big stuff. They were trying to get a hospital and a school up and running on the edge of the Old City. Our guys were mostly playing cards and watching television and staying out of the heat.

Nobody was anxious to go out of what they were now calling the Green Zone. There had been some nasty incidents in town. An IED had gone off near a marine vehicle but no one was seriously hurt. It turned into pretty nasty business when some Iraqi men started cheering and the marines opened up on them. One of them was wounded pretty badly and lay in the street for a half an hour before a Red Crescent ambulance picked him up. A newsman asked some of the guys what they thought about the incident and they all shrugged him off. Later, in the tent, we talked about it again.

"Man, you got to be kidding," Jonesy said, pulling at his crotch the way he did when he was mad. "Don't be smiling and showing your teeth when some sucker is trying to shoot me. You might as well be doing the shooting yourself as far as I'm concerned."

"The ROE for Baghdad says you don't shoot anybody unless they're clearly engaged in trying to harm you," Pendleton said.

"That's not true, Pendleton," I said. "The word this morning was that we're authorized to shoot looters."

"That's not right." Pendleton was shaking his head. "That's just not right."

"Yo, man, come here for a minute," Jonesy leaned forward and whispered to Pendleton, who didn't move. "You take those Rules of Engagement and pin them over your butt and see if one of these dudes running around with a tablecloth on his head don't shoot you through it."

Jonesy was right. The rules counted only for us. The Iraqis who were out to get us could do anything they wanted.

We got clearance in the morning of the game and were rolling toward Al-Uhaimir by 1000 hours. Captain Miller and Jerry rode with Second Squad. We took along three extra balls for the kids and some notebooks and pencils. For the first time in a long, long time I felt really human. I hadn't been down or anything, just tired all the time. Sleep didn't count in Iraq the way it did at home. I always woke up tired.

■ ■ ■

We got to the village and the first kid I see is Omar. He's there and he's got a soccer ball under his arm. There were a batch of guys from the 422nd, some officers, and a photography crew, too. Somebody had leaked the game.

"Man, you guys are going to be on CNN tonight," Marla said. "Maybe Captain Miller and I should strip down to our shorts and shake our booties for the camera."

Captain Miller, who was in a surprisingly good mood, raised an eyebrow.

We met the Iraqi kids. Only they weren't the same kids we had played the first game with; these guys were older, teenagers.

"Hey, Birdy, you getting a bad feeling about this game?" Captain Coles asked.

"Yep."

I got Omar by the sleeve and asked him what was up with all of the new guys.

"People from three villages wanted to play," he said, holding up three fingers. "They all know about the game and want to play against the Americans."

"Who told them?"

He grinned and stuck his chest out.

We wore sneakers and shorts. The Iraqis, for the most part, were barefoot in djellabas. Two had on regular pants and one was wearing sneakers. It was a bloodbath. We were competitive for about three minutes. Then they figured out that Jerry was our only real player, and kept the ball away from him.

The Iraqis had six shots on goal before we had one. They only made four. The score was twelve to nothing before we had to stop it while they argued among themselves. They were yelling at Omar pretty hard and I think he wanted them to have mercy on us. They brought in two more players, teenagers again, and ran the score up to twenty to nothing.

Then Omar got the teenagers to sit out and got some really young kids in to play against us. By that time we were all standing with our tongues out and our hands on our knees and Captain Miller was warning us about dehydration. Meanwhile the camera crew was having a field day, running up and down the field preserving our humiliation for all time.

"I make a motion we should come back and shoot them," Victor said as we lay on the ground afterward.

We voted on the motion and it passed, nine to nothing.

The 422nd served up some lunch and the film crew took pictures of some of the Iraqis and some officers. Miller wouldn't let them take her picture.

"Tribe loyalty," she said.

That was cool.

Omar and three of his friends ate lunch with us.

"Omar, what would you do if you came to America?" Marla asked.

"I would go to New York City and see the tall buildings," Omar said. "And I would go to college and play a horn." He made a movement as if he were playing a trombone.

"Do you play trombone?" Coles asked.

"No, but I would learn in college," he said.

"How did you learn to play football so well?" Miller had been writing down the ingredients on an MRE package.

"I don't play so well, but I am Islam, so I win." He reached over and touched each of his friends on the chest. "Islam, Islam, Islam."

"And we aren't Islam so we don't win?" I asked.

Omar touched each of us. "Infidel, infidel, infidel, infidel, infidel, infidel . . ."

He had to get up and walk around the table to get to me and Pendleton, and he did.

■   ■   ■

"We need us a little old grandmother to sit out on the porch and let us know what the real deal is." Pendleton's drawl had gotten thicker. "This morning they were talking about how this thing is almost over and by noon we were hearing that a bunch of Special Ops guys got nailed up at An Nasiriyah."

"That was supposed to be friendly fire," Jonesy said.

"I don't know why they calling it friendly fire if it kills you," Pendleton said. "A jet wasted a truckload of guys."

"I thought those pilots had to have clearance before they shot anything on the ground." Victor was hanging out more with First Squad. He was sharpening the huge knife he carried all the time.

"How are they going to communicate with our people jamming the radio frequencies?" Jonesy asked. "That's what they were doing last Sunday. Jamming the frequencies so the Iraqis couldn't set off their IEDs by cell phone. You couldn't communicate from the top of your bunk to the bottom last Sunday. If Marla and Darcy were in here begging for some action by radio you wouldn't even know it."

"You guys sweating those chicks when you should be sweating getting home in one piece," Victor said.

"Hey, Victor, who you going to attack with that knife when you got your 16, grenades, and a mouthful of teeth to fight with?" Jonesy asked.

"This knife makes me feel good," Victor said. "I'm thinking, suppose it's just me and Pablo in a dark room. He's scared and I'm scared. I hear him breathing, you know, slowlike. Then I move toward him and he's listening and thinking and getting into position for some hand-to-hand. Then 'Unnh! Unnh!' He feels some cold steel going into his side and he don't know what's happening. 'Unnh! Unnh!' Then he knows but it's too late."

"You saw that in the movies?" I asked.

"No, man, in a drained-out water canal in Albuquerque."

"So what are we going to do about the radios?" Jonesy said.

The radios were a problem because the bad guys were wiring their bomb detonators between the phone and the ring-tone device.

They would wait for a convoy to come along, then call the number. Instead of ringing, it would detonate the bomb. Countermeasures could block their signals but it was messing with our radio communications. Operation Iraqi Freedom had started off with all of the high-tech stuff being on our side, but now the Insurgents, as they were being called, were doing some low-tech stuff that was just enough to kill or hurt somebody every day.

When the God Squad came over, Chaplain Nichols and his bodyguard started talking about how proud the folks back home were of us. Captain Coles asked Nichols point-blank what he thought the folks back home knew.

"They know that the same American army that put itself in harm's way for the sake of democracy is also building freshwater wells and giving shots to the children in Iraq," the chaplain said. "They know that even though there are casualties and deaths there's also a spirit among the men and women over here that wants to help the Iraqis build freedom. Is any of that not true?"

"I just wondered if they knew how many people are getting wounded here," Coles said. "I don't see any of that in the news at night."

"That's because we're still in a war zone," the chaplain answered. "Do we really want to broadcast everything we know?"

All of that was true. A directive had even come down from CENTCOM about what we could put in our emails.

I could see that. The more information our guys put online, the more the bad guys would know and use against us. On the other hand, the more they clamped down on bad news, the more rumors went around. Everybody was edgy and nobody wanted to leave the Green Zone until they couldn't stand the closeness anymore. But even in the Zone we couldn't shake how randomly things were going down.

"Just the way we're playing poker here and looking to see what hand we get — that's the way this war is going down," Sergeant Harris said, looking at his cards.

"I've got two pair, jacks over eights," Marla said, throwing two dollars into the pot. "So it's going pretty good for me."

"Yeah, but the next hand you might get nothing," Harris said. "That's what I'm talking about. You never can tell what's going to come up."

Everybody folded and Marla scooped up the money and laid her cards on the table.

"Hey, you don't have any jacks over eights," Harris said.

"No, but you folded, so I got the money!" Marla said.

"What makes it so random is that we're fighting on three levels." Lieutenant Colonel Petridus was from PSYOP. A tall guy, he played poker wearing a cowboy hat and chewing on a skinny cigar that wiggled up and down when he talked. "There are the big guys in the back with the money and their plans for this country. They're the ones we need to kill, but we'll never see them because they're too far underground or maybe not even in this country. Then there are the people who hate everything American, everything Western, and want to go back to a religious world that never existed in the first place. The last level is all about people who don't have jobs and will plant an IED or take their chances shooting at us because they need the money. And since the big people, the players behind the scene, just want to keep the chaos going until they see a chance to step in, they don't care who they kill. Not really. They'd kill each other as fast as they kill us. Whose deal is it?"

"It's my deal," I said, picking up the cards.

"Yo, sir, this sounds like a crack house operation," Jonesy said. "Not that I know anything about crack houses."

"Just about," the PSYOP guy said.

"You think the people in Washington have it all figured out?" I asked. "If they don't, maybe we should send them a telegram."

"I once played in a poker game in White Sulphur Springs, West Virginia," Lieutenant Colonel Petridus said. "I had a real lucky night and the little girl I was going to marry — I'm still married to her — was sitting there admiring me all the time. But the guy who ran the game was taking five percent of every pot. At the end of the night I was the big winner and went home stone broke. Think about it."

It wasn't what I wanted to hear.

I also lost thirty dollars.

■ ■ ■

Captain Coles was down because his wife had written and said that his three-year-old had been hospitalized.

"How's she doing?" I asked.

"They don't know," he said. "You got a bunch of doctors in a university hospital and they don't know what's wrong with her. All they know is that she's having a reaction from the vaccination she had to have so she wouldn't get sick."

I tried to think of something to say, but couldn't. It didn't seem fair, in a way, that everything back in the real world was still going on while we were in Iraq. Coles was worried about his kids, and wishing he could be there for them. I remembered Pendleton showing pictures of his daughters around. I hadn't looked at them when he did. The next time he brought them out I would.

We turned on the television and watched cartoons for the rest of the afternoon. After about three hours of watching we decided to map out a plan for Wile E. Coyote to finally trap the Road Runner.

"We need a trap that's activated by the beep-beep!" Marla said.

Rooney, one of the construction guys, said that one could be built. All they needed was the specs. Marla, two of the construction guys, Toby Corbin, and somebody they got on the phone from Countermeasures drew up the specs to send to the Acme Corporation. They were going to send for a Burmese tiger trap, a Burmese tiger, a Road Runner costume and makeup kit, and a beep-beep audio trigger.

"So Wile E. Coyote can dress the tiger up in the Road Runner costume and make it look like a foxy Road Runner. Then he puts him in the tiger trap," Marla said. "When the Road Runner comes along and sees her, he goes into the trap and says beep-beep and the trap closes and the Road Runner is in the cage with the tiger, who then eats him."

It was a perfect plan and we spent over an hour in figuring out how the Road Runner was going to get away.

Then we watched a show in which some woman was trying to figure out who the father of her baby was and we took bets if the guy she named was the father or not. I won three dollars by being the only one who didn't think the dude was the baby's father.

I went to the sleeping area and had just pulled off my boots when Jonesy came in.

"We're going out again," he said.

"Where to?" I asked.

"North on Highway 4," Jonesy said.

"Crap!" Highway 4 ran through some of the worst territory for ambushes in Iraq. The 2nd Infantry had spent days fighting house to house clearing terrorists from the small towns in the area. But as soon as they left, the terrorists would move back in.

"It's supposed to be safe now," Jonesy said. "And the Iraqis are taking the area over. We're going up there to give them a big hand, or hand over the keys, or something."

I got my boots back on, grabbed my gear, and went out to where the guys were already in a kind of huddle. They had all been bored twenty minutes before, but nobody wanted to leave the Zone.

"What are we going to be doing?" Marla asked.

"Showing support for the Iraqi police," Coles said.

"You can't get us out of any of this crap?" Marla looked disgusted.

"Kennedy, do you know what insubordination is?" Coles asked.

"Yeah, that's when you mouth off and they put you in some safe stockade so you don't get killed," Marla said.

"The Iraqi police trainees are taking over security for that water project near Ba'qubah," Captain Coles said. "We're going to escort them and show our pretty faces for a camera op."

"I thought that water project was civilian?" I said.

"It is, but we want to show that the Iraqis are taking over their own country and running as many operations as possible," Captain Coles said as he checked his ammo pouches. "We're doing the official show today and they're actually going to take it over next week."

"How come the 3rd ID doesn't make a presence?" Jonesy asked.

We were all glad to see the Iraqis take over security and anything else they wanted to take over. The more Iraqis on the line, the less chance we had of getting hurt or killed. The 3rd ID guys were training the Iraqis and said that most of them weren't interested in what they were doing: "They need the jobs, though."

That was good enough for me.

We mounted up with all three squads and two ugly-butt Stryker vehicles that were around to be up-armored. The Strykers looked like toy tanks that had grown too fast; they had conventional tires instead of tracks. They could carry a whole infantry squad into battle, but the guys had to come out the back when they let the ramp down. I wouldn't want to be cramped into that dark tin can interior and then have to come out into the daylight looking around to see who's trying to kill me. Word was the Strykers could be knocked out with an RPG or a single grenade into the tire well. The army had put a steel grid on the front and sides of most of them. The theory was that if they got hit by an RPG, the rocket would go off before it actually hit the body of the vehicle. The Iraqis saw that and started shooting two RPGs at the same time. The first would blow away the steel cage and the second would microwave the guys inside the Stryker.

We were supposed to convoy up to Ba'qubah escorting a bus-load of Iraqi policemen and a bus of PR guys. There would be a ceremony, and then we would all come back to the Green Zone, except for the Iraqis, who would go back to their training barracks.

We found out that there were only two guys in each of the two Stryker vehicles. A driver and the Vehicle Commander. It was all show-and-tell. We had our three Humvees and the Iraqi trainees were in a bus.

"Probably air-conditioned," Marla said.

"You can ride with them if you want," Captain Coles said.

One of the Strykers led the convoy and the other one was on the tail end. Harris took his Humvee into the two slot. Third Squad was next, then the two buses, then us and the other Stryker.

We got held up while they tried to round up some more news guys for the PR bus.

With the buses it took forty minutes, with all of us sweating and grumbling, to get to the place they were going to have the ceremony. I had got a infection of some kind between my legs; it felt like jock itch, and the bouncing around in the Humvee chafed it more. Technically, it was Ba'qubah, I guess, but just on the outskirts of the city. Good.

The company that was working on extending the freshwater lines had hired private guards, a lot of ex–Special Ops guys, some good old boys from stateside police departments, and just some dudes who didn't mind killing people. They dressed like they had all just come out of central casting: sunglasses, bandanas, beards, earrings, and scowls.

"What they really have going for them is no ROE cards," Captain Coles said.

The Iraqis knew that the private guys did not have Rules of Engagement cards and didn't care who they shot. If you weren't wearing a standard coalition uniform you were fair game.

The media people got out of the bus and I saw that Sessions was with them. They set up a table with a white tablecloth and laid out some food. Then they had the Iraqi trainees line up outside of the bus, do a little marching around, and get their pictures taken. It was cool for our guys to put down the Iraqi soldiers, but I liked them. Better than that, their taking over the operations made a lot of sense to me.

We hung for an hour while the Iraqis ran through some drills for the cameras. I could tell that the official press guys weren't that interested, but they took lots of photographs, anyway.

"Stock footage," one of the cameramen said. "They have huge vaults of this kind of stuff in case they need it as background for a real story."

"Are you saying this isn't a real war?" Captain Coles asked.

"Not this part of it," the cameraman said. "This is about as real as Little Red Riding Hood."

I saw Harris running his mouth with the 3rd ID guys and reminded myself that I didn't like him. He had even come over to Jonesy and made some crack about how lame the Iraqi trainees looked. Jonesy had ignored his remarks. I could tell Jonesy was tense when Harris was talking to him.

Captain Coles went to the PR bus and copped some sandwiches and brought them back. Sessions checked to see if we could split and got the okay.

We mounted up to go back to the Zone and I could see that there was some beer being passed around in the PR bus. Coles must have seen it, too.

"It's probably warm," he said.

The mood lightened and we started singing "Survivor." We had left Yossarian back at the base because we were afraid of running into brass but we sang his theme song, anyway. We were making good time, looping northwest to take a different route, when Marla announced a roadblock a quarter of a mile ahead of us.

"Looks like a bus broken down at the intersection," she said.

"Don't bunch up," Captain Coles said, trying to look out of the side window.

Jonesy had already stopped and had moved the Humvee to the right. The Stryker behind us stopped and the driver popped out and ran up to us.

"You guys got any cigarettes?" The kid didn't look old enough to smoke.

"Nobody in this squad smokes," Marla said. "Check out the film crews."

We looked down the line and saw the Iraqis getting out of their bus and waiting by the side of the road. Marla said they were probably waiting for the film crew to set up before they pushed the bus off the road. Sure enough, a moment later some guys from the PR bus got off; one carried what looked like a camera.

Ahead of us Darcy was climbing out of the turret and I watched her go off toward the side of the road. When she unrolled her poncho and started wrapping it around her waist I had to laugh. She was going to take a leak.

"Yo, Jonesy, check out what Darcy's doing!"

I had my head turned when the bus exploded. The impact went through my body and slammed me against the back of the Humvee. My rifle was between my legs, the butt on the floor; by the time I got it up and pointed out of the window, the second explosion went off.

"Daisy chain!" Jonesy threw the Humvee into reverse and started backing up toward the Stryker.

The guys in the Stryker didn't know what was happening. They figured it out when Jonesy screeched by them.

"Look for bandits! Look for bandits!" Coles was yelling.

"Darcy, get in!" Marla was screaming even though Darcy was way too far away to hear her.

I saw Darcy dive through the side window as Third Squad's Humvee started backing toward us.

Ta-ta-chow! Ta-ta-chow! Ta-ta-ta-ta-ta-ta-chow!

The harsh chatter of the M-240 filled the cab of the Humvee and damned near sent me into a panic.

"Where? Where?" Jonesy searched both sides of the road.

"I don't know!" Marla said. "But there's a ridge over there!"

"Cease fire! Cease fire!" Captain Coles's voice was calmer than ours. Then it went into panic mode as two heads came up over the ridge. "Fire! Fire!"

Marla opened up again and the heads ducked down. Up ahead of us Darcy was back up in the Humvee, the poncho still tied around her waist. The guys from the Stryker were out and racing toward the ridge. Third Squad had the same idea and moved toward it, too. There had already been two explosions and I was hoping there wouldn't be a third.

The Stryker guys were spread out as they went over the ridge; I saw them stand, fire some short bursts, then lower their weapons. As quickly as it had started, the attack was over.

"Check out the damage up ahead. Don't get jumpy," Coles said.

I looked down at my finger, which was wrapped tightly around the trigger — but the safety was still on. I brought the muzzle of the 16 up and sniffed it. Crap. I hadn't fired a shot! I was squeezing a locked trigger.

The bus had been the main blast. The Stryker had been in a direct line and the blast had tipped it over on its side. The Stryker's front was crushed on one side, the side that was off the ground. The driver was hurt bad.

Two of the cameramen were slightly wounded. One had an ugly scrape on his head, more blood than depth. The other wasn't hurt at all. Inside the PR bus they had been scattered, but no one had been hurt too badly.

"They set off the bus and daisy-chained IEDs along the road, but most of them didn't go off," an Infantry officer was saying. "We were lucky."

Third Squad's Humvee was off the road and Evans pulled up to them. At first I thought they had just driven off the road to guard the flank. But Evans signaled us over.

"I'll check it out," I said, sliding out of the Humvee.

"Watch yourself," Marla said.

The front of Third Squad's Humvee looked fine. I looked in the cabin and saw Sergeant Love, his forehead down on the dashboard, his body shaking. Pendleton lay next to him; there was a huge wound in the side of his neck. Victor was on turret and had been hit through the windows. One hand and both of his legs were bloody. We lifted him from the top and let him down the side of the Humvee.

"I've called for medevacs," Major Sessions said. The side of her face was swollen where she had slammed into something. "How are the squads?"

It took a while to get Pendleton's door open. I couldn't help myself when I started to cry. I couldn't help myself when the door opened and we unbuckled him and let the weight of his big body fall against our chests. We got him on the ground and felt around for a pulse.

"You never can tell," Coles started. "You never can tell . . ."

You could tell.

Two A-10s flew overhead and circled us, looking for bad guys. The first medevac chopper came and took Victor and Jonesy, who had a piece of shrapnel cut through his chin, and the two PR guys. A 3rd ID company rolled up and deployed around us. The next medevac took a cameraman and Pendleton.

I felt pressed by a huge weight, like every bad minute you had ever had in your life had come back and was inside your chest and just sitting there. It was like having a huge vulture eat at your stomach and being too tired to do anything about it. I couldn't stop crying as we made our way back through the streets of Baghdad to the Green Zone.

"Stay alert!" Coles said.

"No." I heard myself say the word. I wasn't sure if it was loud enough for anyone else to hear. I didn't want to be alert anymore. I didn't want to be a good soldier. I just wanted to shut down this whole damn war.

"Stay alert," Coles said again.

I straightened up and focused on the low rooftops, barely visible through the dust rising from the vehicles ahead. I wiped my sweaty palm on my pants leg and gripped the stock of the weapon in my lap.

Back in the Zone, Major Sessions got us together in the officers' tent. Her face was swollen badly. One eye was shut and she couldn't talk clearly. Captain Miller was there, trying to get Sessions to lie down.

"We'll have a memorial service this Sunday," Sessions said.

She was crying, too. I was glad to see her tears. I wanted the whole world to feel the pain.

We went back to the quarters and guys started asking us what had happened. We just told them that Pendleton was dead and that we would let them know the rest in the morning.

I was lying across the bed when Marla came in.

"I just figured it out," she said. Her face was twitching in anger. "Somebody knew all the damned details. Somebody knew all the damned details and passed it on."

When we thought of it we realized that she was right. The insurgents had had time to set up the IEDs along the road, waiting for our convoy. We had taken a different road out than the one we had taken going in, but still they were waiting for us. Somebody had called them. Had given them our route.

Later, as I lay in the darkness, I thought about Pendleton's two little girls. How he had talked about sending them to college. I hadn't even looked at their pictures when he was showing them around. Oh, God, why hadn't I looked at the pictures?

■ ■ ■

The memorial for Pendleton was held two days after we watched a plane lift off with his remains from Baghdad Airport. Earlier that morning we had received word that Saddam's two sons had been killed in a firefight. Reporters were running around shoving mikes into faces and getting the responses they expected. Al Jazeera was trying to spice up their stories with talk about whether the sons' bodies should have been displayed.

"They're trying to play it down the middle." Evans was sipping from a plastic cup of coffee. "I bet they're coming off a lot different when they talking to the Arabs."

What was the right way to report a war? A neat list of names in a hometown newspaper? Maybe your picture in *The New York Times*?

That was all that mattered. Nothing was ever settled. It was just who was dying and who was coming home.

Darcy showed up with her plastic mug full of coffee. She sat at the end of the table and cupped it in her hands. She was still standoffish, but drawing closer.

Coles came a bit later and told us that Jonesy was back with a puffy chin, but Victor couldn't make it.

"He wanted to come but they ordered him onto the plane for the hospital in Ramstein," Coles said. "They think they can save two of his fingers. They can definitely save the thumb. That's good."

That's good. I imagined Victor on the streets back home. Would the streets be less hard because he had lost two fingers?

The memorial was in front of the tent we were using for a chapel. We lined up in four rows. First, Second, and Third Squads were in the first row, with other CA Squads behind us. Some guys from the 3rd were there, too. Miller was crying. So was Jonesy.

The ceremony was brief. Pendleton's boots, M-16, and Kevlar were on the small altar. We stood for the national anthem. He asked if anybody wanted to say anything about Pendleton. No one did. No one really knew him that much. Finally Coles stepped forward and took a paper from his pocket.

"Lord, have mercy on us as we feel the pain of loss, and the endless emptiness that marks the passing of Corporal Pendleton; and have mercy on us as we feel sorrow for ourselves, and for all the angel warriors for whom we feel kinship. Let us fear death, but let it not dwell within us. Protect us, O Lord, and be merciful unto us. Amen."

The chaplain spoke of the need to move on, that those who find strength in the Lord would renew their strength and mount up with wings as eagles. They would run and not be weary. They would walk and not faint.

I felt like fainting.

"Roll Call Officer!"

Major Sessions stepped forward. She lifted her clipboard, glanced down at it and quickly up again. "Pendleton!" she called out.

The moment of silence was crushing.

"Corporal Phillip Pendleton!"

Another moment of silence, and then the mournful sound of the bugle sounding taps filled the tent. The final roll call for Pendleton was completed. Two soldiers took his medals and laid them in front of his weapons.

The ceremony was over. We drifted away from the tent and went about the business of trying to walk and talk among the living.

The day began badly. The smell from the river drifted over us like the stink of doom. Nothing was right. I tried to push the vision of Pendleton out of my head but it was impossible. Who was he? Why didn't I know more about him? Why didn't I sit with him and talk to him and try to understand what made him who he was?

"Let's go find Marla," Jonesy said.

We found her in the corner of the dayroom in front of the television. There was a game show on, but I knew she wasn't really watching it.

"You okay?" I asked her.

"No," she said.

May 29, 2003

Hey Mom!

   Go on with your bad self getting online. I'm really proud of you. I know you go down to the Countee Cullen branch with Mrs. Lucas to use their computers but be careful at night. Okay — so first thing, thank you for the dolls. Everybody in the church must have donated one. We gave them out to girls just north of the Green Zone — the safe zone here. And, just as you said in your letter, the little Arab girls really went for the Black dolls. These little Iraqi girls are very sweet. Please thank everybody from the church for me. Jonesy is taking some pictures and I'll get some printed up for you as soon as I can.

   If we weren't at war with these people this would be a great place to spend some time. You would really be impressed by the mosques. If you saw the one up at Kazimayn it would take your breath away.

   Second thing — the women in Iraq mostly don't wear veils. They dress like ordinary businesspeople. Sometimes you see women in veils but they're often from another part of the Middle East. They do cover their hair and mostly don't wear makeup. In a video store they sell tapes of belly dancers and every guy over here has at least one tape. Except me, of course, since I'm not interested in wriggling ladies. Okay, maybe just not wriggling Iraqi ladies. Did you know they also have Christians over here and a Christian church? According to the locals it's no big deal.

   I can't always get online but now that you're on I'll try to find an in and email you as much as possible. Much love to you and Pops.

   Robin

We got an official notification of Victor's transfer and a brief note about Pendleton. Colonel King, from the 422nd, came by and said a prayer with the God Squad. The colonel said he had written to Pendleton's widow.

I don't know why I kept reading the newspaper about what's going on over here. I could just look around but then I'd only see a small piece of it. What I'm seeing is confusing. Marla put it best.

"You go out and you see people shopping," she said. "Women buying onions and bread or people having coffee. Then down the street somebody gets blown up. Jesus, it's weird."

It was weird – weird and unnerving. Somebody buying onions, somebody getting their fingers blown off, somebody dying.

"Hey, Jonesy, how you doing?" I called across the tent.

"I'm good, man," he said. He was lying on his bunk humming to himself. "How you doing?"

"You want to hear something crazy?" I asked.

"Go ahead."

"I was wondering about Victor's monkey," I said. "Whether he should have kept it. Isn't that stupid? I mean, to think that a monkey was going to make any kind of difference?"

"At the service for Pendleton I was wondering if God made a difference," Jonesy said. "I guess if I'm wondering about God, you can wonder about the monkey."

■ ■ ■

The whole place is in an uproar. We got word that nobody is to leave the Green Zone in groups of less than seven and with only up-armored vehicles. Marla told Captain Coles to go find out what was happening and he got pissed because he didn't like Marla's lack of respect.

"Okay, sir, don't go and find out," Marla said. "But they're not going to tell me anything because I'm not an officer."

Coles shook his head but he went.

Jonesy had a toothache but Miller wouldn't give him any pain-killers. She told him to go and see the dentist.

"Captain Miller, I am not stupid," Jonesy said. "If I go to the dentist he might need to drill my tooth or pull the sucker, which will put me in more pain than I'm in now."

"And he might save you some pain down the road," Miller said. "Did you ever think of that?"

"That's all right, Captain." Jonesy lay back on his bunk. "I'll just lay here and suffer because no one cares about how I feel, anyway."

We all knew that Miller would give him some painkillers in the end but a lecture would go with it. With all her bad-mouthing, she was becoming the mother of the CA Squads; I think she enjoyed it, too.

Coles came back with the news. It wasn't good.

"A marine unit found a bunch of civilians dead in a garage," Coles said.

"They think Americans killed them?" Evans asked.

"They don't know who killed them," Coles said. "But they found them with their hands bound behind their backs and all five were shot in the back of the head. And they were all Sunnis, so something is going down that doesn't smell right."

"Were they working with us?" Miller asked. "Maybe they were killed because they were being looked on as traitors or something."

"From what I gathered the thinking is that they were killed by one of the Khalid death squads," Coles said.

We had all heard about the death squads. There was some sort of vague connection between them and the people we were pushing toward the leadership of the new Iraq. Before the invasion the Sunnis had been in power and the Shiites had been pushed around pretty good. Saddam was a Sunni and had put all his peeps in the key positions. Now that Saddam was out and we had put the Shiites in power, there was a sudden explosion of mysterious killings.

"Why aren't we trying to stop these death squads?" I asked Coles.

"Maybe we are," Coles answered. "Your guess is as good as mine."

The whole thing sucked big-time. Every day we were hearing about stuff that had nothing to do with democracy or freedom. There were stories about looting, about some Iraqis being put out of their homes so that others, the ones we were backing, could move in, and stories about Iraqis becoming suddenly rich and nobody knowing why. Now the talk was about death squads.

Coles went on to say that some of the victims had been tortured. There was a whole battle going on around us that we didn't have any grip on, that we really didn't know about.

Some of the construction guys, engineers, started talking about bodies that had been found at the power plants north of Baghdad.

"Those dudes were just executed," one of them said. "It had to be other Iraqis. There wasn't anyone else around."

I thought about a basketball game I had played against Lane High School. Lane had the better team but we had the lead. The coach signaled for a time-out and we gathered around the bench and he started yelling at me because I had kept looking at the scoreboard.

"The game is on the floor!" he had screamed.

Yeah, that was true, but the win was on the scoreboard. I knew when the time ran out, whoever had the most points was the winner. I didn't know if we were winning here in Iraq or not. If we just talked about dead people, about bodies lying in the streets, then we were winning easy. But somehow it wasn't about who was doing the most killing. Jonesy had said it best.

"The only dying that means anything is your own," he had said. "For everybody else, you just shakes your head and keep on keeping on."

So how did we know if we were winning or not? And if we weren't winning anything, what was the dying for?

Coles came over to me on Saturday night. He looked exhausted. I thought the war was finally getting to him.

"So, Birdy, what do you think about this war?" he asked.

"I don't think I like war," I said.

"It teaches you things, though," he said. "What it's taught me is that I love my wife and family more than I knew, and a lot more than I ever told them. Doesn't that suck? I mean, having a wife and family and not getting around to telling them how much you love them. Doesn't that just suck?"

"If you know it now, it doesn't suck," I said.

Captain Coles shrugged, patted my shoulder, and headed off to bed.

I thought of what Jonesy had said about keeping score. I knew there were stories about the Iraqi police we were training, that they were mostly Shiites more than willing to kill Sunnis anywhere in Baghdad. The thing was that killing was taking on a different meaning to me. To take a human life had always been so heavy a deal. It had always meant that some terrible thing had happened, some horrible wrong had occurred that brought people to the far ends of sanity. But now I was willing to kill because I was afraid of being killed, willing to kill people I had never met, had never argued with, and who, perhaps, had never wanted to hurt me. But I was afraid and so I would kill.

And now, when I was hearing about the Sunnis being killed, or the bombs going off in the marketplace, the only thing I could think of was that I was so glad it wasn't me lying in the streets of Baghdad, or Fallujah or Mosul. I was glad that it was not my blood being cleaned off the streets or getting swept up on the roads outside of the city.

Images flicked through my mind. Pendleton's body awkwardly twisted in death, the pictures of his girls still in his pocket against his cooling skin. The parts of the marine on the busy street. Muslim women in black, their hands over their mouths as if they were holding in the screams that would reveal their souls. The old grandmother wailing over the body of the boy.

The amazing thing was the randomness of the dying. If you were American, your picture might be in some daily newspaper. If you died on a slow news day, your mother's grief might be captured in a thirty-second spot. If you were Iraqi, there would be no mention of your dying unless you could be called an insurgent.

"The only dying that means anything is your own," Jonesy had said.

Amen to that.

We stayed in the Green Zone for the next two weeks. All right with me. I didn't want to leave. I took care of a lot of necessary business. I cleaned my M-16, all of my uniforms, and even my boots. I also took out a subscription to *The Source*, mostly to keep up with the music scene.

The only work we did for the entire time was unload a truckload of gifts from the Free Will Baptist Church in Martinsburg, West Virginia. We had a big debate over whether salami was pork or beef, decided it must have been pork, and kept all the salamis, the cookies, and the candy bars for ourselves. We gave out the canned foods, toys, powdered milk, and toothpaste to the Iraqis.

A tribal leader named Hamid Faisal Al-Sadah complained that the Coalition was not protecting his people, and that a number of young men from his area had been killed when they entered Fallujah. A PSYOP major from the 3rd ID was supposed to talk to him, take his complaint, and see if he could establish a liaison. We were going along as backup.

"Security?" I asked.

"They're beginning to respect what we've been doing," Coles said. "The major will be in charge and we'll just stand around and smile at Al-Sadah's people. Captain Miller will see if they need any medical attention we can supply."

"And what is that supposed to mean, Captain Coles?" Miller had her Molle vest and her game face on. "We can't give them routine first aid because we're afraid we're going to be flooded with their sick; we can't give them medical supplies unless it's cleared through thirty-five hundred channels because we don't want them giving those supplies to the insurgents; and we can't refer them to their hospitals because half of them aren't operative. So what do we do? Hold their hands and tell them to take an aspirin?"

"Would you like to shoot me, Captain?" Coles asked. "I mean, if that would make you feel better . . ."

"It might," Miller said.

She was right. Sometimes we could see what was needed but we just weren't allowed to do it. A lot of the guys from the 422nd were talking about sending home for more supplies for the Iraqis.

That was really strange to me. Here we were fighting a war, or at least cleaning up after the fighting, and sending home to our families and friends for supplies for the enemy. When I saw an entire truckload of notebooks and school supplies that had come in from Forrest City, Arkansas, I was impressed. Americans did care about the rest of the world. A lot.

Third Squad was going to Fallujah with us. The plan was that we would talk to the sheik and then spend the night guarding a nearby antiquity site. I was just glad it wasn't Second Squad because as much as I liked Darcy and thought that Evans was at least okay, I was still pissed at Sergeant Harris for his messing around with Jonesy.

"I want to remind you guys that my birthday is August twelfth, so start saving your money for presents," Marla said. She had copped some sandwiches from the unit kitchen and was opening each one to see what they were.

"Yo, that's not sanitary," Jonesy mentioned.

"Shut up or you won't get one," Marla answered.

Marla took the sandwich that looked like turkey and cheese, I snatched the ham and cheese, and Jonesy got the pastrami. That left one sandwich that looked like it could have been tuna fish but Marla sniffed it and so did Jonesy and they couldn't tell.

"Smell it, Birdy."

I sniffed it. It stunk. "It smells like Fancy Feast," I said. "Cat food."

Marla closed it carefully, and then wrote "Capt. Coles" on the package.

Sometimes, when the weather was clear and it wasn't so hot that you thought you were baking, Iraq seemed like the most beautiful place in the world. It seemed huge, with wide open spaces that stretched into forever. When you got away from the rivers it was mostly desert, especially as you went north from Baghdad. You could ride for mile after endless mile and then come across three camels and a donkey going about their business as if there wasn't any war, or any occupation. Guys would stop to take photos and the Iraqis would wave or just stop and look at us the way we were stopping to look at them.

The cities were all crowded, huddled together around whatever plumbing and electrical resources they had, but the people seemed to know how to live their lives. They took things easy, spending a lot of time with their tea or coffee or, if they were men, with the hookahs. When they were calm, they were very calm. When they got excited it was hard to tell if they were angry or just looking that way. One minute an Iraqi would be screaming at the top of his lungs or a woman would be falling down with emotion and the next they would just calm down and continue taking care of their business.

You couldn't really tell who was important in the towns or villages because there wasn't much difference in the way people dressed. In a formal meeting the Iraqis would always wear native dress and I didn't know one unit from the other. Darcy had painted some Iraqi people and scenes using watercolors. They were good and I thought about asking her for one.

We met up with the PSYOP major and six infantrymen, two of whom were black. They were in a truck with a screen around it.

"It's probably a communications vehicle," Jonesy said as we looked at it from Miss Molly. "They're using the whole thing as an antenna."

That seemed on the money and we got into a conversation about all the equipment we had and how cool it would be to steal it and take it home in civilian life. I thought I would like to have the night vision equipment. Jonesy wanted the Kevlar protection gear.

"I just want the squad gun and the Humvee," Marla said. "If I rode into the Wal-Mart parking lot with that bad boy I could park anywhere I damn well felt like it."

We got to the village and the Infantry guys took up casual positions around the cluster of buildings we were visiting. They were supposed to look as if they were just hanging out. That was funny because the Iraqis ran around in long shirts and sandals and we were looking like spacemen with helmets, goggles, vests, and weapons. But the Iraqi kids loved to see us.

Coles was riding with the PSYOP major and they came over. Major Scott was young, maybe thirty, and six-four to six-five. He looked us over and said he was glad to have us aboard.

"You people are doing a wonderful job over here," he said. "Everybody's talking about it. The more friends you guys make, the fewer people we have to kill, and the fewer who will want to kill us."

I never remembered smells before. I would recognize a familiar smell — fried onions or morning coffee — but in the Humvee I remembered one. It was the smell of blood in the cab when we were trying to get Pendleton out. I tried to think of something else to release the tension. It wasn't a crazy kind of tension but a low-level feeling that I was learning to live with 24/7. I kept my eyes on my side of the road, eyeballing every cart or old pickup that we passed as if it might suddenly turn into something deadly.

When we got to the meeting place it turned out to be a huge tent, twenty some feet across and thirty deep. It was dyed a deep red that looked good against the reddish sand. There were smaller tents, black and brown tents, around the large one. We thought we would have to take up positions the way the Infantry guys did but Captain Coles came out and said that both the First and Third Squad could come inside and have dinner with the sheik.

Corbin, from Third Squad, had to stay with our vehicles, which were parked together. Marla gave him Captain Coles's sandwich.

"We'll bring you something from inside," I said. "Maybe some camel ribs, or whatever they're having."

"I'm down with camel ribs," Corbin said. "And see if they got any potato salad."

There was a six-foot gate around the tent and the Iraqis had guys standing near it. Casually dressed, they looked to be eighteen or nineteen years old, but with mustaches and AK-47s. We smiled at them as we went in and they smiled back. They weren't wearing uniforms, but the weapons told me all I needed to know.

The table was placed in the middle of the tent. There was a rug on the floor, and from the edges I could see there was matting under the rug. The sheik was in his fifties, a smallish man with neat, graying hair. He wore a traditional Iraqi garment — the long flowing djellaba with the embroidered front that richer men wore — but I could easily imagine him in a carefully tailored suit. He sat at the head of the ornate table and four of his people, two on either side of the table, sat with an empty chair between them. Major Scott and Captain Coles sat at the other end and the guys from our CA unit sat in the open chairs. Major Scott spoke Arabic but Ahmed, who had come along, sat close to him to help translate.

We were given a bowl of fresh fruit and raw vegetables, served by young women. None of the Iraqi men seemed to take notice of Marla, but the women did, and I saw one of them smiling.

At first the talk was all polite and nice with Major Scott and Captain Coles talking about how beautiful Iraq was and the sheik talking about what a wonderful country America was. I was surprised how good his English was.

"I asked myself what did Adam know of paradise?" said the sheik, who told us to call him Hamid. "He woke up one day and found himself in the Holy Garden and he had never known anything else. That's what I think has happened to America. You are a young people. What have you known but the paradise of peace and security and wealth? It makes your thinking different from the thinking of my people."

"I think most people want the same things from life," Major Scott said. "We want freedom, we want love, and we want a chance to go to heaven when the time comes."

He didn't sound sincere.

"So, you like my country?" Al-Sahad continued.

"I'd love to come back and take a vacation here one day," Scott said. "After things are stabilized, of course. And that's where I think we, you and I, as equals, can make a contribution. Cooperation."

The sheik spoke to his people in Arabic and they all nodded politely.

"Sometimes," the sheik said, "it's better to abandon modern words. When a word falls out of the mouth today it can mean anything. It takes years and sometimes generations for words to be chiseled in history. So, when you talk to me about cooperation between our countries I have to ask myself — Hamid, what does a man who has a thousand jet planes mean when he says 'cooperation'?"

The conversation was getting interesting and going faster than I thought it would.

"It means I will do as much for you, to make your life better, as I can, and in return, you will do the same for me," Major Scott said. "In America we say 'one hand washes the other.'"

"Have you eaten food from the Middle East before?" the sheik asked, changing the subject.

"No, I can't say that I have," Scott said.

"Any of your people have eaten food from the Middle East?"

Scott looked at us and we all shook our heads no.

"Well, then I'm pleased that I've introduced you to the world's best food." Hamid smiled broadly.

"Where have you been in the United States, sir?" Marla asked.

"Washington. New York. California. Once I was in Scottsdale, Arizona. You have a beautiful country. And beautiful people."

"Birdy here is from New York," Marla said.

Hamid spoke to the others in Arabic and they turned and looked at me. One reached out and said something in Arabic as he shook my hand. I felt stupid just smiling and nodding. He could have been calling me a jerk.

"The thing I love most about America is the weather. Here it is either hot or it is raining. My cousin went to live in Chicago for six months," Hamid said. "In six weeks he wanted to come back because it was so cold. He said he watched people standing in the cold looking at the holiday lights and he could see their breath freezing."

"Well, that's Chicago for you," Major Scott said. "But let me ask you, sir — and I don't mean to be rude — but are you still making up your mind about cooperating with the Coalition Forces?"

"Making up my mind?" The sheik turned and spoke in Arabic to nobody in particular and a girl came in, from the next room. Hamid spoke to her briefly and she left quickly. I got the impression that she was just outside the door waiting for him to speak to her.

"When you speak of cooperating," the sheik spoke slowly, weighing his words, "I think you mean helping each other in a common cause. Two strong men can lift a heavy rock."

"Exactly." Major Scott hadn't been eating much, and now put down his fork.

The rest of us had been scarfing down the food big-time and it was great. I was concentrating on eating slower than Jonesy because the Iraqis had hardly touched their plates.

"In this . . . operation, and you know we call it Operation Iraqi Freedom," Major Scott said, "we are in what we call the Security and Stabilization Phase. And there are people out there who don't want that stabilization to work. I'm sure you know that as well, sir, as I do. We can provide additional security for your people, and with that security comes stabilization as we turn over all the operations to the people of Iraq, but to do that we need to free up some of our men from searching for the major weapons systems that we are pretty sure exist. And what I'm saying –"

The sheik had held up his hand for Major Scott to stop. "You mean the weapons of mass destruction?"

"I do," Major Scott replied.

"Go on, sir."

"If you help us find these weapons, we will be able to divert men away from that operation to providing security for your people."

"Major, may I tell you a little secret?" the sheik asked.

"Of course."

"Sir, the war you began is over," the sheik said. "That war you won. It was not beautiful in the end – there were no violins, no birds singing in the sky – but it is over. What is going on now is a completely different war. In this war you merely stand on the side and hold the coats. This war is not about you or America.

"You are trying to stabilize a government in Baghdad. But there are others who are creating – how do the English put it? A *shadow* government? – and which government in the end will rule the Middle East is the new war. Look around you; it is my people who are being killed in the streets of Baghdad and Fallujah. Yes, yes, I know. They kill one or two Americans to make it look good, is all."

"When the insurgents shoot at us we think they're meaning

to kill us," Major Scott said. "But I can appreciate your concerns about your own people and we're certainly trying to stabilize things here."

"Do you really think that we have the problems that your papers are reporting?" Hamid asked. "Do you think that people who have lived together for more years than your country has been in existence suddenly find it impossible? That the hatred has grown so quickly between Sunnis and Shiites that we must shoot each other and bomb each other? No, my friend. Everyone knows that eventually you will miss the warmth of your own bed, the blue eyes of your own wives, and then you will go home. Then who will rule Iraq?"

"It won't be Saddam Hussein," Major Scott said.

The sheik closed his eyes and bowed his head toward Scott. But for the rest of the meal, there was very little said except by Major Scott, who kept insisting that the coalition forces would provide more security if the local people helped us find hidden weapons.

The woman who had come in before returned with two men who served an entire second course. One of the Iraqi men saw me smile and smiled at me.

The dinner ended with the sheik saying that he would do his best and Scott saying that was all that he wanted.

"Sir, what we can accomplish together, the coalition forces along with the goodwill of the Iraqi people, will astound the world," Major Scott said as we stood outside the door. "We're going to have some of our people work with yours tonight at the hospital. We'll assess the needs there and do what we can."

We mounted up and started toward the hospital. Captain Coles rode with the major until it was time for us to split from them, and then he came over to First Squad.

"So what did you think?" I asked Coles.

"I think Major Scott was right in the way he handled it," Coles said. "He had to pin the sheik down into actually doing something. The different factions over here all want our goodwill but they don't want to actually do anything to get it."

"I think the sheik is just one of them uptight dudes," Jonesy said. "You know the type — bomb them once or twice and they get a chip on they shoulder."

I didn't know what weapons Major Scott was looking for. The army hadn't found any big stash of chemical weapons, although they had to be somewhere because they had used them against the Kurds.

There were marines in Fallujah and they were on edge big-time. A marine captain met up with Coles and shook his head slowly back and forth as Coles explained that we were going to assess the needs at the hospital.

"Fallujah is the body-bag capital of the region," the captain said. "Don't spend any more time there than you have to. And don't trust anybody. They killed some contractors here and burned their bodies. Keep that image in your head."

"How do you keep your guys safe?" Coles asked.

"By killing everything that ain't smiling, and half of everything that is," the marine captain answered.

Captain Coles's mouth tightened as he nodded.

We got to the hospital and it looked like crap. There was barbed wire around it and Iraqi guards. We rolled up and a guy came out and directed us toward what looked like an ambulance entrance. I was nervous as Jonesy drove in.

"Hamid called and said you were coming," the man said. "Let me tell you my situation. You are Americans. I am Iraqi. Just talking to you could get me killed. I have to send my people out and say that I am getting supplies from you that will save Iraqi lives. Otherwise I will be attacked for cooperating with you."

"You give us a list of supplies you need," Miller said, "and we'll try to see that you get them. We can't guarantee anything, but we'll try, sir."

"Talib Al-Janabi," the man said. "Do you know anything about hospitals?"

"I'm a Physician's Assistant," Captain Miller said. "I have a degree in biology and enough military training to qualify me for most medical positions."

"Then you don't need a list," Talib said. "We have next to nothing here. We are down to washing bandages. Anything that you can get for us will be appreciated."

We heard mortar fire; Coles called the marines and found that there was fighting in a nearby cemetery. A marine officer told us to stay put and he would try to get us an escort out of the city in a few hours.

Marla found a bathroom and we took turns, all except for Captain Miller.

"I'm going to look the place over with this guy," she said, indicating a heavy man in a nearly white coat. "I'd like to get an idea of how bad it is away from the Green Zone."

"You're not allowed to treat Iraqis," Captain Coles said.

"I've got a few rolls of clean bandages and some antibiotics," Miller said. "I don't think it's going to make a major difference in the war."

"And you know the patients here aren't the enemy?" Coles asked.

"I don't have a good answer for you, Captain," Miller said. "But my gut feeling is that you don't let people die if you can help it. You got a better answer?"

He didn't. None of us did.

Through an open window we got a great view of an enormous moon hanging over the squared roofs of the city. Silver and white against the darkening sky, it seemed bigger and more important than anything below it.

Some radio messages told us about insurgents in the area. We were told to stay on alert. We talked about baseball and tennis and then, as we always did, what we were going to do when we got home. I hadn't known that Sergeant Love from Third

Squad was married. He seemed like a nice guy, but maybe a career soldier.

"You got kids?" I asked him.

"Five," he answered with a smile. "Joined the National Guard in Baltimore for the extra money."

I remembered Pendleton and asked him if he had pictures of his kids.

"Back in my locker," he said. "I don't want them being captured. That's a little stupid, right?"

"I don't think so," I said. "Maybe you'll show them to me when we get back to the base."

"Sure."

Night came in a hurry. The moon lit up the streets and sent eerie shadows across the frosted windows. The night air in Fallujah was fresher than what we were accustomed to in Baghdad and I felt myself relaxing. We could still hear sporadic small-arms fire outside. I thought I recognized the staccato cough of a machine gun and occasionally what could have been a grenade.

"Birdy, you look nervous," Marla said. I was half lying, half sitting on a dark couch that looked as if it might have been a place where patients waited to be seen.

"When the rest of the world is nervous," I said, "you can bet that I'm still cool."

"Oh, you sound so brave!" Marla said. "Now Jonesy over there is fast asleep, probably dreaming about the blues joint he's going to open."

I looked over to where Jonesy was sprawled out; his M-16 across his body looked like a guitar. Very cool.

"So, what were you telling me about some foster family you were with?" I asked Marla.

"My bios — the folks that borned me — if they were ever really together — broke up when I was two or three," she said. "I don't remember. All I know was that I was going from foster home to foster home. Once in a while I would be in a group home. I guess I wasn't cute enough to be adopted."

"I thought that a lot of white couples wanted to adopt kids," I said.

"Yeah, I guess." Marla had her helmet off and was spinning it upside down on the tile floor. "But my folks weren't dead and they wouldn't consent to me being adopted. I think my dad wanted to get a few bucks for me or something. I don't know. Anyway, I knocked around in a bunch of places. Some were good and some weren't. Then I ended up in juvenile court for shoplifting, and this black family took me in. Kept me out of juvy detention. I was with them for a little over a year. Giving them a hard time. They had a kid of their own with cerebral palsy and really wanted a companion for her. It was all good with them. At least I didn't have to fight her husband off. He was okay. Then it was time for me to either go to college or get a job. So I joined the army."

"You going to stay in?"

"No, I'm stronger now. I'll probably get out and go to college," she said. "I'd like to be a teacher if they let me bring my M-16 to school. Keep the kiddie-poos in line."

We talked a while longer and Coles came over and told us that we were going to be in the hospital for the night. I had figured that much already.

It was nearly five thirty when Jonesy woke me to say that we were mounting up.

"I'm glad I'm not married to you as loud as you snore," he said.

Captain Coles said that we were going to start out on our own but go through a part of town that was controlled by the marines. "They'll know we're coming and look out for us," he said.

We got ready and were waiting for Miller, who we figured was making another survey of the place. I started thinking about the guys the Iraqis had caught and hanged in Fallujah and immediately had to pee again. I told Jonesy, who said I was the peeingist black man he had ever met.

The bathroom we were using was down the hall and off to the right. I started walking a little faster because I really had to go. I was just about to reach for the doorknob when the door opened and an Iraqi started backing out. He was pulling something. I jumped back against the far wall. Another Iraqi had his hand over Captain Miller's mouth and was pulling her head back.

The guy facing me yelled something and the one nearest me turned. He had an AK-47 slung over his shoulder and let Miller go as he reached for it. I pointed my piece at him and pulled the trigger. Nothing. Safety! I pulled the safety off and shot a burst into his face. He spun away from me, his hands going to his face as he went down. Captain Miller was on her knees and the other guy was fumbling in his jacket.

I tried to say something. I wanted to say don't move. I wanted to tell him that it was over. Nothing came out. I pointed the muzzle at his chest and he reached for it, grabbing the barrel and pushing it up. Frantically I jerked it away from him and pointed it at him again.

I don't remember shooting again, or any sound the weapon made. All I remembered is the way the top of his head exploded and the way his hands, fingers spread wide apart, went to the side of his face.

Captain Miller was shaking. Her hands were beating flat against her chest and she was sucking in air noisily. I thought she had been shot or was having a heart attack.

"You okay?" I asked.

She looked up at me, then at the two guys on the bathroom floor. Neither of them was moving. She pulled her pants up and buckled them. She was saying something, but either I couldn't hear her or no words were coming out.

The rest of the crew had heard the gunfire; later I learned they thought it was outside.

Miller was stunned. She kept hitting the front of her Kevlar against the tiled wall.

"Are you all right?" I asked.

"No! No! Nooooooo!" she screamed.

She screamed. She cried. She rocked back and forth. She moaned.

"With all the garbage that's going on . . . with all the disgusting garbage that's going on . . . How can they? How can they?"

She was crying again. I put my hand on her shoulder.

Miller turned to me. "You stopped them from raping me," she said. "But you didn't stop them from ripping up what was left of my soul."

"I'm sorry," I said.

"I don't care about sorry anymore," she said. "I just don't care about sorry any freaking more!"

■ ■ ■

Outside the air was clear and crisp, already warm. The sky was slowly turning from a quiet predawn gray to the brilliance of morning. In the distance the bright reddish gold of the Iraqi sunrise began to spread over the horizon. Dark silhouettes brightened into sprawling fields and square squat structures. The foul smell of the Euphrates River mixed with the sweet odors rising from the sands along its banks, adding texture to the rising sun, like a chorus of strings backing up a sad saxophone.

Our crew was going back to Baghdad, back to the base. It was just another sunrise over the city that had seen sunrises from long before men wrote history. But here, on this bright morning, I rode for the first time as someone who had killed. All the times before that, I had fired my weapon into the darkness, or at some fleeting figure in the distance, I could say that maybe I had missed, that maybe it was not my bullets that hit them.

No more. I wanted to be away from Fallujah, away from Iraq. I wanted to be alone in the dark with my grief. I wanted to mourn for myself.

The marines took us through Fallujah and halfway to Baghdad. There we met a patrol from the 3rd ID and tailed them back to the Bubble. We didn't talk about the incident on the way back. When I got out of Miss Molly and headed toward the tent Captain Miller stopped me.

"Thanks, Birdy," she said. "Thank you."

Later Marla came in and sat with me. "You need to be with somebody, let it be me," she said.

■ ■ ■

We had a birthday party for Jean Darcy, who turned twenty-one. The guys in the mess hall came up with a dynamite cake and enough ice cream to feed the entire army. Darcy's parents and friends from Oak Park, Illinois, had made all the arrangements and there were at least fifty presents, cards, and thank-you notes for her service to the country. It blew Darcy away. She sat in the middle of the floor, all her birthday stuff around her, and cried and cried. We were all hugging her and kissing on her and half of us were crying, too. It was crazy cool.

Instead of keeping the presents, Darcy handed them out to us still wrapped in the boxes and so we all got a few odd things.

I got skin lotion and Jonesy got a sponge on a rope to wash his back.

"Y'all trying to say I stink so bad I got to tie the soap down?" Jonesy asked.

The party lasted until way past midnight with guys slurping down Cokes and ice cream until they got sick. I was queasy in the morning when somebody started a whistle going for roll call. We fell out, half awake, half dressed, and half pissed that we had to make roll call at all.

The trek to the mess hall was just reflex. I wasn't in a mood for breakfast or even the hot coffee sitting in front of me. After breakfast I went to the main tent and lay on my bunk. Colonel Rose came by at eleven o'clock with Coles and the women. He waited until everybody had been called to attention and then gave us the "at ease" command with a grin as if he wasn't all into the gung ho crap.

"Boys, I got some good news for you!" he said. "Anybody here want to hear it?"

I looked over at Coles and he was rolling his eyes up. Crap.

"I'd love to hear some good news this fine morning, sir!" Harris, sucking up as usual.

"I'm sending the First, Second, and Third Squads to As Sayliyah for a briefing," Rose said. "A little change of pace. See something different in this part of the world. Major Sessions will give you the details. But I'll tell you this much. When they called down from CENTCOM and specifically asked for men from our unit I was proud as hell. Proud as hell. It means we're taking care of business. And we're going to continue taking care of business. You'll be moving out at 1800 hours this evening. God bless you all."

The moment Rose and Coles left, we started asking around to see if anyone knew where we were being sent.

"Wherever you're going we're not going with you," Marla said. "He specifically said 'men.'"

"He think he's paying us a compliment by including us with the 'men,'" Darcy said. "But wherever it is, it can't be anything good. Did you see Coles? He was definitely pissed."

"What is it with you guys?" O'Crowley, one of the construction guys, came over and sat on Corbin's cot. "You're supposed to be CAs but you're getting into firefights, going on combat missions, getting hit real hard. How come they're giving you the dirty end of the stick all the time?"

"We ain't nothing but some bait," Jonesy said. "They put us out there to smile and see who shooting at us. Then when they pop enough caps in our rear ends they change the Rules of freakin' Engagement so the Infantry can start shooting back."

"I think you're right," Captain Miller said. "We're supposed to be helping our side win the peace and we don't even know what we mean by peace."

"Maybe you don't know what *you* mean by peace," Jonesy said. "What this little brown boy means is sitting home making sweet love to his guitar. It ain't got nothing to do with this foul mess over here."

"We're serving a purpose, I think." Corbin hardly ever spoke. "It could be that we just don't see their purpose. And I think the place we're going to, As Saylah or As Sayliyah, something like that, is where President Bush spoke."

"You think he's there now?" Marla asked. "Because I seriously need to talk to that man about getting the Port-O-Potties air-conditioned."

Sessions came in next. She looked tired, older than she had just a few weeks before. She didn't say anything, just motioned for us to come to her.

"The first three squads and Medical are going to As Sayliyah for a briefing and then going on a special mission," she said. "I don't know what the briefing is going to be about, or the mission. Neither does Captain Coles, but he's going with you."

"Yo, ma'am, from your tone of voice you don't seem to happy with this business," I said.

"Sometimes I feel as if we're being asked to do a lot," she answered. "But I know that if we weren't doing a good job they wouldn't be asking. So . . ."

The army had a way of throwing crap at you in waves, and this just seemed like another wave. We got into a serious group funk for about twenty minutes, but then the word got around about where we were going. Then guys started showing up saying that it was R&R heaven.

"They're building everything down there," an Infantry dude with a bad case of acne and terminal dandruff said. "It's in Qatar and there's no shooting going on, at all. My friend went down there for four days and didn't want to come back. They've got a swimming pool, lounges, beer, everything you can think about."

"How come he was only there for four days?" Jonesy asked.

"That's what it's about," Dandruff Dan answered. "It's wind-down city for guys in combat. Four days of chill and thrill in Q-8 and then back to bang-bang city."

Combat? That didn't sound good.

Marla went over to HQ Company and begged a guy to let her send an email home. She came back ready to blow somebody away.

"The creep said no!" she said. "Something about all the area being jammed for security. I don't believe him. I asked him to check my emails and he did and he didn't have any problems. I should go back and shoot him."

"Emails are coming through?" Corbin asked.

"Yeah, I got one from Victor," Marla said. "He wants us to take care of Yossarian until he gets back."

We were told to turn in our weapons to supply and to put most of our gear into our bags until we returned.

"Just take enough for four days' change of underwear," Coles said. "And take any civvies you have."

My one pair of jeans smelled musty and the two shirts were wrinkled but I packed them, anyway. On the way to the bus Miller was cursing up a storm. She was really good at it, too.

"What you thinking, Birdy?" Jonesy was next to me in the

crowded C-3. We were hip to hip with our legs stretched out and touching in the center of the plane.

"I'm thinking that we might be getting reassigned," I said. "But if the women are going, then we probably won't be getting reassigned to the Infantry. What you thinking?"

"That sounds good to me," Jonesy said. "I'll think the same thing because I promised my mama I wouldn't get into no out-and-out combat."

It took an hour and a half from wheels up to touchdown in Doha, Qatar. It felt good to get out of the bus and not feel the weight of a vest full of ammunition. The ride to As Sayliyah was short and it was still daylight when we reached the camp. We were taken to our quarters.

"Yo, Birdy, I been here before," Jonesy said. "This is hog heaven. You know, just before they kill the hogs they bring them out to the pen, let them wallow in the mud a while, then rub their backs."

"Then?" I had to ask.

"Then they gets their choice, bacon and eggs or Hoppin' John!"

There were people to greet us, to check us in, and to tell us where everything was. A girly-looking lieutenant told us that we had the next day off.

I got up at eight thirty in the morning. We had been given printouts with the layout of the camp but what I saw right away made me feel good. There were guys just hanging out and relaxing on the front lawn of our building. There were women in robes and bathing suits sitting in lounge chairs and a volleyball game going on. I thought it was great.

"I bet the gladiators had a place just like this that they could cool out in before they fought the lions," Captain Miller said when I met her coming out of one of the coffee shops with a huge cup of orange juice in one hand and coffee in the other.

We found some lounge chairs near the pool and stretched out. Marla and Evans found us and flopped down, too.

"Did you see that we're allowed so much beer per day?" Marla asked.

"Yeah, but I don't drink beer," I said.

"That's another thing you need to work on, Birdy," she came back.

What I was supposed to do was to chill, and I realized I was working on it way too hard. I kept reaching for the weapon I had left back in Baghdad. Some men from the 101st Airborne were dressed in desert camouflage uniforms but everybody else had managed to scrape together a few civvy units. Sometimes it was only shorts and a T-shirt, but it was civvy.

The food was good, but not much better than in the Bubble. The difference was that you could buy as much junk food as you wanted and everybody was lining up to get at it. I wanted to see if Miller, who was all into science and health, would go for it, too. She did.

Darcy slept most of the first day. Love found a religious group and had Bible study. The rest of us played pool or just hung out in the rec room and watched one of the four big televisions. A heavy sergeant from Kansas City — his name tape read DONGAN — told me that the place had originally been set up for the media.

"They've got every kind of transmission device you want right here," he said. "Studios, radar connections, the works."

"They got any amps?" Jonesy asked.

"They have a whole professional setup for visiting entertainment," Dongan said. "They even have guitars and a few horns. Once in a while somebody comes in who can play them."

Jonesy checked everything out and I figured he would try a hook-up but he said he was too tired. "If I seen two chords and a big-butted mama walking down the street between them, I'd have to wait until I got online before I could send them a shout-out," he said. "This war is wearing my black butt down to a freckled nub. Yo, Birdy, did I tell you I had freckles on my butt?"

Jonesy's freckles were not what I needed to hear about. I thought about hitting on Marla. She was looking really good in a beige sweater she had brought with her and some dark slacks. I asked her how she was doing.

"I'm sitting here wondering what Victor is going to do with the rest of his life," she said. "How many guys you know out there in the world kicking it with two fingers on one hand? What are you thinking about?" she asked.

I knew I didn't want to answer her. I shrugged and looked away and she asked me again.

"Yo, Marla, I'm trying not to think about the war," I said.

"You just want to relax here?" she said. "I can understand that."

"No, that's not it," I said. "If I think about the war enough, if I think about Pendleton and Victor and some of the other things I've seen over here, it might become part of me. You know what I mean? I'm afraid of that. I've always thought of life as being precious and wonderful and all about the great things you were going to do with it. I don't want the images of body parts lying in the streets in my head. I don't want to think about shooting somebody and seeing their life . . . seeing their life twitch and jerk away from them.

"Maybe it's all a part of me already. I don't know. Look, I'm trembling. My hand is actually trembling. Jesus, Marla, it's me I'm scared of. Does that make any sense?"

"It makes sense, Birdy," Marla said. "It makes sense."

The second night at As Sayliyah went badly with me banging around the bed and waking up a hundred times trying to figure out where I was. I dreamt of being in a firefight. Crap. I dreamt of shooting people. It was like I was shooting and couldn't figure out who the enemy was and just kept on firing. Who the hell was I if I was dreaming about shooting people?

Everybody watched the news in the morning. It was as if we were in a game without rules and we had to watch the scoreboard to see how we were doing. We watched the president say how we had accomplished the primary mission and were well into the last phase. A reporter asked him when the troops would be coming home and he said they would be home when the time was right to bring them home. Most of the guys cheered that.

Somebody noticed it was Sunday and Marla and Barbara went to early mass. Jonesy and I went to a music store and bought a copy of the *Survivor* CD and a CD player. There were two machines. One for eighty dollars and one for nineteen. I wanted to pool our money and get the eighty-dollar job but Jonesy was all against it.

"Go cheap," he said. "That way when things go wrong you know why."

"Don't you ever buy good stuff?"

"Only in wine," he said. "In wine I stick with Petrus Clandestinus."

"I don't know anything about wine," I said.

"You probably know it by its street name," Jonesy said. "Sneaky Pete."

At 1500 hours we were rounded up and told that the CAs had a formation at 0800 in the morning. I wondered if there were other CAs besides us and Dongan said no. In the afternoon Captain Miller bought a map and we gathered around as she showed us where Qatar was. Marla asked her where she had been and she said she had been hanging in the officers' club.

"Trying to get a fix on this war," she said. "Trying to see if we're really kicking as much butt as we say we are."

"Are we?" Jonesy asked.

"A lot of people are dying," Miller said. "Is that the same thing?"

■ ■ ■

Monday morning formation. Mucho casual. There was a table set up in the lounge with coffee, doughnuts, danish, and OJ. A thin lieutenant colonel with a thousand lines in his face spread a tablecloth over one of the pool tables. In the middle of the table he put a small orange, two figs, and a handful of raisins.

"My name is Lieutenant Colonel John Kelly. I'm a career soldier, and my father before me was a career soldier. Folks, there's not much on this table to eat," he said. "When you give it to one person, you have a chance to make a friend. When you divide it between two people, you're liable to make two enemies. That's what we're facing here in the Middle East. There's so little to go around and so many people who need both food and spiritual substance that no matter what contribution we make we're going to create more enemies than friends. You've been here awhile and you've seen it in the streets and in the countryside, so you know what I'm talking about."

He went on and on, but he was right. We knew what he was talking about. There wasn't one war going on in Iraq, there were a dozen. The invasion had made a power vacuum and different groups were rushing in to fill it. There were Shiites and Sunnis and tribal groups and Kurds, and political parties. Our guys, our army and our marines, were in the middle of it.

"Basically, I'm saying that we believe in democracy, and in the American way of life, and we are trying to export that to the world. We've done a fine job of it so far," the colonel went on. "In 1776 we were the world's only true democracy. Now most of the world's leadership has followed our example. I don't want to sound utopian, but if we can bring 1776 to the Middle East we can change the world. You young people can take an important step in that direction. You can show us the way. That's what I'm asking of you, that's what America is asking of you. Thank you."

The lieutenant colonel snapped to attention.

"Ten-hut!" Captain Coles stood and saluted.

Kelly snapped off a salute, nodded, and left. From the back of the room another officer, this time a major, came forward. He was Asian, short, and very muscular. Everything about him was spit-and-polish.

"Troops, we're going to be sending you on a mission that's a little out of the ordinary." The major spoke slowly, deliberately. "Your unit has been in Iraq for some months now and you know that the enemy — and by the enemy I mean anyone who is trying to do us harm — plays on the edge of the playing field. Sometimes they change the rules and that gives them a marked advantage. We're going to be selecting a team from among you to work with some other players in the area to complete a mission. You're going to be playing on the enemy's turf, on the edge of the field, and you're going to play with whatever rules work to complete the job.

"If you're successful you will save lives. American lives, yes, but also Iraqi lives. Let me change that to 'other' lives as well. Okay, from now on what you do and where you go will be on a need-to-know basis. When you finish the mission there will be very few people in the world who will know what you have accomplished, but the army will know, the president of the United States will know, and most important, you will know. I don't see this operation as being very risky. You should be able to move in, do what has to be done, without shots being fired. If there is a need to have shots fired, you can rest assured that your security detail will be amazingly proficient at doing just that. My read is that it won't be necessary.

"Finally, I want to tell you why you are being asked to do this. Your unit has dealt very efficiently with the civilian population. You've built bridges and relationships that the 422nd, which is now taking over the bulk of the Civil Affairs function, will be using. In other words, you get the job done. That's all we want. Every time you people make a friend, help a sick child, you create the possibility that we'll get some little piece of information or cooperation which will help us win the minds and hearts we need to prevail. At the end of this mission your entire unit will be reassigned. Many of you will be returning to the States to train other CA Special Ops. Most of you will have interesting choices. Thank you."

The major snapped off a salute and he was gone. We headed back to the rec room.

■ ■ ■

"Captain Coles, what was that about?" Miller asked.

"I have no idea," Coles answered.

"Okay, here's where the blues come in," Jonesy said. "When you come home and call out 'Hey, sweetie!' and your sweetie ain't there but you see a note on the table next to a bottle of wine, right away you know ain't nothing good is in that note. This here R&R is like that bottle of wine and they sent two officers to deliver the note and neither of them told us what the sucker was all about. What I say is, put a dollar in the jukebox and push J-7 four times because the blues is definitely coming down!"

I was excited about the whole thing. Kelly and the Asian officer were both being gungy but they were letting us know they were serious about the importance of the mission.

"What bothers me about this bad boy is that crap about it not being risky," Marla said. "If it's not risky, why doesn't he get his little butt on the stick and do it himself?"

"I think it's because we're good," I said. "You read some bad crap in the papers about what's going on over here and you don't read about us or the 422nd or any of the CA operations."

"I feel some bad mojo working," Jonesy said. "Some bad, bad, BAD mojo!"

"I don't feel it," Marla said. "Our unit is being given a lot of jerk details but we're getting it done. This might be a little hush-hush but I bet we work it."

Sessions called us together that evening and told us that what she called the "insertion team" had been picked.

"Ma'am, is this 'insertion team' about sex?" Marla asked.

Sessions acted as if she didn't hear her. Then she announced the team. It was going to be the First and Second Squads. "Everyone else is excused from this meeting."

At first the others didn't know what that meant, but slowly they got it and stood up and left. I felt excited. My stomach was jumping and I was nervous, but I was also excited.

"Where are we going?" Barbara always seemed to have a hair coming down into her face that needed pushing up and she was brushing it back as she spoke. "Outside of Baghdad?"

June 8, 2003

Dear Uncle Richie,

 Things are going well. There's a lot of talk about us being reassigned. The thing is that we are officially attached to the 3rd ID. Some of the older noncoms are saying it's all part of Rumsfeld's yo-yo concept. We're all on strings and he jerks us around where he wants us. I don't know if I will be reassigned to the 422nd or another CA unit or back to my original unit from Fort Dix. That would suck because they haven't been over here yet.

 I can use some Harlem. One thing I miss over here is the music you hear walking down the streets at home. We got one of the construction guys to rig us up a little portable amplifier so we can blast out the Humvee as we go down the street. They have a lot of amplifiers over here that they use to aggravate the Iraqis.

 A car bomb went off near a Sunni mosque yesterday. The marines call the car bombs "Mist Makers." They say that when you're hit with one of those major explosions all that's left is a pink mist. There's more and more fighting between the Sunnis (not that many of them, really) and the Shiites. I don't really understand the differences between them, they all follow Islam. Still, if they blow each other up and you're too close it doesn't matter if there's a big difference or a little one.

 I had the chance to speak to Mom the other day and we were having a good conversation and all of a sudden she started crying. If you see her will you tell her that I'm actually okay and not just putting on a brave face. I don't think I have a brave face. They don't send the CAs into areas they expect resistance, they send the marines and the Infantry and man, those guys are deadly. They go after everything with such confidence and joblike determination. I'm glad I'm not going up against them.

Don't get me wrong, I don't want to go up against the Iraqis, either. I just want to do my bit to make this place a little bit safer before I leave.

Give everybody my love. Robin

"Yo, Birdy, you know what we need over here, man?" Jonesy had bought a cheap guitar from a guy in supply and was trying to tune it.

"What?"

"An Arabic dictionary so we can see if the names of places we going to mean anything," he said. "Al Amarah could mean the Gaping Ghetto or something."

"I found it on the map," I said.

"Yeah, I seen it, too," Jonesy said. "About an inch away from Iran. I got a bad feeling about this mess."

I looked at him to see if he was kidding. He wasn't. "How come?" I asked.

"They giving us some time off, and they handpicking people instead of just sending out some numbers. Somebody thinking this is some serious business."

"They think we can handle it," I said.

"I hope they right," Jonesy said.

We picked up new gear from the supply sergeant in As Sayliyah. It was all the same stuff except for the pistols. I hadn't carried a pistol but we had shot them in training. I didn't want to be so close to anybody again that I had to use a pistol. The M-16 at a hundred meters was fine with me.

We got a final briefing from Kelly that didn't sound good. I kept checking Jonesy and he looked worried.

"The whole area between the southern tip of Iraq north through the Maysan province is supposed to be held by the British," Kelly said. "They're way undermanned and trying to work with the civilians to keep things cool. They've had a lot of success with their Civil Affairs ops and we're hoping for the same thing."

"If they had so much success, how come we're going?" Marla asked.

"We've got some people in the area, too," Kelly said, smiling. "They're just more used to working with Americans."

"We only going to be there for this one set?" Jonesy asked. "Who coming to hear us play?"

"There are two main groups in the area. The good guys are the ones who have always lived there. They're good people but they rose up against Saddam in the early nineties and he tried to wipe them out. This was a marsh area and they made their living off the water and rice farming, which demands a lot of water. Saddam drained the marshes and mined the area. They hate his guts," Kelly went on. "We just found out that some of their children have been kidnapped and are being held for ransom. Kidnapping's big business over here. We think we can use that to our advantage. The local tribe that the children belong to has been — or at least we think has been —

dealing with some of the Badr fighters who are coming across the border from Iran. The Badr fighters are the bad guys in this picture. Many are former Iraqis. They're all Shiites and all anti-Saddam. But the intelligence is that they're being supported by some foreign elements."

"Iran?" Captain Coles asked.

"We haven't verified that," Kelly said. "And we haven't verified that they're absolutely the ones bringing in the new detonators we're finding throughout the country, either. If we get our hands on a supply of the detonators, we might be able to trace them directly to the source. If we can do that, we might be able to exert enough behind-the-scenes pressure to stop the flow. What we think is that the Badr fighters are bringing in the detonators and selling them to the locals, who then bring them into the suburbs around Baghdad."

"Yo, let me get this straight, sir." Jonesy was deep into his gangsta lean. "The bad guys are bringing in detonators so we know they bad, right?"

"Right," Kelly answered.

"And the good guys are dealing with the bad guys but we know they the good guys because they was hating Saddam first?"

"They need to eat, soldier, the same as everybody else over here," Kelly said, his voice going flat. "But they want their kids back and we're offering you guys up as first-class negotiators. The guys we have in the area now will help you get the kids and, hopefully, we'll make a lot of friends."

"And you asked for women because . . . ?" Miller's head was turned to one side.

"If you need reasons, Captain, I'll give them to you." Kelly had gone from flat to pissed. "The first is that I've seen what the new detonators and the new shaped charges we're finding can do to our people. I've scraped the pieces of flesh from the sides of burned-out vehicles so the insurgents don't get them and feed them to their dogs. I've seen the blood of guys I respect change the color of the air around a vehicle. I'd send my mother if I thought it would do any good."

I didn't like Kelly sounding off to Captain Miller, and I knew he didn't like us questioning him.

"I hope they at least have the good sense to wear white hats and black hats so we can tell them apart," Marla said as we headed back to our quarters.

■ ■ ■

0300 hours. We were driven to an airfield where an old, dull-looking C-3 transport plane crouched on the runway. The night was hot and the interior of the C-3 stifling. I felt myself sucking in air through my mouth.

"Birdy, you're sucking in bugs," Darcy said.

"I need the protein," I answered.

Captain Coles was being quiet and I wondered if he knew anything the rest of us didn't. "Hey, Captain, what you got to say?" I called to him.

He undid his straps and stood up. "I just think everybody needs to get their game face on for this mission," he said. He stepped over Miller's legs and headed to the john in the back of the plane.

"Look at it this way," Miller spoke up. "They wouldn't be sending four women on a mission if it was all that dangerous. Not that they give a crap for us, but it'll look bad in the papers."

"Did I ever tell you about the time my cousin Jedediah was on the front page of the *Memphis Appeal* for robbing a Piggly Wiggly on New Year's Eve?" Jonesy asked. "He got all the way to Panama City, Florida. When he called back home and found out he was on the front page he went back to Stone Mountain. Got arrested, got six months, served three, but he been a celebrity ever since."

Coles got back from the john and was just settled in when the hatches were shut and the C-3 took off.

The flight to Al Amarah took nearly two and a half hours. Coles said the pilots must have been flying around hot zones. We had a vote and it was agreed seven to nothing that flying around hot zones was a good idea.

"I'm supposed to tell you, once we get in the air, that we're going to be working with some Special Ops troops who are already in place in the marshes," Coles said. "They've been there since the first of the year."

"Who are they?" Marla asked.

Coles shrugged.

0620 hours. Al Amarah was hot and stinky. We deplaned and got into trucks for the bumpy ride to a long stretch of wall. There were towers along the inside of the wall at intervals of 100 yards. The truck was checked by a British marine who actually looked under the carriage for something. Then we were taken through a yard the size of a supermarket parking lot to a squat, dirty building that stunk even more.

"The Coalition took out the electricity before we arrived," an officer said. "So it's all a bit backed up."

We were given a room to sit in for the next hour and a half. The Brits and a few Japanese were sitting at computers in the compound. All of the computers were laptops and none plugged into anything. Compared to Baghdad, this was pure crap.

We waited in full gear until nearly 1200 when a young-looking Brit lieutenant asked Captain Coles if we were ready to go. Coles said no, that we wanted to eat first, and the lieutenant said we could eat when we landed.

"Lieutenant, my soldiers need to eat first," Coles said slowly, deliberately.

"Captain, you have about fifteen minutes to get your people on your transport," the lieutenant said. "If they're not on, you're going to be quite sorry."

Captain Miller, who curses better than anyone I have ever heard, said some wonderful things about the lieutenant's parents that I wish I had had the time to write down even though I didn't really believe that a human being could be conceived by sand crabs under a flat rock.

1230 hours. According to the chopper pilot we were landing five miles southeast of Al Amarah. "Good luck!" he chirped.

The place looked desolate. To our left there were huge patches of dark green soil. To the right there was fog. We had been dropped with our gear and two crates of medical supplies in a clearing. Coles was on the radio asking the pilot if he was sure that this was where we were supposed to be when the choppers took off.

I could hear the pilot's voice in Coles's headset as the wind from the rotors blew dust in my face.

"Company," Marla announced.

There were three vehicles coming toward us. I couldn't see the drivers and I didn't recognize the trucks.

"Easy! Easy!" Coles said.

I felt the weight of my piece and toyed lightly with the trigger.

As they drew near we saw one guy standing on the sideboard waving. He was wearing camouflage gear, and a bandana around his head. We were all frozen in our spots when they reached us.

"You guys bring any beer?" the first guy out of what looked like an up-armored SUV asked.

"'Fraid not," Coles said.

"Man, we've been waiting for the beer run for six months," the guy said, extending his hand. "Pile into that second wagon and we'll take you to the camp."

We loaded the medical supplies in the second vehicle and tried not to stare too hard at the men — we could only guess that they were soldiers — who were staring at us. They were a motley crew. Big, muscled, in a variety of uniforms. Some wore bandanas around their heads, others wore earrings.

"Who are you guys?" Coles asked.

"Fifth Group," one guy said. "We work with the local tribes."

These were the guys that Marla had called "Hoodlums" back in Kuwait. They had left camp back then before us and nobody knew where they had been headed.

We got into the trucks and headed to their camp at a speed that I was sure was gong to kill us all. I looked at Marla across from me and she looked tense.

When we arrived at the camp it wasn't what I expected. It was a small village. There were dark tents huddled together on one end of a field and small round huts made out of sticks and mud at the other.

But most of all, there were people that I knew were not soldiers. We were in a tribal camp and I was hoping that I hadn't misread the guys who picked us up. I was hoping that they were really American soldiers. We trailed the guys who had picked us up into the camp. I stopped once to see a dark woman, dressed all in black, staring at me with eyes that looked a thousand years old.

I smiled. She didn't.

We were led into a slightly larger tent where a bare-chested white guy sat in front of a low fire. A woman, slight with quick, nervous movements, sat next to him.

"Make yourself at home," the white man drawled. "Y'all eat?"

"I'm Captain Coles. My people could use something to eat."

"Colonel Roberts" was the reply. "We'll get you some food and you can lay up until it gets dark. We got some work to do tonight so you need to be rested. Sorry our hospitality couldn't be more considerate but we got us a situation, so to speak. People working before you — including us — haven't got the job done. That's why you folks are here. We understand you're pretty good."

"We're trying, the same as you," Captain Coles replied.

"Yeah, well, that's good, Captain," Roberts said. "So, what we're going to do is to have you meet the locals this evening."

"They're coming here?" Captain Coles asked.

"No, we'll send in all of your people to their camp with four of ours for security," Roberts said. "I don't think they'll try anything rough with your people, and with ours there they won't try to intimidate you. They've been told that you're a crack negotiating team from CENTCOM and that you're willing to spend our government's money to ransom the kids from a rival tribe. These are the kids of one of their religious leaders. So it's important for the chief to get the kids back to show he's still got juice."

"If it's that important to him, why do we have to convince him?" Coles asked.

"Because they don't trust anybody who isn't a blood cousin. They've been betrayed by the Iraqis, by the Iranians, by anyone who has anything to gain in this area," Roberts said. "The only difference between this place and everywhere else in this country is this place doesn't make the news."

Roberts gave us a map and pointed out a place that we would meet after dark to make the exchange. "We'll give you one kid to take with you to show we can get them out," Roberts said.

"You already have one of them?" Marla asked.

"We have all of them," Roberts said, glancing toward Miller. "They were kidnapped as a favor to us."

"So it's true, we can't be trusted?" Miller asked.

"After the war we can sit down and have a drink someplace," Roberts said. "We get a good enough buzz on, we'll talk about the philosophy of war. Until then we'll do what we have to do to keep our people alive."

We were fed. The food was good. I thought it was lamb with carrots and couscous. The stick-and-mud hut we were in looked something like old pictures of American Indian homes.

"The funny thing is . . ." Captain Coles was holding a piece of meat on the end of a stick. "In a way we are getting closer to the people we're dealing with. I don't trust Roberts, either."

"What are we going to do?" Miller asked.

"What we're told and hope he gets us out of here alive," he said. "And I hope he's right about the detonators and that we're actually going to be doing some good."

Roberts came in with a young man dressed in black. He moved into the shadows against the wall and almost disappeared. Roberts had a dark green sack with him which he tossed down in front of us. We shut down the conversation as he sat.

"The food's good, huh?"

"It's okay," Marla said.

"If we thought we could pull this off without you guys, you wouldn't be here," Roberts said. "But we think you're going to do just fine. Fadel here is going to translate for you. He was a student at Basra College."

"Is there a chance they'll try to reneg on the deal and just off our people and take the kids?" Jonesy asked.

"That's what I would do if I was them," Roberts said.

I was scared out of my freaking mind. These Special Ops guys were physically and mentally as tough as they came, but there were stories about some of them not being wrapped too tight. From what I had seen of them, I believed it. Roberts opened the sack and showed us the money we were going to be using.

"You'll tell them that you're going to be using the money to buy the kids' safety," he said. "And try to hang on to it."

■ ■ ■

2030. Was an hour after sunset when we mounted up. The stink from the marshes was mixed with sewer smells and cooking. My stomach was queasy and the aftertaste from the meal didn't help any.

Two of Roberts's people were in the first SUV. Me, Jonesy, Coles, and Marla were in the second, with a driver chewing on an unlit cigar. Miller and Owens and the translator were in the last vehicle with the fourth security guy and a kid. They had put a sack over the kid's head. I felt sorry for him, or her, I didn't know which.

What I was wondering was whether the security guys were there to protect us or to watch us. The guy driving our vehicle — he said his name was Gambarelli — was short and wide, with a big head that seemed to come out of his chest. His teeth were perfectly lined up so when he smiled — or *maybe* he was smiling, it was hard to tell — they lined up like teeth in a kid's drawing.

"I ever tell you about doing stuff you don't want to tell your mama about?" Jonesy asked.

"That what we doing?" Marla asked.

"That's what we doing," Jonesy said.

Gambarelli got a big kick out of that. "That's good! That's real good! I'm going to tell all the guys about that!"

I thought about my father. An image of him sitting on his chair near our front room window came to mind. He didn't know how much I wanted things to be okay between us. What I wanted was for him to look at me and see me in the moment, and not worry about what I was going to do or how I was going to kick it ten years down the line. I hoped if anything happened to me he would be all right with it. I knew Mama would be sad, but she wouldn't feel mad. Mama wasn't like that.

We drove west for a while and then made a right turn toward the east. We were on the road longer than I thought we would be, maybe twenty-five minutes, maybe a half hour. I knew that Al Amarah was only thirty miles from the Iranian border, but I didn't know how we had traveled to get to the tribal camp. After a while I saw the flicker of lights ahead in the darkness. Torches. I thought I could see figures. I felt my testicles shrivel.

"I think they know we're coming," I said.

"Yeah, you don't want to surprise anybody out here unless you plan on killing them," our driver said. "Don't get spooked. Everything's cool, just don't get spooked."

He was spooking me out all by himself.

A string of clouds drifted across the three-quarter moon, sending shadows everywhere. The driver slowed the vehicle down and then we stopped in front of two guys who pointed their AK-47s in our direction. They said something and Fadel told us all to get out.

The air was still and there was a swarm of tiny bugs flying in front of my face. I saw Owens taking the hood off of the kid. He was wide-eyed, and slight, but good-looking.

We were led through a maze of tents and small groups of men, huddled together in the darkness. I knew I was walking stiff-leggedly, but I couldn't help myself. My mouth was dry and I wondered if I would be able to speak when the time came.

We were led into a tent that was up against a hill. We went through the tent into a one-story semi-square building. For some reason I expected Osama bin Laden or somebody to be sitting inside of it.

They had electric lights set up and it was fairly bright. There was a rug on the ground and rugs along the wall. We stopped inside and the men who had brought us in, two older guys dressed in caftans and sandals, pointed to the ground. We started to sit. I saw Miller with her arm around the shoulders of the child we had brought along. The Iraqis didn't even glance in the kid's direction and I wondered if there had been some mistake.

We waited nearly ten minutes in silence until four more men came into the cave from the same way that we had entered. They were followed by a man carrying pillows. The pillows were put down and the four new guys sat on them.

They looked us over and spoke among themselves. They looked at the boy and one of the men nodded. That was a relief. He said something and one of the men with a gun took the boy by the hand and led him out of the cave. Then they continued talking among themselves.

Fadel leaned toward us. "They are saying that the women are probably prostitutes," he said softly. "Remember that they probably understand English, too. So you tell me what you want."

Coles sniffed twice and started talking. He spoke in a low voice and I thought it was probably because we were all so close together. He said we were willing to talk to the people who had taken the children.

"We believe we can get them back without any harm coming to them," he said.

"And what do you want?" The guy speaking was my complexion, at least he looked brownish in the dim light, and maybe a hundred years old.

"We understand you have some detonators that interest us," Coles said.

The old man shrugged, and spoke to the others. They all shrugged. It reminded me of hanging out in the barbershop on Saturday and the old dudes wanted to mess with the young bloods. He spoke to Fadel, who turned to us slowly.

"He says he doesn't know what the American is talking about," Fadel said. "What are detonators?"

Coles shook his head slowly, then stood. We all stood and watched as Coles extended his hand to the elder Afghani. The two men shook hands briefly and we started out of the cave.

"Wait!" Fadel stopped us just as we reached the flap that covered the entrance. "The chief has something else to say."

We stood for what seemed forever. My right leg was aching. I had never noticed that before.

The old man I thought might have been a chief spoke very softly to the man on his left. He was also ancient-looking and wore a kind of half turban the same silver-white color of his beard. The fire reflected in his beard and eyes and gave him a mystical look. The chief went on for a while but the other man didn't speak. Occasionally he would raise his hands, then turn the palms up and out, as if he weren't sure of himself. My stomach was hurting now. Then I realized that if we were suddenly attacked, I wouldn't even be nearly ready. I looked at Jonesy and Miller and they were just as absorbed in the conversation between the two men still seated on the floor as I was.

Finally the chief spoke to Fadel, who in turn asked Coles for the map. Fadel got down on his knees and showed the old man the meeting place.

"Show them the money," Coles said to me.

I fumbled with the bag, finally got it opened, and folded my hands so no one would see them shaking. None of the Iraqis looked at it. They were so cool.

Another of the men spoke to Fadel, who answered in a different tone of voice. The man spoke to him again and Fadel bowed his head and did the same palms-up gesture as the older man had done. Then there were nods all around and Fadel told me to pick up the money. A minute later we were out of the cave and headed back to the vehicles.

"We do it?" Marla asked.

"We did it," Fadel said.

"What was that last bit of conversation?" Coles asked. "When the other guy spoke to you?"

"He wanted to know who my people were, and if they knew I worked for nonbelievers."

I thought of the kid walking around touching all the Americans saying, "Infidel, infidel, infidel."

We were supposed to meet in one hour and we would just have enough time, if we tore through the darkness at a clip fast enough to kill us all, to make it.

"Roberts timed this too closely," Coles said.

"There's an old proverb they say in the marshes," Fadel said.

"'Chiefs sleep on anthills.' If he sleeps on it he's going to be bothered all night and by the morning he will have changed his mind five times."

We were elated on the way back. I was worried about IEDs on the road but I didn't think too much about them.

"The thing that gets me," Marla said, "is that if either side blows us away, they're going to think they at least got something out of the deal."

Fadel radioed ahead and Roberts and his team met us on the road.

"Fadel, they buy our story?" Roberts asked.

"No, but they think we can get the kids," Fadel said.

"I thought bringing in decent-looking people might help the situation," Roberts said, grinning. "We pull this off and I'm putting myself up for general."

Roberts had the other kids brought out and put them into the vehicle with Miller.

"Is that kid . . . ?" Miller squinted.

"Blind," Roberts said. "We build ourselves another life, Captain, and I'll come back over here with you to help these people. In the meanwhile if anybody has to pee or anything, do it now and get on your way. If it starts going down wrong, get into your vehicles and bug the hell out. Our vehicles have armored plates on the sides and if you don't get a direct hit with an RPG or take a straight-on shot from a AK-47, you have a good chance of making it. These people shoot and run quick; they don't want to tangle with my men. We lack sympathy."

I felt like I had to pee but couldn't go.

There was an eerie sound coming from the camp. I thought it was chanting and asked Fadel if they were praying for us.

"That guy's buffalo is sick," Roberts said. "He's singing to it to make it feel better. He's only got that one buffalo so he gets priority."

Great.

"Birdy!" It was Jonesy.

"I get that blues club, you going to come down to Memphis to check it out?"

"I get free drinks?"

"All your narrow butt can handle." Jonesy put his hand up and I slapped him five.

"Bet!"

I was more relaxed as we set out. Having the kids to deliver made me feel better. I could tell Marla was more relaxed, too. She was running her mouth about how she hadn't made it on the debating squad at Half Hollow Hills.

"What I should do is get me a Humvee and hook it up with a sound system and a squad gun," she said. "Then I'll put on the *Survivor* cut and blast it up to decibel heaven as I blow away all the old biddies picking the debating team."

"It won't be the same ones that didn't pick you," I said.

"Birdy, the whole deal's symbolic; don't be so lame, man," Marla said.

Driving through the night was spooky, scary, but we had done okay so far. We were actually dealing with these people far off the beaten track. I hoped we were saving lives. Even Miller looked okay. Or at least as okay as Miller ever looked.

We got to the place on the map where we were supposed to meet the Iraqis and Gambarelli pulled off to one side.

"They're here," he said. "I can smell them!"

I looked at him to see if he was kidding. He wasn't.

Roberts's guys got out first and quickly disappeared into the darkness. For a wild moment the thought came to me that I wasn't sure if they were really good guys after all.

Put it out of your mind.

Coles and Miller were getting the children out. It was beginning to rain and had grown cool. I wondered if the children were cold. I pulled down my night-vision goggles, couldn't see crap, and pushed them back up.

Miller and Coles pushed the kids forward. Fadel was with them.

"Birdy! Move up with us." Coles spoke in a loud whisper.

We walked toward what looked like a shimmer in the fog. As I got nearer I could see the outline of a rifle; from the angle it was on someone's back with the sling across his chest. A shift in the moon and I could see three figures. Each one stood behind a box.

Fadel stepped forward and greeted them in Arabic. I checked the safety on my weapon.

The three figures were young men. They piled the boxes down in front of Fadel.

"Take a look, Birdy."

Crap, I didn't want to look away from the guys. Stepping forward as I fumbled for my flashlight, I realized I wasn't sure what I was supposed to be seeing. I lifted the first box. It was lighter than I thought. For some reason that was reassuring. At least it wasn't going to be a 105-mm shell rigged to mist me.

The box was unsealed and I put my hand in it. I felt something in plastic and put the flashlight on the contents. There was a row of blue tubes, two, maybe three inches long, each with two wires sticking out of one end. A quick guess said there were at least a hundred in the box.

"They look like detonators to me," I said.

"Take them back to the truck," Coles said.

I could lift all three boxes easily and was glad to be moving away. I got the boxes into the vehicles I had come in. By the time I turned, Coles and Miller were almost back with me. Behind them I saw the children disappear into the darkness. I heard one of the Iraqis speak and saw the children squat down quickly.

"The kids are —"

I didn't have a chance to finish the sentence before the first shots rang out. The flame from the muzzle of the AK-47 lit up the figure for a hot moment and I could see the guy sliding off to the right.

"The children!" Miller was screaming.

From behind me I heard the answering fire from Roberts's men.

"Move it out! Move it out!" Coles was shouting.

The sound of a machine gun came from our side of the road and a grenade went off a short distance from where the Iraqis had been standing. Then there was a sudden and awful silence.

"Mount up! Mount up!" Coles's voice was higher, more urgent.

We were getting into the vehicles when we heard another sound. It was one of the children. He was crying.

"One of them is hurt!" Miller.

"Leave him!" Coles.

I could see the child. It was the blind boy, his hands up in front of him, pushing against the darkness. Then I saw a figure – it was Jonesy – running toward him.

"Jonesy's out there!" I called out.

Crouching, I headed toward them. Jonesy had grabbed the child around his chest and was covering his body with his own.

"Get out of here! Get out of here!" One of Roberts's men.

For a moment I lost sight of Jonesy. Then I saw him get to his knees.

"Stay low!" I yelled. "Stay low!"

I felt a sharp pain and my foot slip out from under me. More bullets hit the ground to my left and suddenly I was firing into the darkness.

Then an explosion, it had to be fifty yards in front of me, lit up the night sky. The impact of it lifted me off the ground and backward. Then I was being pulled to my feet. I looked up and saw Gambarelli, eyes staring straight ahead, a pistol at arm's length pumping bullets in the direction the explosion had gone off.

I half walked, half got dragged back to the vehicle and slid in. Marla was behind the wheel and as soon as the door closed, she spun it around.

"Where's Jonesy?"

"They're taking him to the other truck," she said. "He's hit! He's hit!"

I was sprawled across the backseat of the truck as we spun in the road. We started after the first truck with Marla pushing within ten feet of its rear. Twenty seconds down the road, we saw the rest of Roberts's men in SUVs and Humvees lining the road. I glanced at the rearview mirror. There weren't any lights following us.

It took forever to get back to the camp. There were torches lit everywhere and guys running around with automatic rifles as Roberts was setting up some kind of a defense.

I stumbled through the confusion looking for Jonesy. Then I saw two guys carrying someone into one of the huts. Miller was pushing her way past us to get to him.

They were putting him down on the ground as I reached them. Jonesy's eyes were open and his hand was moving near his neck, as if he were trying to brush something away. I looked and saw a bubble of blood swell and disappear.

"Give him some air!" Miller was on her knees next to him and cutting away his uniform. "Give him some air!"

I hobbled outside and tried to breathe. A burning pain seared through my left leg. There were streaks in the sky and the first signs of morning. What to do? Where to put my eyes? What to think? It had been so long since I had prayed. So long.

O Jesus God, please don't let him die. Oh, please don't let him die. O God, please don't let him die. Oh, please! Oh, man, God, please don't let him die. Not Jonesy, God. Please.

I sat down on a pile of sandbags and realized how tired I was. There was a lot of activity around me and I looked up and saw Roberts's guys stringing concertina wire around the perimeter of the camp. I figured they must have been expecting an attack. The M-16 felt heavy in my arms.

Two deep breaths gave me enough energy to head back to the tent where Jonesy lay. I envisioned him sitting up, telling some story about his blues joint. When I got into the tent he was still lying at the far side, the flames from the low fire casting a reddish glow to his skin.

"You were wounded," Miller was on her knees near Jonesy's feet and started toward me. "Let me take a look at you."

"Deal with Jonesy," I said. "I'm okay."

She stopped where she was, still kneeling, head down, hands folded in front of her thighs.

"Captain Miller?" I called to her.

She looked up at me. Her face, pale and drawn, looked as if she were in shock. "I'm sorry," she said. "I'm so sorry."

She began to sob, and then to wail. It was as if something horrible and ugly were pouring out of her. "I'm so sorry! I'm so sorry!" She was shouting the words. Moaning the words. They were coming from deep inside her and filled the tiny space we were in. They broke against the walls in a thousand tortured shards that said that Jonesy was dead.

Several of the Iraqi women came to her. They began to put their arms around her. Now they were talking softly to her. Now they added their wails to hers.

Jonesy was dead.

Somehow she got herself together and looked at my leg. There was an ugly cut just below my knee and a huge swelling that bled lower on the side of my ankle. The leg looked different, raw and ugly, as if it was something other than a leg. I was ashamed of the fact that it hurt so much and that I could still feel the pain when Jonesy couldn't. Miller gave me a shot in the leg that eased it quickly and told me to get some rest.

I didn't want rest. I wanted to be outside if we were attacked. I wanted to hurt something, to make something right. But what?

Roberts. His mouth moving. He babbles on about the success of the mission.

Sorry about your buddy. He said. We're calling in a bomb strike.

Keep their heads down. He said. The detonators were just what we thought they would be. They're traceable. He said. There are parts numbers on them which encode the country of origin. Babble. Babble. He said. Detonators and photocells. Don't know what they're for. But you guys did well. I don't think they'll attack. He said. Babble. Babble. I see he is elated with the detonators. They will save lives. But not enough lives. This I know for sure.

I found Marla. She was bent over, her arms around her shoulders, rocking from side to side.

"Marla." I put my arm around her. She turned to me, the tears streaming down her face.

"If there's a God." Her face was stretched tight in her anguish. "If there's a God, Birdy, where the hell is He hiding?"

■　■　■

There was no attack. A day of waiting and watching. A night of bad dreams, of living again the moments that flashed wildly by and that I was already not sure really existed as memory danced them in my tired brain. Those moments and countless images of body bags holding my friend, my blues-loving friend.

A chopper to Al Amarah. A transport to Baghdad. Marla sat next to me, leaned against me, and put her hand on my leg. Miller sat apart from us. She was miserable, but we were all so equally miserable that we couldn't comfort her. I thought of the Iraqi women. How long had they known the griefs they shared?

In Baghdad there was packing going on. I put clothing into

my duffel bag, deciding what to take, what to leave behind. There were questions. What happened on the mission? How did Jonesy get it?

There were many questions and I tried to answer them with some logic. But over and over I thought that we were in a war of complete randomness. Death was hiding in every shadow, lurking along every roadway, flying through the midday air. It came suddenly and randomly. There was no logic except the constant adding up of numbers. How many are dead? What are the names? Where are the pictures for the hometown papers?

As we line up for the memorial service I think of the blind child, his arms outstretched as if he were feeling for answers in his eternal darkness. And I am glad for him, that he lived for those frantic moments, even though I believe I will forget him with the passage of time. For Miller running toward him, and Jonesy giving up his dreams for that child, was what lifted all of this above fear and loathing. In that one last desperate moment, there was actually something for the blind child to reach, some higher point of humanity.

"Does anyone know what religion the young man was?" the chaplain asked.

"He was a blues man," Marla answered.

"And an American," Miller added. "A damn good American."

The questions stopped. The service went on.

"Lord, have mercy on us as we feel the pain of loss, and the endless emptiness that marks the passing of our brother, and have mercy on us as we feel sorrow for ourselves, and for all the angel warriors for whom we feel kinship. Let death be swallowed up in the victory of righteousness. Let us fear death, but let it not dwell within us. Protect us, O Lord, and be merciful unto us. Amen."

"Roll Call Officer!"

Major Sessions, at the back of the tent, marched forward, stopping in front of the first row of chairs. She looked down at her clipboard, and then up.

"Jones!" she called, her voice wavering.

Again, the unbearable silence, the longing to answer.

"Corporal Charles Jones!"

The stillness between heartbeats held for what seemed an eternity before giving way to the grieving melody of taps.

There weren't enough tears within what was left of our squads to wash away the moment; and all the prayers and words of comfort were not enough to hold the griefs we shared. Still, we had to summon the strength to walk out of the memorial tent again, and into the brilliant Iraqi sun with the getting on of our lives.

When Miller saw me she stopped, looked up at me, with her head tilted slightly back, and covered her eyes from the brightness as if to see me more clearly. We looked at each other for a moment, and then she nodded and went on. There was nothing that needed to be said.

■ ■ ■

We got new assignments. All the specialists, the construction people and the plumbers and the electricians from our flying squad, were reassigned to the 422nd. They were given some time off and the option to apply for other units. The rest of us, Coles, Evans, Jean Darcy, Harris, were being recycled back through a training process center. I had been wounded and received a Purple Heart. Marla told me to stick out my tongue to see if that was purple, too.

"If your tongue is purple it means you can poison them when you bite them," she announced.

We turned in our weapons to supply and then there was the coming together and the saying of good-bye. It wasn't complete, wasn't over in any real sense. I looked at Marla and hugged her for as long as we could stand it.

"Birdy, you're a trip," she said.

We swore that we would always be in touch. I would call her a thousand times and she would write to me and we would huddle together over the years. I told her, for the first time, that I loved her.

"Birdy, when people shoot at you," she said, "you automatically love everybody that's ducking down with you."

"Is that all there is to it?"

"No, but it's all I have the courage to deal with right now." Marla put her arm around my neck and kissed me lightly on the cheek. "But I'm thinking heavy on you, Birdy Boy. I'm giving you a lot of thought."

The good-byes were hard and filled with tears and promises. We were all going to stay in touch forever, and to keep one another in our prayers and thoughts. There were handshakes and hugs. And

Marla coming back to me and putting her fingers to my lips so that I wouldn't speak and holding me for a long moment.

Then we were at the airport again. Marla was going to Incirlik Air Force Base in Turkey and from there back to the States to train new CA ops. Captain Coles, Sergeant Harris, and Darcy were going to Doha and I was going to Ramstein, in Germany, to have my wounds taken care of and then I would be reassigned. Everybody else was assigned to the 422nd and, for the most part, they were happy.

I wondered what Jonesy's blues place would have looked like. If he could have pulled it off. I wanted to think he could.

June 17, 2003

Dear Uncle Richie,

There's no way that I mail this letter off. Coles and Marla and Evans and all of my squad buddies are gone to their new assignments. Captain Miller left last night before I had a chance to say good-bye to her. Her original unit was rotated back to the States and she went with them even though they never left Qatar. Uncle Richie, I just wanted to write down that I did what I thought I had to do over here. I did it for my country and for the people I love and for myself, too. At least that's what I'm telling myself. But there's a distance between what my brain says I'm doing, which is more or less what the missions tell us that we're doing, and what I'm feeling inside. I think you probably know that, too.

I got The New York Times *today. It was several days old but there's nothing on the front page about the war, or about Iraq. Inside there is a small square with the names of two more KIAs. I touched the names with my fingertips but I couldn't feel the people they represented. I'm sorry about that.*

Mama said that I shouldn't be the hero type. I don't know. Maybe you have to be a hero type to deal with the bigger things that happen to you. At least you have to be bigger than life to fit all the things inside that you didn't know you could absorb before. I never thought I would see the things I have seen. So many people dead. So many with their parts blown off and them bleeding and crying. I've had to cram all of these images into my head, and it's not easy.

I tried to think about how I would tell people about my experiences over here. I was thinking that if there comes a day when someone says that we have won this war I know that I'll have doubts inside. The ones who make it home are just survivors. If there's any real winning it's that, once we get home, we'll know for sure the things we're living for. And, hopefully, we'll be more thankful for all those things.

If there comes a day that someone says that we have lost this war, I'll know that they are wrong, too. Because once you have seen a Jonesy or a Pendleton desperately reaching for the highest idea of life, offering themselves up, you don't think about losing or winning so much. You think there is more to life and you go on and you want to find that something more.

The funny thing is that the people I loved over here — my guys — could become strangers to me. What I mean is that I saw them here, and was afraid with them and cried with them here, but would I even recognize them if I saw them out there in the world? Would Marla be the same without her body armor? Or without her blond hair tucked up under her Kevlar? How about Coles or Jean Darcy? Would they look different to me in the supermarket?

What was Captain Miller about? How big is her heart? If I saw her riding a bus — maybe reading a newspaper — would I recognize her? I don't think so. I don't know if I will ever know anybody again.

Can I ever hear the blues again without crying?

Uncle Richie, I'm glad I won't mail this letter to you. Because the hardest thing to say is that I don't know if God and I would recognize each other. Why would He let such crap go on like this? How come there's so much *pain in the world if He has anything to say about it? What kind of a God is this?*

The thought came to me that all of this — the training and the bombing and the people being shot, children and old people, and women and crazy-ass guys on drugs — all of it might have been part of God's plan. I'm not saying it was or even if I believe in any of it anymore. I don't know.

If I do talk about the war maybe I'll try to tell people about a blind Iraqi kid stumbling across the field, bullets flying around him, lost in his dark world.

Uncle Richie, I used to be mad with you when you wouldn't talk about Vietnam. I thought you were being selfish, in a way. Now I understand how light the words seem. If I ever have kids, I think I won't tell them much about what I did here, or what I've seen. I'll tell them something because I'll want them to know about war. But are there really enough words to make them understand?

Your favorite nephew, Robin (AKA Birdy)

GLOSSARY

A-10
A U.S. jet fighter bomber used for close air combat

AK-47
The first true automatic assault weapon; manufactured in Russia during the Cold War; widely, often illegally, traded and used in conflicts throughout the world

Al Jazeera
A worldwide Arabic satellite and cable network, based in Doha, Qatar, that has widely expanded the availability of media in the Middle East; commonly gives the viewpoints of the Islamic world

Al-Qaeda
A loosely organized, radical, international terrorist organization whose goals are to get rid of foreign influences in Islamic countries and establish a world order based on strict, fundamentalist Islamic laws. Al-Qaeda was founded in 1989 by Osama bin Laden, among others. The United States,

with its worldwide influence, has been particularly targeted by bin Laden and Al-Qaeda, which uses bombings and other forms of tactical violence to further its goals.

CENTCOM

The United States Central Command, under the control of the Secretary of Defense, is in charge of coordinating military affairs for the U.S. Armed Forces in the Middle East, Central Asia, and East Africa. CENTCOM is headquartered in Tampa, Florida.

Civil Affairs

Branch of the U.S. Armed Forces that acts as a liaison between the military and the civilians in a war zone or disaster area

Coalition

The military forces deployed from other countries to join the U.S. military in Operation Iraqi Freedom. At various points during the Operation Iraqi Freedom campaign, more than 30 countries have been listed as part of the Coalition, although the great majority of combat forces are from the U.S., followed by the United Kingdom. Most countries sent significantly smaller forces, which were often limited to support roles, rather than combat or engagement.

Detonator

A device used to trigger an explosive

Fedayeen

A group of guerilla fighters loyal to Saddam Hussein

Final Roll Call

A military ritual in the memorial services for slain personnel

FOB

Forward Operations Base; a military base that is located near the front lines of combat

Green Zone

The heavily fortified area in central Baghdad from which Coalition command decisions are made

Gulf War

Iraq invaded neighboring Kuwait in August 1990. In January 1991, United Nations–sanctioned troops, in a coalition led primarily by the United States, waged the Persian Gulf War to liberate Kuwait, which was accomplished by February 1991.

HMMWV

A hybrid vehicle, outfitted for a number of different military purposes, with a top speed of 80 mph; commonly called a Humvee

IED

An Improvised Explosive Device

Insurgents

People fighting in armed revolt against a civil, military, or political authority

Islam

A religion based on the teachings of the Prophet Muhammad. Followers of Islam are called Muslims.

Jihad

A system of protecting Islamic beliefs. There are traditionally four methods of practicing jihad. 1. With the heart: doing what is right under Islamic law. 2. With the tongue: speaking the truth and propagating Islam. 3. With the hand: correcting what one sees is wrong. 4. With the sword: defending Islam against its enemies.

Kevlar

A dense material that resists penetration by bullets and can be woven into many forms. U.S. troops wear Kevlar vests with ceramic front plates inserted into specially designed pockets. The U.S. military helmet is also made of Kevlar.

KIA

Killed In Action

Kurds

A tribal people of the Middle East, most of whom live in Turkey, northeast Iraq, and Iran. Kurds are the second largest ethnic group in Iraq, where they maintain an area of autonomous control.

LOC

Lines Of Communication. LOC ensure combat soldiers have essential access to supplies, intelligence, and advice from rear services and commanders.

M-16

The standard infantry rifle of the U.S. Army

Medevac

The abbreviation for medical evacuation, the process by which wounded soldiers are quickly moved by helicopters or ground vehicles to hospital centers

Molle

Moduler Lightweight Loadcarrying Equipment. A Molle vest has special webbing and loops that can hold personal armor and upon which other equipment can be fastened.

MOS

Military Occupational Specialty; the job a soldier has been trained to perform

MRE

Meals Ready to Eat; individual rations carried by soldiers in the field

NCO

Non-Commissioned Officers; any soldiers above the rank of private, for example, sergeants, corporals, etc.

POW

Prisoner Of War

PSYOP

Psychological Operations. PSYOP military units are specially trained to give useful information to local inhabitants to encourage their cooperation and influence their support of U.S. objectives.

Red Crescent

Middle Eastern equivalent of the Red Cross. A white flag with a red crescent moon on it denotes an organization or vehicle that's on an errand of mercy and, according to international treaties, should be immune to attack.

ROE

Rules Of Engagement are established by U.S. military authorities and define when and what kind of force U.S. soldiers can engage in.

RPG

The Rocket Propelled Grenade is a shoulder-fired weapon with an effective range of up to 500 yards. It is favored by Iraqi insurgents because of its light weight.

Rules of War

Internationally agreed upon laws and treaties, such as the Geneva Conventions. Rules of War define humanitarian issues, such as the protection of civilians and how prisoners of war and war-wounded are treated, and outline which war activities are prohibited, such as attacks on hospitals or Red Cross or Red Crescent vehicles or the deliberate killing of civilians who are not directly involved in combat.

SAW

Squad Automatic Weapon; a light- or medium-size machine gun

Sheik

An Arabic term applied to a tribal elder, wise man, leader, or highly respected person

Shiite

A follower of Islam who believes that the leadership of the Islamic religion should have been the descendants of Ali, the cousin and son-in-law of the Prophet Muhammad. Shiites are the second largest branch of Islam; the majority of Iraqis are Shiites.

Squad

A group of soldiers. Squad size may vary according to the needs of the mission.

Sunni

A follower of Islam who believes that the caliphs, or rulers, who took control after the death of the Prophet Muhammad were the rightful leaders of their religion. Sunnis make up the largest branch of Islam but are a minority in Iraq.

Tribe

A group of people who have family, religious, and language ties

Up-Armored

The additional armor added as needed to vehicles in the field

WIA

Wounded In Action

WMD

Weapons of Mass Destruction

Acknowledgments

Andrew Carroll, author of *Operation Homecoming*, offered encouragement and helped in finding suitable readers for this manuscript.

Ryan Kelly, Edwin L. Jordan, Jack Lewis, and James Rimensnyder were willing to share their insights and experiences of our war in Iraq. I am grateful for both their commentary and the pride with which they approached this book.

My son, Michael, gave his views of the Middle East when serving in the first Gulf War, and my daughter-in-law, Major Spring Myers, briefed me on some of the problems facing the returning veterans.

About the Author

Walter Dean Myers grew up in Harlem and now lives in Jersey City, New Jersey. A beloved and outstanding author of children's and young adult literature, his many awards include two Newbery Honors, five Coretta Scott King Awards, and the Michael J. Printz Award. His most recent books for Scholastic Press include *Harlem Summer* and *The Beast*.